THE BALLAD OF SCREECH AND FRIDAY

Piney Falls Mysteries

JOANN KEDER

Cover Art: Molly Burton

Editor: Chrisandra Johnston

ISBN: 978-1-953270-43-6

For Dinah

Acknowledgments

This is a season of change. I've been carried through by the kindness of others, and I don't take that lightly. Paul—thank you for helping me find my smile. To the friends I've accumulated on social media, your messages lit the dark—you mattered more than you know. And to my family, near and far, you are woven into every part of who I am—your love is my grounding, my compass. I'm still finding my way, but it means everything to know I'm not walking alone.

"Oh, what a tangled web we weave, when first we practice to deceive!"

— *Sir Walter Scott*

Characters

MAIN PLAYERS

Pepper Plantz Friday frizzy hair, questionable fashion, and a growing list of reasons not to trust anyone.

Sybil Screech Sharp of tongue, sharper in stilettos never say no to dairy.

Lanie Anders-Hill narrator and reluctant sleuth. Quiet backbone of the story. Smart enough to keep receipts.

November (Vem) Bean Master of dramatics, interpretive moaning, and sardonic commentary.

PINEY FALLS TOWNIES

Cosmo Hill- Baker, antique shop owner, and Lanie's devoted husband who loves her despite her dubious choice in best friends

Piper Moonlight-Hill Adopted daughter of Cosmo and Lanie, she's sugar, sass, and just sharp enough to frost you if needed.

Obie Lumquest Honest to a fault police deputy who is engaged to Piper Moonlight Hill

Boysie Lumquest Police Chief of Piney Falls and Gladys Petrie's favorite son-in-law, Boysie knows where all the bones are buried—literally and otherwise.

Gladys Petrie Mother-in-law to Police Chief Boysie Lumquest and the oldest person in Piney Falls—if you believe her—Gladys is a dark-web-surfing, casserole-slinging legend whose steely smile and suspicious side dishes have kept the town in line for decades.

CULT CLUB

Moonbeam Cloaked in flowing robes and vague philosophy, Moonbeam conducts his off-key Mooners while masking shadowy intentions.

Derek za'Dimwit abandoned his family to serve Sybil Screech and the Mooners with blind loyalty and zero critical thought—what he lacks in brains, he doesn't make up for in anything else.

ROOTS AND WEEDS

Dill "Pop-up" Plantz Cult escapee turned tyrannical father. Loves order, seaweed smoothies, and himself. Will trade affection for obedience. Maybe.

Sage Plantz Soft-spoken and deeply strange. Pepper's mother. Might be victim, believer, or both.

Ginger Plantz Too cute to be dangerous. Too smart not to be.

Mr. Gumb Always in velvet. Always one step ahead. Claims to love children. Might mean it. Probably doesn't.

Maribel Chafe Greenhouse matriarch. Straight spine. Frosty eyes. Hates glitter.

Prelude

Chapter 1

Lanie

"Lanie," Vem hisses without opening her eyes, "do you think that browless battle-ax is going to sing? I'm not sitting through THAT again."

I glance at the karaoke stage, where Sybil Screech, wearing a sparkling gold gown better suited for the Miss Piney Falls pageant than a karaoke club, appears to be readying a song.

"Syballus…Syballus…Syballus," Sybil says as her microphone test word without one note of irony.

"Yeah, you're right. She's so rude even my sourdough starter wouldn't rise around her. And it's survived three power outages and my meaty ex-boyfriend Brick."

"Shh." I point toward the stage.

Sybil reaches for the mic—and Pepper Friday yanks it back.

"I'll take an apology first."

The acoustics in the old Scheddy Opera House are impeccable. A word whispered onstage will carry to the back row of the second balcony. At least where it used to be.

I smile.

"She knows how to take care of herself," I whisper to Vem.

"You'll never get an apology from me!" Sybil snarls, then lunges. They wrestle for a brief moment, a tangle of gold lamé, polka dots, and righteous indignation. Finally Pepper pulls the mic high overhead like a victory torch.

"Derek is tired of being your lapdog too," she announces. "He told me he wants to be known for his *expertise*, but all you do is berate him."

Sybil's laugh is enough to peel wallpaper.

"Neither of you could unscrew a lid without instructions. You're both USELESS. Moonbeam and I have decided to fire you! You've outworn your welcome, Ms. Friday!"

"I'm afraid not. I QUIT!" Pepper yells. The mic in her hand screeches in protest as she drops it to the floor. She storms offstage, her frilly skirt bouncing with purpose.

There is an audible gasp in the audience of

local dignitaries and the wealthy who procured tickets through underhanded means.

Sybil doesn't flinch. She waves toward the booth. The music begins—something jazzy and unearned. There is a hush over the audience and tension thick as blackberry jam as we wait for off-key evil to pour from Sybil's mouth.

Sybil starts slow, a croony almost-whisper that lulls us into a sense of calm. Her vibrato flutters like a mosquito. There are chuckles around the room. Then she signals the sound booth again.

And that's when the performance goes off the rails.

What follows can't be classified as music. Not even generously. It begins in a register only accessible to malfunctioning flutes, plummets to something resembling whale distress calls, and ends in what I can only describe as *operatic shrieking*.

Somewhere, I imagine a wine glass cracking on its own out of fear.

Across the room, napkins are being ripped and rolled into makeshift earplugs. One elderly gentleman folds his entire program and shoves it in his hat like a makeshift helmet.

Sybil's voice jackhammers the rafters. Every note is a personal attack on the concept of harmony.

Then come the lyrics.

"Screech was a legend with coal-black eyes

And beauty that stopped traffic.
She saw through lies and resolved the issues—so graphic.
Then came Friday, loud and unsure,
Dressed like a tantrum in discount couture…"

Vem gasps so loudly, three people turn.

"She did NOT just say that!" she growls.

"Shhh. We're here for one purpose, remember?"

The Mooners aren't allowed phones, so they raise miniature flashlights above their heads as they sway and hum as though they know this song.

"She tried to glow like a sparkler bright,
But fizzled fast like a two-for-one light…"

I see movement.

Off stage right, Derek, her clueless lover, watches her intently. His expression is strange. Arms crossed. Leaning forward, mouthing something. Not admiration. Not hatred. Is it a word?

Nerves.

Vem whispers, "This is slander with jazz hands."

Suddenly Sybil gasps and reaches for a high note. Instead, her face contorts—red, bulging—like someone attached a bicycle pump to her nostrils.

"Is her body having a reaction to her squaller?" Vem asks. "If so, her nervous system is working well."

Foam spills from her lips. Red lumps rise from her face like a cheap horror film. She collapses, twitching.

"I was a trained medic during the Mommies, where I won International Moaner of the year. I know CPR!"

Vem leaps over two rows of chairs with the kind of grace only adrenaline or decades of interpretive moaning produces.

Out of the corner of my eye, I spot Pepper. She's slipping through the emergency exit with her glasses askew and tears rolling down her cheeks. A man in a red velvet suit follows.

Odd.

I bolt upright.

Lanie doesn't run. It's practically law in Piney Falls. But tonight, I break every personal precedent. I walk with purpose down the steps toward the exit.

"Pepper!" I shout. "Wait! No judgment, hon! I just want to talk!"

She pauses, wild-eyed. Then she kicks off her polka-dotted Mary Janes into a bush and sprints barefoot away from the building.

I fumble for my phone to call Boysie when I hear a bloodcurdling cry:

"LAAAAANIE! LAAAANIE!"

Pepper Plantz

2

Went to a Garden Party

The cash register jingled every time it opened or closed. "Thank you for shopping with us at Dill's Plantz!"

Pepper Plantz handed a customer a half-box full of herbs along with her change.

"Well aren't you a smart girl!" the woman remarked. She leaned over so that she was close to Pepper's face. "And how old are you, miss?"

Pepper sensed her father standing behind her before she opened her mouth. The rules were clear: no sharing with customers unless it involved something in the greenhouse. Dill Plantz squeezed his eldest daughter's shoulders protectively. "We don't normally allow our children to share private information with customers."

"Oh. I didn't mean—"

"But I can tell you're trustworthy," Dill continued. "Pepper is nine. My other daughter, Ginger, is seven. They've both worked in the greenhouse since they could walk."

The woman stood and frowned. "I'm on the local school board. We generally don't approve of children working at their family business until they're old enough to handle homework as well as physical labor. I haven't seen either of your children in Hugh G. Laff Grade School before. I would remember your unusual last name."

"Run and fetch your mother, Pepper," Dill said firmly. Usually this tone was reserved for her punishment. Even though she'd done nothing wrong, Pepper still trembled as she took the steps upstairs to their apartment two at a time.

"Sage?"

Her mother, a beautiful woman with soft green eyes and waist-length honey brown hair, appeared wiping her hands on a kitchen towel. "What is it, daughter?"

Pepper wished for once her mother would call her by her name, but one of her father's endless rules was that only he was allowed to call the girls by their given names.

"You're supposed to go downstairs. Someone is asking too many questions."

Her mother blinked hard. "Go finish the dishes for me."

Pepper was relieved to have a few minutes without the scrutiny of both her parents. "Ginger? Are you done with math problems?" she whispered when she heard her mother on the last very squeaky step.

"What?"

A bright red head peaked around the corner.

Ginger was never bothered by the urgency of completing unsanctioned tasks the way Pepper was. Maybe it was because she usually escaped the worst of the punishments. A round-faced girl with curly red hair and dimples, Ginger was everything her frizzy-haired, homely sister was not.

When Ginger finally sauntered into the kitchen, Pepper used one wet hand to pull her close. "Ow! Stop!" Ginger complained.

"Did you print out the pages on the office printer like I told you last night?"

Ginger nodded. "They're under my mattress."

"Good. We can learn more about our siblings tonight, then."

Ginger's expressive brown eyes narrowed. "Why do you even care, Pepper? It's not like we'll ever see them. We're trapped here forever."

A silence overtook them as they contemplated the truth in that statement. A brisk tap on the front door startled them both.

"I'm going to answer," Pepper said with unusual bravery. "It might be important."

No one came to visit them. The only person who knocked on the door was Dill's good friend, Mr. Gumb. All customers entered through the greenhouse, making life feel very isolated for the Plantz girls.

When Pepper opened the door, she was surprised to see the customer who'd just left the store.

"Did you forget something, ma'am? Pop-up is downstairs, I can go—"

The woman reached out quickly and grabbed Pepper by the sleeve. "No, I want to talk to you," she whispered. Ginger used this moment to find her way to the front door. The woman gasped when she saw her. She bent down at eye level, marveling at the genetic good fortune that was Ginger Plantz.

"Aren't you a widdle cutie?"

Baby talk was wasted on the Plantz girls. They'd been treated as adults since they were two.

"I'm concerned you girls aren't receiving a proper education. Do you have an actual home-school curriculum?" She stretched her neck, attempting to survey the small living room and kitchen as though she might discover outdated text-books lying around.

"Yes, we do our studies every day from ten until two-thirty. And then from midnight until—"

Pepper clasped her hand over her sister's mouth. Though she didn't know much about the outside world, she knew enough to keep their odd hours private. "She gets confused," she explained.

The woman stood and sniffed the air like she'd

smelled moldy lunchmeat. "I believe I've seen enough." She softened her tone. "It's not your fault, girls. My job is to protect you when other grown-ups aren't doing their jobs. Tell your parents to expect a visit from the local police and truancy officer soon."

She marched out the door like a monarch doing a ceremonial procession. It had barely creaked shut when Sage appeared.

"Daughters!" she clapped twice, the signal that if they chose to disobey, they would lose computer privileges. "Who was at the door? And why would you open it?"

Pepper opened her mouth to reply, but Sage's response stopped her,

"And before you make up a story, Pepper Plantz, remember how poorly things went when you lied about eating all of the pudding!"

"No dessert for two months!" Ginger giggled. She was enjoying this a little too much.

"It was the wrong house," Pepper blurted out. "They thought we sold pies."

Pepper thought of that one on the fly, making her quite proud of herself.

Sage nodded. It was her "I'm too tired to deal with this" nod instead of "I know you're making this up."

"To your room!"

Their mother clapped her hands together, the only form of discipline Sage used. If they were banished to their bedroom in the middle of the day, there was only one reason—Mr. Gumb was coming for a visit.

"Can I show him how I curtsy just like the court of King Henry the VIII?" Ginger asked. "He wanted me to learn."

"Maybe. Hurry up now. You know how Pop-up hates to be interrupted when he meets with Mr. Gumb."

Once safely in their bedroom with the door shut, Ginger pulled out the two pages she'd printed off. One was a Google search for former members of the Fallen Branch Cult. Dill and his first wife raised their children in the cult before it disbanded.

The second page was a wedding announcement for November Breeze and Chester Flushmore Bean, of the Flushmore Toilet Paper Dynasty.

Pepper marveled at the exquisite silk dress. This November person had curly hair just like her sisters. It was piled high on her head, barely contained in a wreath of delicate flowers. Her glasses frames were white, matching her dress. Pepper couldn't say that November was beautiful, but she was certainly fancy looking.

"The happy couple will make their home in San Diego, California, where Chester continues as president and CEO of the toilet paper company founded by his mother. His bride, November, will work at Nothing But Guts Vitamins and Supplements."

She sat the page down. "Our sister is married to that guy, Ginger."

Ginger grabbed the paper from her sister's hands. "She seems nice."

It was hard not to feel jealous. Here she was, doing something other than selling plants and seeds. November was married to a handsome, rich man. Pepper and Ginger would never be allowed outside of their homes, much less to marry anyone.

"Girls!"

Instantly Ginger dropped the paper behind her. Pepper, sizing up the situation quickly, stepped in front of her. "What is it, Sage? We were practicing our daily mantras."

"Mr. Gumb is here. He wanted to say hello."

After using one foot to scoot the papers under her bed, Pepper practically skipped out the door. As she reached the bottom step, it occurred to her that Mr. Gumb wasn't appearing in his usual location, the plastic-covered couch. Instead, they spoke in the kitchen in hushed tones.

"You'll take care of the situation, then?" Pop-up whispered.

"Don't I always?" Mr. Gumb replied, his boisterous voice echoing.

Pepper entered the kitchen on tiptoes, unsure if her presence would be welcomed. Mr. Gumb turned. "I think I heard a mouse. Dill, we need a trap."

He winked at Pop-up. Pop-up nodded. Winking wasn't really his thing.

Pepper knew she was too old for this game, but it didn't matter. She tiptoed over to Mr. Gumb and yelled, "Boo!" as she wrapped both arms around his neck.

The only visitor welcomed into their home was a friend of Pop-up's. A jovial man who enjoyed Pepper and Ginger's company, Mr. Gumb smelled like cedarwood, bergamot, and a touch of dried sage, as though he'd just stepped out of a very tasteful apothecary hidden deep in a forest—or perhaps out of someone's dreams. His scent was grounding, warm, and just a bit smoky, with the faintest trace of citrus hovering beneath the surface.

He was also the most handsome man Pepper had seen in person. Like James Cagney from the black-and-white movies they were allowed to watch once a month. Always clean shaven, with a series of small scars across his chin. His eyes were dark green, the kind that held both mischief and melancholy.

The best part about Mr. Gumb was his attire. He always dressed in crushed-velvet suits. Pop-up said it was a sign of his prosperity and style. Pepper and Ginger never thought to ask what exactly made him prosperous.

Mr. Gumb seated himself at the kitchen table and patted his lap.

Pepper jumped in his lap and stuck one hand in

the pocket of his jacket. She pulled out a large sucker and immediately unwrapped it and shoved it in her mouth before her father could force her to wait until after dinner to enjoy it.

Sage entered the room timidly. "Dill?" she asked softly.

He used two fingers to wave her in. She waved nervously at Mr. Gumb before whispering in Pop-up's ear.

Pop-up leaned forward and focused his sharp gaze on Pepper. "She was at the front door? Why didn't you say anything?"

he asked Ginger.

Pepper pulled the sucker from her mouth. "I was going to—"

"Dill, leave the kid alone. I told you I'd handle the problem didn't I?

Pepper never saw the woman from the school board again.

3

Those Were The Days

Dill Plantz swept one arm toward a long, weathered table with the grandeur of a man unveiling a sacred relic. "And this is where we ate. All together, all the time. Though I was always one to gain Zion's favor, so I ate at the private table inside a colorful tent."

Pepper looked at him with wide-eyed reverence, the same expression she'd worn since childhood. "Pop-up, I thought you were the only one who escaped and became… well, normal."

Pop-up was the name Dill had insisted on being called since Pepper and her younger sister, Ginger, were toddlers. No one ever asked why. Dill had little patience for questions—he allowed exactly three per week, submitted in writing, with no spelling errors. Their mother, Sage, once whispered that she had given up everything—her home, her family, even her real name—to marry him.

Pepper could have asked why. But she'd never wanted to waste one of her precious questions.

"Well," Dill said, puffing up his chest, "most who left couldn't assimilate. I'm one of just a handful of Fallen Branch survivors who thrived. Probably the most successful."

He cleared his throat—an unfortunate side effect of the seaweed cocktail he swore by—and raked his fingers through his thick brown hair. Pepper had once caught him applying dye to his roots. He'd offered her an extra weekly question in exchange for her silence. She had agreed—only after looking up the word *discretion* in the dictionary.

They strolled past empty cabins and leaning sheds, the air sharp with pine and damp earth. A chill crept over Pepper's shoulders—not from the cold, but from that peculiar prickling sensation she sometimes got when something wasn't quite right.

"Once you children are out in the world," Dill said, lowering his voice, "you must never mention our trip to Piney Falls or the Fallen Branch Compound. Understood?"

Everyone nodded. Even Sage.

"Ow!" Ginger jabbed Pepper in the ribs as she darted past. "Race me!"

Ginger, with their mother's deep brown eyes and red hair, looked like every hidden family photo Pepper had ever seen. Pepper envied that resemblance. Ginger barely seemed to notice it.

"I don't want to run," Pepper said softly. "I'm going to sit and meditate."

Dill nodded in approval and gestured toward the long table, its yellow paint peeling in tired curls. "Down on the end, right-hand side—that's where I sat. You'll certainly feel my intense energy and charisma if you sit long enough."

Sage reached for his hand, but Dill slipped it neatly into his jacket pocket instead.

Pepper eased onto the bench, careful to avoid bird droppings and splinters. She closed her eyes and tried to picture her father here as a boy—Zion's prized disciple. But nothing came. Just blankness.

She shifted, preparing to stand.

"You haven't given it enough time," Dill snapped. "A proper meditation takes twenty minutes. Sit until I release you. Show me your self-control."

Pepper huffed softly but stayed where she was. She thought about inventing something—some grand vision he'd believe. But before she could, an image crashed into her mind:

A narrow hiking trail.

A woman ahead with frizzy hair like her own.

A strange sound—not words, but an odd, tuneless hum.

The woman bent to pick weeds, then spun around so fast Pepper stumbled backward.

"*Excuuuuse me!*" the stranger said, shoving her glasses up her nose and planting one hand on her hip. "I've been expecting you, but I'm far too busy for chitchat. And you've stepped right in the middle of a perfectly formed pile of Jamaican Blue Beetle dung."

Pepper blinked—and the vision disappeared.

Her father's voice echoed somewhere in the trees. The group was moving on.

Pepper slipped away.

Instead of following the marked trails, she wandered off-track, drawn by a narrow path swallowed by weeds. Branches whipped her arms and tall grass scratched at her shins. The trail narrowed to barely a foot wide, and a thrill sparked inside her —like no one had walked it in years.

Then the light began to fade.

Her stomach turned. She realized she didn't remember how to get back.

"Hello?" she called.

Silence. The stillness she had admired moments ago now felt heavy. Like someone was watching.

A tug at her ankle made her yelp. Vines had snared her shoelace. She bent to free it, tugging and muttering under her breath. One foot came loose, but the other stuck. When she finally yanked it free, the ground beneath her shifted.

She fell.

The drop wasn't far, but it was enough to knock the wind from her chest. She landed hard and stayed still, waiting for her breath to return. Around her, the dark settled like a blanket. Insects flickered through the gloom, their tiny bodies glowing like embers.

The light above was fading fast.

A voice, close now, said, "I'm sorry, Miss—"

Pepper looked up.

The woman from her vision leaned in, sniffing the air beside Pepper's face.

"Hmm. A little fear… and is that cult? Girlfriend, Daddy isn't just growing plants. You'll never be happy until you're far, far away."

Pepper's face burned with shame. Her father was a revered cult survivor—wasn't he?

"Who are you?" she whispered.

"I'm your sister, silly bones. Tell Darling Daddy that you had a vision of him receiving the Zion's Favorite Award for his exemplary service. He was wearing green and gave a ten-minute acceptance speech on the many ways he'd improved the lives of everyone there. That oughtta make him happy. Now open your eyes, sissy-poo!"

Pepper's eyes flew open. For a moment, she forgot where she was.

"Pepper, you're not in trouble, honey. Just come out and let us know you're safe!" It was her mother's deceivingly comforting voice. Of course Pepper would be in trouble. She'd taken the initiative to think on her own.

She took her mother's hand, and they walked in silence back to the rest of the family. Ginger was smirking. She knew what was coming.

"You ran away," he said quietly. "There will be punishment."

"I had a vision," Pepper said boldly and without concern for his reaction. "It was about you."

Dill uncrossed his arms and arched an eyebrow. "Well? What did you learn?"

She cleared her throat, desperate to know how long she'd been in this dreamlike state. But it would have to wait until she was home and had pen and paper. "Yes, Pop-up. I saw you receiving the award for—"

"Best member of the cult. I still remember the speech I gave…"

While he recounted his self-aggrandizing speech, Pepper tried recreating the dream, or whatever it was, that had just taken place. Who was that? Was she real?

4

Be True to Your School

Despite little contact with other children, Pepper and Ginger understood that Dill's version of home-school was a strange one. A surreal patchwork of Dill's obsessive rituals and Sage's scattered memory of basics, classwork was often inconsistent and easily disproven. This year's classes, created wholly by Dill, included *Czar Beets: Russian History in Root Vegetables and Seasonal Plant Math: How Long Until It Dies?*

Both topics required two semesters, so when Dill abruptly declared, "You're ready for graduation," neither girl believed him.

Pepper had been fifteen. Ginger only twelve.

Sage beamed with pride and presented the handmade graduation gowns she'd stitched at night after meditation. They were beautiful—soft cotton and shimmering lace, too delicate to wear and too sacred not to.

The ceremony itself unfolded in a daze. After dressing, Dill ordered them to march down a makeshift aisle in the greenhouse while Sage played something haunting and unfamiliar on a pan flute.

Dill offered some heavy-handed encouragement about life beyond the garden and potion shop, but neither girl really listened. They were too stunned. Too unsure.

Was he… suggesting they leave home?

"*And now you applaud,*" he'd instructed, clapping his own hands to demonstrate. "We've discussed polite actions before."

Startled back to the moment, both girls began clapping—loud, frantic, and far too enthusiastically.

Sage had set out refreshments in the tearoom: carrot cookies for Ginger, cucumber-kale punch, and a tomato cream cheese mousse that trembled ominously in crystal cups.

It was the first time they'd ever been allowed in the prized corner of the greenhouse. The white-painted wrought iron furniture was typically off-limits—too close to Dill's most valuable herbs and far too precious. That space was reserved for patrons who paid over $100 a head to sample his carefully curated teas while birds chirped from hidden speakers in the foliage.

But today they were guests at the grandest table—the legendary "eight-legged moneymaker," as Sage affectionately called it. Dill had outbid an entire family at an estate sale to secure it. The losing grandchildren had glared like they'd lost a throne.

After every last crumb had been devoured, Dill stood, cleared his throat, and addressed Pepper with the weight of someone delivering a sentence, not a speech.

"Graduation means a start to the next chapter of your lives. Pepper, please rise."

She stood, legs trembling, her gaze locked on a pink geranium in desperate need of pruning.

"Your mother tells me you've been spending unapproved time on the computer at night."

Pepper's eyes flicked toward Sage. The betrayal stung more than expected.

"You've broken too many rules," Dill continued.

"I said I was sorry about the—"

He raised a hand. "Yes, I know. But you never learned your lesson. When your mother informed me of your transgressions after I trusted you, I went through your search history. No history of the ficus or the best climate for marigolds."

Dill stood, his body swaying as it did when he was excited to lecture them. "Oh no, not the schoolwork you told me you were researching. I discovered you've been using the family computer for unauthorized web searches."

"I... I was just trying to find out more about our brother and sister in Piney Falls. They're really successful, and I want to meet them! Well, at least

Nochturn lives in Piney Falls, but our sister lives in—"

"Silence!"

His fist crashed down on the table. The sound made the entire family jump. His hand turned red and pulsed with the impact, but he didn't flinch.

For a moment, Dill's face looked like a storm rolling over prairie land—furious, wordless, heavy.

Then he straightened his shoulders. "Your mother and I have discussed it. Since you find yourself bored with your schoolwork, we found a way to challenge your intellect."

Pepper could hear the sarcasm dripping from his voice, though she didn't have a word for it. She hung her head, waiting for the punishment to come.

"You've been enrolled in St. Slackjaw Preparatory School for the Mildly Gifted. I spoke with the headmaster today."

"What?" Pepper's eyes filled with tears. Though Pop-up was strict, nothing could have prepared her for this unusually harsh punishment. She couldn't look at her, but the sound of tiny sniffles confirmed Ginger was just as shocked.

"For…how long?" she asked, suddenly wishing she'd followed Dill's rules.

"Until you graduate! I thought that was clear. When you've completed your studies, we'll find a suitable university to teach you how to run a business. Our business."

Tears ran down her face. Pepper felt a hand

nudging her, and when she looked over her shoulder, her mother was handing her a tissue. Ginger stood up suddenly, pushing back her chair with a screech. "I don't agree with this arrangement."

The silence that followed was instant and sharp. She hadn't been granted permission to rise, let alone speak.

Pepper looked at her with both admiration and dread, waiting for Dill's fury to land.

"It's not your decision, Ginger," he said coldly. "It's already been finalized." He glanced only briefly in Ginger's direction before returning his sharp gaze to Pepper. "We leave in the morning. Go help your mother pack your things.'"

Pepper felt strangely numb. Not hurt. Not angry. Not human.

Truthfully, part of her was curious—maybe even excited. She knew she wasn't ready. Her late-night searches proved that. Math, reading, history? All foreign languages. But maybe… just maybe, this was her chance to meet someone new. To discover who she could be *outside* this strange, fragrant prison. Maybe she would become richer than November Bean. Marry someone handsome. Be in the newspaper.

But then she thought of Ginger. Left here. Alone.

"I can wait," Pepper said quietly. "I'll go when Ginger can come with me."

Dill smiled and crossed his arms like a man

without enemies. "Don't upset me or you'll leave tonight."

"Pop-up, you always say we have to live frugally," Ginger began. "Isn't school expensive?"

At least the kid was trying.

"You're both old enough to understand now. This nursery isn't entirely self-sufficient. For years, Sage and I worked on a product that would revolutionize the way we see greenhouses. St. Slackjaw's School for the Mildly Gifted agreed to test its efficacy for us."

Pepper's mind was reeling. How could they do something like this without ever mentioning a word? "Is this why we have to do schoolwork in the middle of the night, Pop-up? So you and Sage can work without worrying that we'll interrupt you?"

He nodded. "I'm proud to say that after years of tweaking, Dill's Moonroot is near perfection. The teachers reported less cursing in the breakroom, and staff absences due to 'personal matters' dropped to almost zero."

Pepper blinked. "You've... been planning to get rid of me? Without saying a word?"

She looked from her father to her mother, searching for some trace of regret. But they stared back at her, passive and unreadable.

"It troubles me that you would openly defy me," Dill said, shaking his head like a disappointed coach. "If you'd simply come to me and asked about your siblings, I would have told you what little I know. They and their mother played a very small role in my life. When the Fallen Branch Cult disbanded, their mother took them and disappeared. Now that they're adults, they've made no effort to contact me. Or you. They aren't worthy of our time."

Pepper's face burned. Her fingers gripped the edge of the table.

"Maybe they don't know about us," she whispered. "Did you ever think of that?"

"I suspect their mother poisoned their minds with mistruths. If you were to meet them now, they'd be bitter. Dangerous, even. You wouldn't be safe. The fact that you're openly defiant is proof that these miscreants are purveyors of evil. Don't give them one more thought."

But she *had* thought about it. Every night. Every time she read another glowing article about Chester Flushwater Bean—the "Toilet Paper King," standing proudly beside his wife, November. Pepper saw it. The shared frizzy curls, the same mischievous bend in their smiles. Her sister wore bright colors and a sky-high bun. Her brother was the mayor now, entering his second term. With his slicked-back black hair and square jawline he must've gotten from his mother's side, he grew more handsome every time Pepper saw a picture. His wife posted photos of their two children—laughing, loved, *real.*

Later, after their parents left them alone, Pepper took Ginger's hands in hers.

"Don't leave me, Pepper!" Ginger pleaded as the tears cascaded down her angelic face.

"I promise I'll find a way, Gingie." Pepper's words didn't match the feeling of despair on her inside. "I'll have more freedom once I'm gone. I'll contact Nochturn and November, and then we'll all come and sneak you out. The four of us will live our happily ever after."

5

Sing a Song of Slackjaw

Pepper's years at the St. Slackjaw Preparatory School for the Mildly Gifted were mostly happy. She learned how to behave in social settings, how to politely show interest in the endless sports stories of her boyfriends and how to avoid detection when consuming alcohol.

Dill refused to allow her to come home for school holidays and summer break. Pepper wracked her brain, trying to remember when she'd committed a grievance so severe as to deserve this treatment.

Every week she wrote letters to Ginger. There was no indication that Ginger received them, as Pepper's mailbox remained empty for her entire tenure.

Instead of focusing on her loneliness, she began obsessing over images of her wealthy sister. Her jealousy became something darker. She hated this sister who'd escaped Dill's punishments and seemingly lived without boundaries.

Amidst her loneliness, she saw a man in a crushed velvet-suit coming in and out of Headmaster Hollowhead's office. She knew him as the seed supplier for their greenhouse. He always brought crisp dollar bills for she and Ginger when they were younger. It had been years since she'd seen him now that she thought about it. "Mr. Gumb?" she called when she saw him the first time. It felt good to finally see a familiar face.

"Mr. Gumb?" she called again, as he continued walking down the long, shiny hall. "It's me, Pepper Plantz!"

He paused, turned, and tipped his hat to her. That same scene replayed itself many more times during her stay. Pepper never said a word to anyone, choosing instead to believe that her father sent him as a bridge between Dill and his wayward daughter. Mr. Gumb spoke with Headmaster Hollowhead about her behavior and grades. Satisfied, he left without saying a word, as was dictated by Dill. That's how it worked in her mind.

Once, Mr. Gumb paused at the trash can, crumpling a paper before disposing of it. After the heavy sound of his feet was gone, Pepper ran over to retrieve it and found a flyer for the opening of a karaoke club.

🎤 *Pitch, Please Productions* presents…

Karaoke: For Warblers, Warblers-at-Heart, and Shower Divas Alike!

Where every note counts (but we won't hold it against you if it doesn't).

Coming soon to Portland—bring your pipes, not your pride.

Free drinks for all opening night!

Mr. Gumb… liked *karaoke?* Pepper had only just learned what that meant when the boys basketball team hosted a karaoke night for the school. Musical Magical Mushrooms was only one semester, and the songs were all of Dill's choosing and accompanied by mushroom tastings that left her with a horrid headache. Pepper knew nothing about popular songs, so she sat in the back and admired those who sang their hearts out no matter if they could carry a tune.

WILMA JABSWORTH, granddaughter of the heir to the Jabsworth Punching Bag fortune, had attended St. Slackjaw since kindergarten. Wilma's family found out right away that she wasn't going to be the family genius (that role was reserved for the twin boys—Boxer and Bounce), when she was caught eating tea bags and have to have her stomach pumped. Twice. Her parents sent her off to boarding school to prevent any further embarrassment. She was very plain looking, with long, straight black hair and bangs cut too short. She always wore two green barrettes close to her scalp. Poor Wilma had a pronounced large nose which curved unnaturally at the end. Her face was in a permanent state of angry zombie, and her long, thin arms and legs made her appear frightening to new students.

But not to Pepper.

She'd seen so little of the world that Wilma's odd look and the way she salted everything until it formed a thick thrilled the food novice. Pepper felt a kinship with another girl who had been kicked out of her home.

Though Wilma had no future in punching bags, she did have an unrecognized talent as a hacker.

Wilma routinely broke into the school's instructor-only website and changed grades. Not hers, because despite her family's opinion, she was a straight-A student who never had to study for tests. Instead she found kids who were trying hard but just not making the cut. Those straight-B students. She gave them As for a semester grade.

The bevy of beautiful but evil students found themselves with surprise Ds or Fs. Wilma locked the site so that their teachers couldn't see the grade they'd posted. Once the hullabaloo died down, Wilma changed the grades back, temporarily, and unlocked the site.

“I’d like to help you, Pepper. I can tell you’re a real peach,” Wilma said as she gulped down her second egg salad sandwich.

Pepper nodded. She noticed others giggling when Wilma burped so loud everyone within a three-table radius jumped. It didn’t bother Pepper any, given that during one of Dill’s middle-of-the-night lessons he belched for ten minutes straight, trying to get them to break. Ginger was first, but because she was adored by her parents, the punishment was minimal.

“You’ll help me find my brother and sister?” Pepper asked, her voice rising. “My sister seems to have dropped off the face of the earth. She looks just like me, you know.”

Wilma cocked her head to the side, examining Pepper with curiosity. Her sudden head movement caused egg salad to fling across the table. With a mayonnaise covered hand, she grabbed Pepper’s phone and searched through her photos. “Ohh. I see what you mean. Same hair, same jawline. Kind of weird looking, just like you. Have you considered hiring a private detective? I could help. My mother sends me so much money every month that I've stashed it under my bed. Bags and bags."

Pepper stared at her in disbelief.

"You don’t think I'm telling the truth?" Wilma stood, allowing a cascade of breadcrumbs to tumble to the ground. She picked up her tray and turned to face the jeering students. She produced the loudest, juiciest belch yet. Even Dill would have been impressed.

"Dump your tray and follow me. We're going to find the best detective that money can buy. But first, you're going to do something for me."

6

That's What Friends Are For

Two weeks. That's how long she followed Wilma like a lost puppy, picking up trash she purposely dropped, watching her favorite cheesy black-and-white horror films, and cutting her meat. Wilma felt how much Pepper wanted information, and she was going to milk it for every last drop.

"What do I have to do?"

Pepper dreaded whatever sinister plot Wilma had in mind. She got chills every time they were together, and something in her stomach didn't feel right. Of course poor Wilma had a right to feel upset, ignored, unloved. Did Pepper have to be the one to fill that bottomless hole?

On top of that, Pepper's resentment of her sister's perfect life grew. November didn't have to follow someone around, cleaning up after them.

Wilma crossed her arms. "Tired of being my friend already?" she asked without emotion. "I pegged you for at least a month of coziness. Guess I was wrong."

Something about that dig made Pepper feel even worse. "No, I—I've just been wondering what you want me to do. If it's something that requires skill, I need to—"

A forced laugh and a hard squeeze of Pepper's arm felt far too intimate. "I was just joshin' ya, kid." Wilma turned and sat on her spider-printed bedspread. She patted the space beside her. "Sit," she instructed.

After two weeks of doing everything Wilma said, Pepper almost declined. Almost.

"Okay. So you know how Brittany Snobwin is awful to everyone?"

Pepper nodded, though she wasn't entirely sure who this girl was. "Yeah. I heard she hit some poor kid in the back of the head." Improvisation at its best.

Wilma's glare told Pepper she saw right through her.

"Anyway. I found out that she has been forcing the poor kids to do her homework for money. If they don't agree, the kids have to stay here on the weekends. No movies or candy in town."

Neither Pepper nor Wilma went into town for movies. Pepper had no money, and Wilma had no interest in being around other humans.

"What can we do?"

"Brittany applied to enter Bigbuks Finishing School. I'm sure you've heard of it."

Pepper nodded.

"I want you to slip a series of letters into her mailbox. It will have to be done at night, while no one is watching and the cameras are off."

"What do these letters say?"

Wilma slid a drawer open without leaving the bed. She pulled out a letter, printed on thick paper that Pepper had never seen at their school. At the top was a stylish gold-and-pink letterhead that read, "Bigbuks Finishing School." And underneath, "We turn Preening Teens into Darling Debutants."

Pepper swallowed hard. "Why do I have to do this? You seem to know everything about the mailroom. And how would I even get in her box? I don't have a key."

Wilma opened another drawer in her opulent dresser and pulled out a large wooden box with dozens of small dividers. Inside each divided space was a room number and a mailbox number. One key only was needed for both. "Let's see…ah. Here it is. Number 112." She held the key in thc air like it was a thing of beauty.

Pepper didn't dare ask how Wilma had acquired these. With each passing day, Pepper felt more that Wilma's pain became evil that consumed her. The sooner Pepper was able to escape her grasp, the better. "What if I just tell you to forget about the information? I can find it myself."

Wilma grabbed her arm and squeezed. Hard.

"Ouch! Let go of me!" Pepper shook free and stood. "I'm done."

"Pity. I've found all sorts of interesting information about your family. They aren't as innocent as you led me to believe."

Wilma's smirk made Pepper's blood run cold. "How many letters?"

"Three. One telling her the essay she submitted was received and being considered. It also tells her she is dressed inappropriately in her submission photo. She has to start wearing mismatched earrings and bright yellow eye shadow to prove she's willing to go the extra mile." Wilma paused to giggle, or maybe it was more of a cackle. "The next one says her grades arrived and its clear she hasn't been creative enough. In order to gain entrance to finishing school, she has to re-write history. They'll expect proof."

Wilma gazed at Pepper, perhaps expecting praise. Instead, Pepper looked away.

"And the third ," she continued, "is her rejection letter. Yummy."

When the silence built an icy wall between them, Wilma said, "you know, I don't HAVE to research your brother and sister. They've probably got pretty swell lives without you, right?"

Pepper took the key and the first letter and stormed out. After giving herself time to cool off, she opened the envelope. Wilma's logo was all wrong. It needed to look professional, not like a kid with markers for the first time.

She spent most of the night studying the actual logo before creating her own. Luckily, there was a printer on her floor that wasn't in use at 3 a.m. Finally, Dills odd hours of study paid off!

She deposited the letters every four days, as per Wilma's instructions. Evidence Brittany read the first letter was swift. Everyone stared as she walked down the hallways with a thick frosting of yellow above each eye. Her socks were expensive, but different colors.

The effect was immediate.

Every girl with aspirations to popular copied the look. Those without the means to purchase expensive makeup stole mustard from the cafeteria and use it instead. Sixteen girls ended up in the infirmary with eye infections. Wilma made a point of walking by the nurse's office every day, proud of her accomplishment.

The following week, Pepper was taking the garbage out for Miss Quizzman when she encountered Brittany and Dr. Thinkback, the history teacher, standing in the hall. "Ms. Snobwin, I've come to expect exemplary work from you. Replacing 'we' with a random bodily function in your study of the Declaration of Independence is beneath you."

Pepper averted her gaze and scurried down the hall, her cheeks burning with embarrassment.

Once the final letter was received, Pepper finally discovered who Brittany Snobwin was. A tall blonde wearing a microscopic skirt and tall clogs wailed for two days. She roamed the echoey halls of the school sobbing, "How could they reject me? I'm perfect!"

While Pepper could understand Wilma's need to avenge the underdog, she still felt guilty. It gnawed at her day and night, and it became virtually impossible to think of anything else. She began sleeping in class and forgetting homework.

"Pepper, dear," Ms. Bummer, the Practical Problems teacher whispered.

Pepper lifted her head and looked around. She was the only one left in the room.

Wilma kept hedging. Over the next two weeks, she slipped cryptic notes under Pepper's dorm door like she was feeding a raccoon in the woods. Each scrap of paper offered the tiniest breadcrumb:

"Your sister is exactly twenty years older than you."

"Your brother has dark brown hair and three children."

"He had a pet goat named Buster."

But nothing more. No last names. No contact info. No explanations.

Pepper thought she'd earned Wilma's trust—or at least her sense of fun. But just when she began to believe the clues might lead to something real, love and adoration turned to icy dread.

A harsh knock rattled the dorm door.

"Come with me, Miss Plantz," snapped the tight-lipped secretary to the administrator, her words clipped like pruning shears.

They were waiting for her in the headmaster's office: Sage staring at her hands, and Dill as impassive as granite.

This couldn't be good.

The air in the room felt colder than usual. Clinical. Even so, Pepper wanted to hold them both in her arms and never let go.

She bent over to hug her mother, whose lines around her eyes had become craters and her once-rich brunette head was now half gray. When she reached her mother's head, she felt a hand, familiar for its use of punishment, push her away.

"Tell me," Sage began, her voice barely above a whisper, "how did you discover it was our daughter again?"

It was impossible to tell whether her mother was confused, ashamed, or simply rehearsing lines she'd said a thousand times in her head.

Headmaster Hollowhead jabbed a long, pointed fingernail toward the ceiling. "We have cameras in all public spaces. You signed a form acknowledging that fact during your student orientation. Perhaps you remember?"

Pepper's face flushed. Of course she hadn't remembered. She'd been too numb from being dumped here without warning or affection to pay attention during the tour.

"I thought they were turned off at night?"

The adults in the room gasped at her admission.

"Usually we turn off the cameras in the office and mail room, that's true." Headmaster Hollowhead cleared his throat and jostled in his chair. "But someone turned them back on every four nights for two weeks."

Wilma. She set her up. People were just pawns to that nut.

"Miss Snobwin discovered the letter almost immediately. Suspicious phrasing, she said. Strange formatting. And then—confirmation via surveillance."

Pepper struggled to keep a straight face. Sixteen cases of pink eye said differently.

The headmaster slid the letter across the desk toward Sage.

Before her mother could take it, Dill snatched it up and unfolded it quickly. His eyes scanned the page, and for a moment the room seemed to deflate, the air disappearing until Pepper wasn't sure it was worth breathing anymore.

"*You* made this?" Dill asked with an insulting amount of surprise. "When did you learn to design logos?"

It wasn't the response she expected. If anything, it bordered on... impressed?

"I found it online," she lied. "I just copied what I saw—"

"Disgraceful," Dill cut in. He tossed the letter

across the desk and folded his arms and leaned back, his trademark punishment stance. "This proves I was right to limit your internet access."

Headmaster Hollowhead cleared his throat. "You understand then, Mr. Plantz, why our options are... limited."

Pepper's stomach turned.

"When she left the letter in Miss Snobwin's mailbox, she clearly intended to deceive."

"I didn't mean to hurt anyone," Pepper mumbled.

The silence that followed told her it didn't matter.

Headmaster Hollowhead let the moment stretch until her heart beat like a kettle drum in her ears.

"You'll need to have her items cleared from her room by the end of the day tomorrow. We'll discuss additional consequences later."

Dill stood as though the words had released a trapdoor beneath his chair. "I'll go pack her things now. We'll be out in an hour."

He gave Pepper's shoulder a sharp squeeze—not comforting, just enough to assert control.

Headmaster Hollowhead raised a hand. "I'd like a moment alone with Miss Plantz. We conduct exit interviews with departing students to improve our... methods."

Dill nodded. Too quickly. "Of course. Thank you for your patience. My daughter may not appreciate this school, but I do."

He turned to Sage. “Come.”

For the first time since they’d arrived, Sage caught Pepper’s eye. There was something in her expression—fear maybe? *Regret?*

It made Pepper ache. More than anything, she wanted her mother to hug her. To smooth her hair and ask in that gentle, gardening-lesson voice: *“What did you learn, my sprout?”*

But there would be no hug today. No forgiveness. Only retreat.

As the door clicked shut, Pepper stared down at her pink sneakers and whispered, “I’m sorry.” It hurt being dumped here, but it hurt just as bad being thrown away again.

“Shh,” said the headmaster. “I know you’re a good kid.”

His voice shifted upward, almost cheerful. “You've never been a troublemaker. However, my instructors tell me you’ve been spending time with Wilma.”

Pepper hesitated, then nodded. “She’s... helped me.”

“Wilma’s parents are generous donors,” he said. “So you’ll understand when I say, in any other situation, she’d be expelled. She’s hacked our gradebook six times in three years.”

Pepper’s jaw dropped.

“She didn’t change Brittany’s grades?” she asked, incredulous.

“She framed you for sport.” His tone remained

even. "Wilma doesn't go home for breaks. This place *is* her life. And like many lonely people, she enjoys making others just as miserable as she is."

Pepper's chest tightened.

"I'm sorry," she said. "Will you tell Brittany the truth?"

He gave a slow nod. "Of course. But that's not your concern. What *is* your concern is what happens next."

She braced herself. Surely, she was going home to the greenhouse. To Sage's endless rows of lavender and Dill's punishment meditations. A future of carrot cookies and controlled breathing.

"I'm going home," she said aloud, hearing the sadness in her own voice. "To run the greenhouse."

"No," Hollowhead said gently. "Your father made it clear—he's not taking you back. He's already enrolled you in the Blackwell School for the Hopeless."

Pepper gasped.

"That's a reformatory," she said. "With—criminals."

"Yes," the headmaster said. "But I convinced him to give my plan a shot."

She blinked, unsure whether to feel grateful or terrified. "What plan?"

"My sister contacted me last week. She's looking for an apprentice to help with greenhouse management for Grady's Gardening Supplies. You know them?"

"Do I!" Pepper's eyes lit up. "We used to order all our seeds from them!"

"She wants to mentor someone who understands plants and has potential. You fit the bill."

Tears welled in Pepper's eyes. It was too good to be true.

"But my father—he'll never agree."

"Leave your father to me," Headmaster Hollowhead said, smiling for the first time. "He and I go way back."

7

A Hollow Goodbye

Dill insisted he should drop Pepper off no matter how much Headmaster Hollowhead pleaded with him. Pepper assumed it was because Dill hated handing over control. She shook as she got in the back seat of the silver sedan. Glancing at St. Slackjaw one last time, she noticed Wilma standing in the floor-to-ceiling windows of the library. Pepper waved. Wilma smirked as though she was happy to see Pepper go.

The drive to Maribel's Greens and Teas had taken longer than Pepper expected. It wasn't just the twisting back roads or the endless miles of fence-posted fields—it was the silence in the car. Her father didn't speak once. Not when they stopped for gas. Not when she offered him half her sandwich. Not even when they passed a billboard with Maribel's face on it, advertising "Herbs in Harmony. Become the best you."

He pulled up to the edge of a long gravel driveway and killed the engine. "They're expecting you," he muttered.

"Father, I—"

Dill raised a rough hand, weathered by too much time digging in the soil. "I don't want to hear it. You're a disappointment to both your mother and me. The next time I see you, I expect a polished professional who is ready to do as she is told."

That was it. No hug. No goodbye. No parting wisdom.

The car rolled away before she'd even reached the porch.

It was for the best, she reasoned. An even cut of a branch was the best way to let it heal. And she was just that branch.

Maribel's home wasn't what she expected. The house was rambling, old, and partially overrun by climbing ivy and trumpet vines that clung like gossip. Windchimes tinkled from every corner, some metal, some made of bones—or at least they *looked* like bones. Spooky didn't fit Headmaster Hollowhead's persona. He kept a rotation of Pez dispensers on the shelves around his office, telling the students during morning wrap about them. "The newer the better!" he'd say.

A carved wooden sign above Maribel's porch read:

"WE GROW MORE THAN PLANTS."

Pepper hesitated. Was that a slogan or a warning?

Before she could knock, the door creaked open.

A woman stood silhouetted in the dim hallway, a watering can in one hand and a mechanical parrot on her shoulder.

"You're late," the woman said.

Pepper blinked. "It's 3:59."

The woman narrowed her eyes. "Then you're *exactly* on time. Come in."

She had the kind of presence that made people lower their voices instinctively, as though they'd just stepped into a library or a cathedral—or both. She stood just under six feet tall, with a posture so erect it made your back hurt to look at her. Her hair was a perfectly controlled cascade of ash-blonde waves, gathered at the nape of her neck in a style that hadn't changed since 1983 and probably never would. Her eyes, pale gray and flecked with glacial blue, were identical to her brother the headmaster—sharp as sleet and twice as unforgiving.

Like her brother, she had a round face, a muscular body, and a mouth that always seemed halfway through a disappointed sentence. Her thin eyebrows arched unnaturally, giving her a look of perpetual suspicion or bemusement. While her brother wore his age like a uniform, Maribel had weaponized it; not a wrinkle out of place, not a hair left to whimsy. Her wardrobe wasn't anything like the casual jeans and t-shirts worn in Dill Plantz' greenhouse. Strictly monochrome—a charcoal skirt, dove-gray blouse—all cinched and buttoned with military precision.

And yet there was something elegant in her severity. A quiet strength in her restraint. You wouldn't call her beautiful—not unless you had a thing for cryptic headmistresses or operatic villains—but you couldn't deny she commanded a room the second she stepped in.

She stepped aside. Pepper moved cautiously into the house, nearly tripping over a large, suspiciously mobile pile of moss. On the wall hung a portrait of three blond children. The oldest, a girl, was smiling. The younger boy and girl were decidedly unhappy.

"Are you Mrs. Chafe?" Pepper asked.

"No one calls me that anymore," she said, her voice as crisp as her suit. "Around here, I'm Maribel. That picture you're staring at was taken when I was five, brother six and my sister, Mystic was twelve. That's the last time you'll hear me utter her name, so don't ask, understand?"

Pepper nodded solemnly.

"Now let's get something straight—this isn't your average apprenticeship. You'll learn soil pH, heirloom crossbreeding, and how to make a compost pile sing 'Moon River' if you do it right. But that's not *all* we grow."

Pepper frowned. "What else do you—"

"In time," Maribel said, glaring at her new charge. "We're going to change the future. Through further testing, our serum will be refined until it's..." Maribel's voice trailed off.

"Until it's what?"

"Something for a different conversation. Our boss likes to stay anonymous, but once in a while, he and his entourage will show up. That's why you'll need to be on your best behavior. Always."

Did Maribel know? Of course she did.

Behind her, a curtain swayed despite no breeze.

"My brother and the rest have high expectations, young lady."

Pepper glanced up quickly. "Who are 'the rest?'"

"People you'll meet when the time is right." The corners of Maribel's mouth lifted slightly into what could have been a smile. Or indigestion. "You have lots of homework for tomorrow." But first let's see if you're worthy of the dirt you're standing on."

Pepper pushed herself upright and took the brochure Maribel offered. The cover showed a bright-eyed young woman holding a seed packet: *Seeds for a Brighter Tomorrow.* The girl looked like she had slept eight perfect hours and woke to purpose.

"Marketing?" Pepper asked. "I thought this was greenhouse management."

"It is," Maribel said, gliding to the tiny desk. "Different soil, same growth. We cultivate markets, not marigolds." She drew a ladder on Pepper's notepad with a thin black pen. "Rung one: attention. Rung two: trust. Rung three: purchase. Rung four: loyalty. Your story is the seed we plant to climb."

Pepper nodded, but her eyes flicked to the courtyard below. Two strangers stood near the back door—matching leather jackets, sunglasses in the predawn gloom. Watching, but pretending not to.

Maribel followed her gaze. "Ignore them," she said lightly. "Daylight marketing partners. They're here to observe."

"Daylight?" Pepper asked.

"A polite word for distribution," Maribel said, voice too even. She flipped the brochure, revealing bright mockups—seed packets with poetic names: *Renewal Blend*, *Second Chance*, *Encore*. When Pepper reached for one, the desk drawer slid an inch. Inside, nestled in velvet like jewels, lay six glass vials filled with a faintly glowing green liquid.

Pepper's breath caught. The light seemed to throb.

Maribel snapped the drawer shut and set both palms on it. "Distributor samples," she said. "Not for handling."

"What's in them?"

"Essence," Maribel said with the kind of smoothness that meant the conversation was over. "The formula isn't our job. The story is."

She kept the lesson brisk. Pepper wrote slogans in tight, careful script while the sky went from cobalt to gray. *Grow Wonder. Plant Magic. Seeds for Every Soul.* Good copy, Maribel said, nodding.

Clean. Aspirational. Pepper felt a small spark of pride, then the quick, guilty thought that she was enjoying something she didn't fully understand.

By mid-morning, the strangers came upstairs.

They didn't knock. The taller one moved like a metronome, precise; the shorter one had a smile that didn't touch her eyes.

"This is Nelson," Maribel said, tone tightening by a millimeter. "And Sylvia. They're here to guide digital growth. They're connected to the network."

Nelson shook Pepper's hand. Warm grip. Held a breath too long. He slid a thin booklet into her palm: *Secrets of Viral Growth*. "Engagement drives belief," he said. "Once people believe in you, they'll buy anything. Keep the packaging sealed. No leaks. Ever."

His eyes didn't blink enough. Something about him seemed familiar, but Pepper couldn't place him.

Sylvia leaned in, scent of spearmint and something metallic. "Green Thumb says you have potential," she said. "You've got the look. The story. People trust you without effort. That's… useful."

"Who's Green Thumb?" Pepper asked.

"Supply chain oversight," Nelson said, as if that answered nothing and everything.

Pepper's head buzzed. Her story. Her voice. It should have felt flattering; instead it felt like a pair of hands measuring her shoulders.

Maribel moved briskly to the tray of mock seed packets. "We'll demonstrate at Teatimefest this weekend," she said. "Pepper will speak. Nelson will capture. Sylvia will coordinate."

Nelson nodded once. "We'll also need a few short videos. Close-up, eye contact, thirty seconds each. 'New beginnings' theme."

It was still so hard to believe they had faith in this clumsy girl who'd been kicked out of the boarding school with the lowest qualifications of any in the country. "Why me?"

"Because people look at a wide-eyed homely child such as yourself and they see their own vulnerabilities," Sylvia said. "They give you permission to sell them hope."

"Sylvia, you'll be in charge of her script. I'll expect you back in..." Maribel brought a shiny gold watch up to her face. "Two hours. That should give you sufficient time to craft something."

Sylvia nodded, and the duo left without so much as a goodbye. The air felt a degree colder.

Pepper turned back to her desk and found a new mockup on the top of the stack. A hot-pink packet stamped with a word in laser-cut script: *Moonbeam Enterprises*. It glittered unnaturally, the edges too sharp for paper. She lifted it by the corner. A dusting of shimmer fell to the floor and caught in the light.

"Careful," Maribel said, snatching it from her. "Old promo. The glitter gets everywhere."

Pepper crouched and brushed the floor with her fingers. The shimmer clung like static. "Why would you use a kid's grade school art project product instead of something more...professional?"

"We're selling hope in every form, Pepper," Maribel called from another room. "Glitter, gold dust, fairy droppings, call it what you want. It means hope for things to come."

A cough broke the air. Harsh. Tearing.

Pepper spun. Maribel stood in the doorway of her office, one hand braced on the jamb, the other pressed to her mouth. On the desk behind her, a vial lay tipped, a small emerald puddle spreading in a halo. The smell hit—sweet and clean like cucumber, edged with something biting that made Pepper's eyes water.

She darted forward. "Let me—"

"No." Maribel's voice cracked. She snapped on thin gloves, grabbed a folded cloth, and blotted the spill with practiced motions. "Only for weeds," she said breathlessly when Pepper froze. "It's caustic to unwanted growth. That's why we package carefully."

Pepper stared. The cloth darkened, then bleached faintly. The place where the puddle had been looked... scoured. As if the desk had been scraped of a layer of itself.

On the floor near Maribel's heel, a vial of hot-pink glitter labeled *Moonbeam Enterprises* winked again. Pepper reached. Maribel stepped on it and ground it to dust.

"Enough samples for one morning," Maribel

said, cheerful voice restored by force. "Go get lunch. Clear your head. Your afternoon will be full."

Pepper went, only because leaving felt like obeying and staying felt like drowning in information she had no way to absorb.

On the stairs she passed Nelson, phone to his ear. "—Yes, sir. You can count on us," he said, low. "Yes, voice-forward. I don't anticipate a problem. Innocence will play in our favor."

Pepper kept moving. A second later, Sylvia appeared at the bottom of the steps with a to-go bag and that same too bright smile. "Turkey on wheat? We thought you might have skipped food." She pressed the bag into Pepper's hands. "Workshop tomorrow. Seven a.m. Bring a plain blouse, no logos. We're filming in natural light."

"How did you know I—"

"Your intake form," Sylvia said, as if Pepper had signed something she couldn't remember. "Also, we pay attention. It's our job to take care of you." Her eyes flicked briefly toward Nelson. "And to use you well."

Pepper's stomach tightened, the sandwich suddenly heavy. "Use me?"

"Your voice," Sylvia said, drawing the words out like silk. "Don't overthink."

They left her on the landing with the bag in her hands and a small, hard knot under her sternum.

The afternoon slid by in useful tasks that

pretended to be neutral. Pepper wrote copy, scheduled posts, organized sample packets into "story stacks." Maribel praised her for being efficient, disciplined, precise. Nelson set up lights in the corridor and stood Pepper in the wash of a window, coaching in a patient baritone. He showed Pepper a prompter which displayed a speech that Sylvia somehow had time to write over lunch.

"Say it like you're saying it to one person," he instructed. "Look into the lens and give the lens permission to believe you."

Pepper swallowed hard. "New beginnings are messy," she began. "They don't look like the brochure. They look like dirt under your nails. But you plant anyway. And then you wait."

The prompter stopped. Pepper looked up, waiting for Nelson's direction. He was handsome, in the same way as the gangsters from the 1940s black-and-white movies she and Ginger watched. Dangerous. Dangerously gorgeous.

"Good," Nelson said. "Again, slower."

They did ten takes. Twice he moved in close, gently removing hair from her face. He smelled good. Not like Dill Plantz, who smelled like soil and weed poison, but a scent that reminded her of the tall trees in Piney Falls, Oregon. The family's one and only vacation.

Between takes, Sylvia drifted in and out, counting beats, sliding Pepper small notes with phrases like *hold the eye contact* and *make the smile land on the last word.* She asked questions that sounded like compliments.

"Where did you go to school?"

"Do you have family nearby?"

"Have you ever done public speaking?"

"Would you wear a brand color if we asked?"

"Would you dye your hair if we asked?"

Pepper laughed at that last one, then stopped when Sylvia didn't.

"Don't worry," Nelson soothed. "Green Thumb won't change your hair. He likes the whole 'approachable genius' thing."

"Green Thumb is watching these?" Pepper asked, marveling at her sudden fame.

Sylvia's smile softened. "Green Thumb watches everything."

At five, Maribel called it. "Enough. Pepper, draft five more thirty-second scripts tonight. Sincere. Close to the bone. We'll pick the best tomorrow." She squeezed Pepper's arm, gentle, almost motherly. Then her phone buzzed and she slipped into her office, voice dropping. "Room seventeen, ten o'clock. Yes, I'll bring them."

Pepper stood very still until the door clicked shut. Then she exhaled and realized she'd been holding her breath for minutes.

Later, the two women sat in silence as they consumed a rich vegetable soup and homemade bread. Pepper wanted to ask about the message but couldn't find the words. Maribel pressed a lavender tea latte into Pepper's hand and said she needed to step out "for a short compliance meeting." Her heels clicked down the stairs, unhurried. All of these secrets were getting to Pepper. What kind of spy movie had she stepped in?

Pepper waited thirty seconds, then took the back staircase, silent on stocking feet, and eased into the alley.

She kept two buildings between herself and her host. Maribel cut across the dark lot of Muchless Community College, a place the city had promised to renovate eight budgets ago. One window glowed on the second floor. Room seventeen.

Pepper scaled the outside stairs, breathed shallow, and flattened herself against the brick. Voices slipped through the cracked pane—an old radiator hiss, then a man's low murmur. She recognized it: Mr. Gumb of all people. What was he doing here? Maribel, still polished, let her eyes dart sharp as knives. She was on alert for…*who, exactly*? Mr. Gumb stood before her, wearing his trademark velvet suit, and gripped Maribel's elbow firmly. They both glanced around nervously before exchanging passionate kisses.

Pepper's hand flew up to her mouth. It seemed so out of character for Mr. Gumb, a man who loved children but claimed he never wanted to get married and deal with a wife. He never seemed to give Sage attention, leading Pepper to believe that was true. She wanted to feel happy for them both. But something about it was…wrong.

"Stick to the schedule," Mr. Gumb began. "Green Thumb wants the launch synchronized. The Atlanta club opens Saturday. You hire someone to place the *Renewal Blend* in the duct work, as per orders. At the same time, we'll be testing in Phoenix. Genius, really. Anybody else have thoughts?"

"Pepper isn't ready," Maribel said, as she passed small bags around the group. "She needs boundaries. She's… soft."

"Soft sells," Gumb insisted. Paper rustled. "Never thought of you as cracking easily."

"She's not a prop."

A pause. Then, "Everything's a prop."

Pepper pressed her forehead to the cool glass. The word *prop* burned.

"Fine," Maribel said quietly. "But I choose the words that go in her mouth."

"Green Thumb chooses the words," Gumb reminded her. "You forget who pays you. Well."

"If she doesn't work out, we could always use her as a test subject. No one would miss her."

Nelson's words stung. She knew he was right though. Her father was relieved to be rid of her. Sage didn't care. And Ginger was too little to help.

Silence. Then a sound like an envelope passing from one hand to another.

Pepper backed away, pulse loud in her ears, feet

finding the steps without looking. She made it home before Maribel, heart punching her ribs, and stood in the kitchen pretending to read analytics until the key turned.

Maribel walked in alone. Her face was smooth, her mouth careful. "Late night," she said. "Don't wait up next time."

Pepper nodded, throat too tight to answer.

She went to her room and closed the door. There, on the rug, lay a small hot-pink shard she hadn't noticed before. Laser-cut script: *Renew*. It caught the lamplight and threw it in a hundred directions.

She picked it up and the glitter dusted her fingers. It wouldn't rub off. She tried water. It smeared and shimmered.

A soft shift of air moved behind her.

Pepper turned. A woman stood in the doorway, half shadowed by the mid-century shelving. Late thirties, hair pulled back tight, eyes tracking like a cat's.

"Who are you?" Pepper whispered.

"Not who," the woman said. "What." She stepped forward and pressed a plain white envelope into Pepper's hand. No logo. No return. "They're not teaching you. They're tailoring you."

Pepper glanced at the hall. "Tailoring me for what?"

"To speak," the woman said. "To front. To launder belief." She touched Pepper's forearm, quick, almost kind. “Your story is the solvent. Stop letting them pour it over poison. I can help.”

A knock rattled the front door. The woman moved—not fast, exactly, but with an efficiency that made Pepper blink—and vanished behind the shelves.

“Pepper?” Maribel called. “Who are you talking to?”

Pepper slid the envelope under a notebook and opened the door. “Nobody.”

Maribel’s gaze traveled the room, landed on Pepper’s glittered fingertips, then on the empty patch of corkboard where *Grow Wonder* had hung. “Tomorrow’s big,” she said softly. “Get some sleep.”

Pepper nodded. Maribel withdrew. The house went quiet except for the faint hum of the espresso machine cycling itself clean.

Pepper sat on the edge of the bed and opened the envelope. Inside was a printing of one of her videos from the afternoon, still frames tiled in rows. In the margin, a neat hand had written, *Count the cuts*. Below that, *Count the lies*.

She watched the frames in her head: the way Nelson had called “cut” before she finished a sentence, the way Sylvia had slid in a new line, the way her mouth had kept moving around words that weren’t hers.

She went to the sink and scrubbed her hands until the glitter lifted in pink flakes. When she returned to the bed, she pulled a scrap of paper from the nightstand and wrote four words in block letters. She folded it twice and tucked it under the pillow like a talisman.

The room felt smaller after that, as if the walls had leaned in to listen. She lay down fully dressed, shoes on, and stared at the crack of streetlight under the shade. She thought of the scoured patch on Maribel's desk. Of Nelson's patient baritone. Of Sylvia's inventory of her life, question by gentle question. Of Gumb's voice in the dark classroom, calling her a prop. And of Nelson saying no one would miss her. Of the woman who had come and gone like a warning.

Pepper closed her eyes and saw a seed packet—hot pink, glittering, the word *e* cut with a laser so sharp you could split a hair on it. The packet didn't hold seeds. It held a mirror. When she opened it, her own face looked back, smiling on command, promising the world something she could not name.

She slept in jagged pieces. Twice she awoke to the shape of a shadow at her door. Once she dreamed she was speaking into a camera lens so wide it could swallow her whole. November Bean watched from the side, judging.

At 5:12, gray light seeped into the room. Her phone pulsed with a new message.

From an unknown number:

Meet me on the corner of Whistler and Blossom in fifteen minutes. Don't be late.

She stared at the screen until the words blurred. Then she deleted the text and went to the window. The courtyard below was empty, but she knew Nelson and Sylvia would arrive by six.

She brewed coffee strong and bitter. She set her scripts in a neat stack and then deliberately shuffled them out of order. Feeling cocky, Pepper pulled the scrap from beneath her pillow and read the four words again, tasting each one like medicine.

Had they seen her last night?

Good, she thought. Let them.

She buttoned the plain white blouse and pinned her hair without product, without shine. No brand color. No borrowed glow. In the mirror, her face looked stark and serious, the face of someone stepping onto a narrow bridge.

When she opened her door, the hallway smelled faintly of cucumber and bleach. Somewhere below, the espresso machine hummed through its cycle, faithful as a heartbeat.

Pepper took the stairs without making a sound. There were more oddballs in Maribel's world than had lived at St. Slackjaw. Whoever was waiting was sure to be another piece in this confusing puzzle.

8

Branding, Bonds... and Betrayals

Her eyes and ears opened to the hum of Maribel's espresso machine. The second was the creak of hallway floor as a business card slid halfway beneath the threshold.

Pepper picked it up, reading the neat print:

Pepper Plantz. Junior Marketing Executive.

Her chest tightened. It should have made her proud. It felt official. Final. Like she'd been branded.

Had she been dreaming earlier this morning? The note telling her to meet five blocks away?

To her surprise, it was Joseph Friday, a handsome dock worker with curly brown hair and big blue eyes waiting in a beat-up Ford pickup to tell her she was in danger.

Pepper Plantz, there are people pulling your strings. You're not safe here.

How do you know that?

People talk. I was curious so I stayed late after my shift one night. The things I found…

Maribel thinks I have talent. I'm not going to mess up a chance to become a marketing executive because of someone I don't even know. Goodbye.

Whenever you're ready to leave, just text me. I'll pick you up, no questions asked.

She'd cursed herself for agreeing to meet a complete stranger. He could've killed her. Her mother gave them a week of "stranger danger" lessons. Apparently Pepper learned absolutely nothing.

By the time she reached the kitchen, Maribel was perched on a tall stool in front of her laptop, fingers clicking through charts with the confidence of a sea captain steering through storm fronts.

"Morning!" Maribel chirped, sliding a lavender latte toward her. "Engagement is up thirty-five percent since your demo. Viral lift like that? Bigtime agencies bark at your door all night."

In all her years working at Dill's Plantz, her father never complimented her once. She held her head high. Pepper sipped, the warmth easing her nerves. Still, she felt swallowed whole by Maribel's approval.

Then Maribel's phone buzzed. Pepper caught the flash across the screen:

Tonight. Room 17. Voice maters.

No name. No number. Just a directive.

Maribel's eyes flickered. "My coworkers are

always sending weird messages that mean nothing," she said too quickly, shutting her laptop.

That night, when Pepper begged off to "study materials alone," Maribel left in a brisk click of heels. It was too hard to resist. Pepper waited ten minutes, then slipped out into the lavender-dark night.

She followed at a cautious distance, heart hammering.

Maribel entered Muchless Community College. Its windows glowed, like it had been kept alive by ghosts of dead students.

Pepper crept to a cracked pane. Inside, four figures stood in a loose circle, their voices rising and falling:

The last person to enter took her breath away. After all these years of studying him, Pepper would recognize her brother anywhere. Nochturn was tall —taller than their father and much handsomer. He bore the hooked nose of the Plantz family and the same half-smile her sister Ginger used to charm her parents into one more helping of cheesy potatoes. But he had a suaveness about him, a movie star quality that couldn't be captured in still photos. Pepper's breath hitched. She wasn't meant to see this.

Through the broken glass, she caught words: *voice… metrics… control.* Mr. Gumb slipped Maribel an envelope. Nancy passed out flyers. Nochturn simply observed, smiling faintly.

Pepper squinted, trying to read the flyers and hear the conversation, but it was no use. She thought she should get home anyway. After sneaking out twice, Pepper didn't want to press her luck. She stumbled away, unsure of what she'd seen, but when she turned the corner, another woman was waiting—the woman she'd seen in her room the first night at Maribel's place.

"Who are you?" Pepper whispered.

"Not *who*," the woman said softly. "*What.*"

The woman pressed a small envelope into her palm.

Pepper's pulse jumped. "Why do you keep showing up? If you think I can change anything, you're wrong. I'm nobody."

"No one is nobody. Pepper Plantz has survived where others would fail. You have a voice and it is powerful. But they'll twist it to achieve their vicious deeds. Read this and then destroy it." She vanished into the evening with impossible speed.

Moments later, Maribel's heels clacked on the broken pavement, causing Pepper's throat to close as she stuffed the note in her pocket. "Pepper? What are you doing here?"

Pepper turned around with a fake smile plastered on her face.

She couldn't breathe. Behind Maribel stood Nochturn. The handsome older brother she'd dreamt about meeting since she was old enough to use the computer. He caught Pepper's gaze and smiled knowingly. *Does he recognize me? Does he know we are brother and sister?* She smiled back and waved, wishing she knew how to tell him. To hug him and feel safe in his arms.

"Who is this pretty young lady?"

His voice boomed loud and deep, and for a second, Pepper thought it was her father speaking.

Maribel gestured towards her without looking. "This is my apprentice, Pepper."

Nochturn stuck out his hand, and Pepper took it immediately, squeezing too hard.

"That's quite a grip you have there, Pepper!" Nochturn withdrew his hand and shook it, hopefully more for show.

Her cheeks burned with embarrassment. "Sorry." Her mind raced, trying to come up with some reason to stay in his company longer. "You like… licorice!"

He cocked his head to the side. "Now how would you know that, Miss Pepper?"

Maribel huffed, clearly annoyed with her charge. "Let's go, Pepper. You have a big day tomorrow."

Pepper paused. She wanted to wrap her arms around him. Tell him she'd been waiting her entire life to find him. Instead, she gave him another little wave, turned, and walked behind Maribel.

"I know what you're thinking," Maribel said after they'd walked one block.

"Oh?" *Play it cool, Plantz.* "My brain goes all over the place."

"You're thinking that Nochturn is very handsome. It's nothing the rest of the women in our... group...haven't thought. But no amount of daydreaming will change the fact that he is married. And I don't want you saying derogatory things about yourself again. You are the face of Moonbeam Enterprises now."

Back at Maribel's, Pepper slipped into the guest bedroom and closed the door. Before she could remove the envelope from her pocket, there was a knock at her door. Without waiting to be asked, Maribel marched in.

"Yes?" Pepper said with as much self-control as she could muster.

"We need to have a discussion tomorrow about your sneaking out. And I don't appreciate your following me. It's not safe for a young woman to wander the streets alone."

Pepper nodded. "I'm sorry. I was...curious."

"Be that as it may, let's decide this was a learning experience that won't happen again."

Maribel paused momentarily before closing the door.

Pepper's hands shook as she opened the envelope.

A picture of a woman, eyes half-open fell onto the floor along with a note.

Does this scare you? It should.

They are creating dangerous drugs and will use you to market to the younger generation. I can help you escape.

She turned the page over and found it was written on the back of a flyer:

SAVE OUR SALOON!
An Otter's Run Community Fundraiser to Reclaim the Historic Sassafras Saloon
Bake sale. Silent auction. Pie Bingo.
We must preserve our landmark!

At the bottom, in the tiniest type:

Cult reprogramming offered.

9

The Ease of Unease

Maribel's tea shop had become a strange kind of sanctuary—safe, warm, and saturated with her presence. The air always carried undertones of lavender, lemon verbena, and something darker—like toasted fennel that lingered in the throat. Corkboards crowded the walls with cheerful affirmations in neat handwriting. In the corner, a tidy box of trading cards sat untouched, gathering dust.

But beneath the scent of herbs and the hum of the shop, Pepper felt unease. She'd followed Maribel's directive and stayed in her bed every time her mysterious boss disappeared into the night.

The only time she felt comfortable was when she ran into Joe. His dimples, his disarming laugh, his curly hair, they drew her in unlike any other relationship she'd had. Who was she kidding? This was the one and only time she'd had conversations with a boy.

The tea festival loomed, and Maribel had promised a full day of marketing prep. Pepper expected spreadsheets, photo staging, maybe a few choreographed social posts. Instead, Maribel waited at the bottom of the stairs, hair twisted sharp and perfect, a leather folder under one arm.

"Morning," she greeted. The brightness in her voice did not match her eyes. "Come. We've got something important today."

They crossed the courtyard, gravel crunching beneath their steps. Maribel kept glancing over her shoulder as if shadows followed. At the far edge, a seldom-used gate opened onto a narrow alley that smelled of mildew, wet brick, and stale citrus.

A storage unit hid in the wall. Maribel unlocked it with a padlock that looked like it belonged in a museum. Inside, the air was cool and damp. Cardboard boxes loomed, their corners soft with water stains. A faint tang of dried oranges and mold threaded through the dim light.

"This," Maribel said, crouching beside a crate labeled *Misc. Decor,* "is where the real magic happens."

The crate groaned as she opened it. From inside, she pulled a small black case—metal, cold, its hinges squeaking as she unlatched it. The inside smelled faintly metallic, like warmed wires.

Neatly stacked hard drives gleamed under the dim light. Each was labeled with numbers and cryptic terms—*Mist-A, Batch K, Surv. Raw Data.*

Pepper's throat tightened. "What's all this?"

"Data," Maribel said smoothly. "Belonging to our sponsors. It must be moved to a secure location before inspection."

Pepper stepped back, palms clammy. "Moved where? Inspection? What inspection?"

"Tillamook. Tonight. I can't go. You'll deliver it. Tell them it's promotional material."

Pepper's voice faltered. "You want me to drive this? Alone?"

"You're not alone," Maribel said with a tight smile. "You'll use my car. GPS. And my promise that if you follow directions, nothing will go wrong. You have a license, right?"

"Learner's permit." Her voice cracked. She remembered Wilma's parking lot "cookies" and the snow spinning under the tires. No highways. No practice.

Maribel's tone hardened. "If you refuse, the internship ends. No housing, no meals, no recommendation. I hear that dreadful boarding school makes students read the same textbook aloud, in turn. All year. Before a dinner of powdered eggs and sour milk."

The alley wind lifted a scrap of torn paper, slapping it against her leg. Pepper's heart raced.

"You can't do that," she whispered.

"I can. And I will." Maribel leaned in, her perfume—sweet anise and bitter cloves—making Pepper's eyes sting. "People who want to matter do the uncomfortable things. You're bright. Ready. Or was your headmaster wrong?"

Pepper's mouth was dry. She nodded once.

Maribel's smile returned, serene. She shut the case, its latch snapping shut like a verdict, and pressed it into Pepper's hands. "Good girl. Leave at sunset. If you're stopped, say you're scouting tea booth space on the coast. Instructions are in the envelope."

At sunset, the sky painted itself in rose and amber as Pepper gripped the wheel with clammy palms. The black case lay strapped into the passenger seat like an ominous guest.

Every sound amplified—the squeal of tires on asphalt, the rattle of loose gravel, even her own uneven breathing. Tillamook was only two hours away, but every mile stretched long. The head-lights of oncoming cars seemed too bright, too watchful. Each taillight became a red eye in the dark.

She almost ran over someone.

A man waving his arms wildly on the outskirts of town. She pulled over, uncertain if she had the know-how to tend to an emergency. When she got close, she recognized the face.

"Joe? What are you doing here? Do you need help?"

It was more of a declaration than a question. She was so relieved to see him.

"I...um... my car broke down. The tow truck

can't come until the morning. Could you give me a lift?"

Pepper stared at the setting sun. "I would, but I have to drop some stuff off in Tillamook. I'm on a deadline."

She held back the tears that wanted to stream down her cheeks. Maribel asked the impossible of her, but she couldn't back down now. "Unless…you want to come with me?"

Joe grinned. "Thought you'd never ask."

They were only three miles outside of town when he asked her to pull over.

"Why? Did I do something wrong?" Pepper asked as the gravel crunched underneath the wheels.

"No, but I can tell you haven't driven much. You said you had a deadline, right? If you let me drive us, we'll make it. If you continue driving twenty-five, we won't make it until Thursday."

Pepper laughed with relief. "Yes! Please!"

She scooched over to the passenger side, and instantly her stress melted away. For the rest of the drive, they exchanged stories about their weird families—Joe's family owned a trucking company in Texas. He had a thirst for something different so he left in the middle of the night without looking back.

After Pepper finished her story, he stared at her, incredulous. "Is that all real, or are you making this up?"

"Real. I promise."

The drop site reeked of fish brine and salt.

"Do you want me to come with you?" Joe asked.

"No, I have to be brave tonight. I've already failed the driving test but I won't fail this one."

A shuttered seafood plant loomed nearby, its rusted siding creaking in the wind. Unit 117. The lockbox's metal was slick with condensation. She slid the case inside, fingers shaking.

Close it. Walk away. Don't look back.

Someone was watching. She was sure of it.

When she opened the locker a familiar smell hit her nostrils. Was that ...potting soil?

The creaking sound of a door opening made her jump out of her skin. "Hello? I'm just dropping off the information. I'm nobody!"

She waited a split second. That was all the courage she had. As she turned to leave, she ran squarely into an unwashed man with no teeth and eyes that pointed in two directions. "Sweet juice from a sweet prin-thess," he hissed.

As he reached for her, another person came up from behind him. It was the woman who'd lurked in the shadows and offered to help her. "Go!" she commanded. "Leave quickly!" That last beams of daylight seeped in through the door frame and for the first time, Pepper got a good look at the woman's face. "Maribel?" she whispered.

"Go! Go now! This place isn't safe for you!"

Pepper turned and ran as fast as she could back to the car. She heard the man scream in pain and then silence. She slammed the car door, the smell of brine clinging to her clothes, her skin.

"You look like you saw a ghost! Is everything okay?" Joe asked.

"Just drive. Fast. Drive fast!"

Joe obeyed. Once they were safely on the highway, she shared her experience with him. Something about Joe made her want to open up. "I don't think it was Maribel now that I'm calm. But the woman looked very similar. I can't understand why someone would follow me around."

"I can," Joe said softly. "You're one of a kind, Pepper Plantz."

"We can all be grateful for that!"

Joe laughed in a way Pepper decided was cute. "I'm sure there's a logical explanation for all of it. And Maribel has a pretty basic look. I bet there are a hundred women in this town you could easily mistake for the boss lady."

She nodded, comforted by his logic. Pepper's nerves calmed eventually. To her surprise, she was so relaxed she fell asleep. The next thing she knew, Joe was gently shaking her shoulder.

"Hey there, Pepper Shaker. We're at my place," he whispered in her ear.

Pepper sat up quickly. So quickly that her head hit Joe's chin. "I'm sorry!" she said quickly. His mouth was dangerously close to hers. Take the lead, guys like that, Wilma taught her.

Pepper grabbed either side of Joe's face and kissed him. Hard. It felt right.

Joe kissed her back and time stood still. When he pulled away, he said, "Thank you, Pepper. I've never enjoyed a sketchy trip to the coast this much!" before slipping out of the car.

It didn't matter if she drove in inches, Pepper's spirit soared as she drove back to Maribel's place.

That night, in the false safety of Maribel's home, Pepper couldn't sleep. Her pulse still carried the rhythm of Joe's lips against hers. At midnight, she opened her laptop.

She searched: *Mist Study*

An obscure result surfaced—an academic scan titled *Inhalation Responses. Induced Performance Environments: A Pilot Study*.

Author names: S. Screech. M. Beam. and anonymous contributors.

Her stomach flipped.

The file detailed induced performance responses, karaoke scenarios, chemical diffusions, aerosols, voice strain. Mist compounds. Physiological triggers. Graphs of heart rate, blood pressure, vocal endurance. S. Screech was someone named Sybil, and her name appeared again and again.

Pepper sat frozen, the faint hum of her laptop fan the only sound. She had delivered drives connected to *this.* Not marketing. Not branding. Experiments.

Her reflection wavered in the black screen, eyes

wide, face pale. What had she just delivered? Data used to poison people?

She backed the file up to three hidden drives. Then she packed a go-bag. Socks, water, granola, cash.

Now all she needed was a plan. But she forgot that help was on the way.

10

Work Like No One is Watching

She could barely keep her eyes open. In addition to her attempts to uncover Maribel's secrets, Pepper began to experience anger towards her elder sister and brother. It grew like a field of dandelions and before long, it had taken over her entire brain. It wasn't just anger either. She was jealous. Those two never had to worry about saying the wrong thing or confusing a Yarrow plant with Queen Anne's lace. They didn't have to memorize twenty facts about the proper soil for growing roses. But the worst offense of all was living their lives like they *enjoyed them.*

Nochturn's dismissal of her was the final straw. Though he was handsome and charismatic, he was just like his sister. After she left Maribel's home, she was going to track them down.

And do what?

She was going to track them down and…end them. They didn't deserve their easy lives. Maybe Pepper and Ginger would inherit a large sum of money after their deaths. They wouldn't share it with Dill or Sage. They'd open their own place for kids to come and feel safe. Kids who didn't feel safe anywhere else.

The knock on the door startled her.

Luckily, Maribel was out.

The face was elongated, perfect and aged, but the bright red hair was still the same.

"Ginger? What are you doing here? You're all grown up!" They hugged tightly. Pepper had pushed away her feelings for her family for so long that it was hard to retrieve them now.

Her sister smiled. "Mr. Gumb told me where you were. It took lots of convincing."

Pepper's cheeks burned. "Ginger, I have to tell you about him. He's not the man we knew."

It took a matter of minutes to describe Mr. Gumb and his secret relationship with Maribel, his involvement with this group; he wasn't the good guy who brought them sweets anymore. Maybe he never was.

Ginger looked at her with concern. "I know. I've overheard conversations between them. There is something they're working on for the government. I think it's just private."

Poor kid. She knew nothing of the real world.

"No, no," Pepper protested. "You don't understand, Ginger. He's evil!"

Her sister's eyes softened. "I promise you he isn't."

Being at an impasse, Pepper changed the subject. "I've actually met Nochturn. He's—"

"YOU DID?"

Ginger jumped around the room like a child. "I can't believe this! What did he say? Did he know about us? When can we visit him?"

Pepper stiffened. "He's a terrible person. I'm afraid we won't be spending time with him. At least of a civil nature."

"What? How can that be? He smiles in all of his photos. They had such easy lives without the taskmaster."

Pepper gave her a once-over, then pulled her into another hug. "You look like you haven't slept in a week," she murmured.

"I haven't," Ginger said flatly.

Pepper stepped back, concern lining her face. "You got out. How?"

Ginger glanced toward the darkened hallway behind her, something they'd. "I didn't sneak out," she said, voice low. "He kicked me out. For three days."

Pepper's eyes widened. "Dill did what?"

"I caught him," Ginger whispered. "Out in his shed. Mixing something. It wasn't just fertilizer or plant food. He was wearing gloves and one of those old masks Mom used to use when she painted. And there were these little bottles—dark glass, no labels. He didn't hear me at first, but when he turned around and saw me watching him through the slats in the door..." Her voice caught. "He lost it."

Pepper crossed her arms. "And then what? What'd he say?"

"He told me I was too curious. That if I wanted to survive in this family, I needed to learn respect." Ginger let out a breath. "So he locked me out. No keys. No money. Just a pack with a toothbrush and one of those fake protein bars."

"And you came here?" Pepper asked, a flicker of something tender softening her face.

"I figured if he wanted to teach me a lesson, I'd teach him one back. He thought I'd come crawling after a night. He didn't expect me to make it all the way across town." Ginger's voice held a quiet triumph. "He definitely didn't expect me to find you."

Pepper sat heavily in the chair by the window, absorbing the weight of Ginger's words. "So that's it," she said finally. "We're all just pieces to be moved around his little garden."

"There's something else," Ginger added. "He's not just messing with dangerous plants or strange chemicals. He's hiding something bigger. That shed—he's reinforced it. I heard something whirring from underneath the floorboards. Something mechanical."

Pepper raised an eyebrow. "You think he's making something?"

"I don't know."

A heavy silence fell between them.

Then Pepper exhaled. "When I said I was going to find our other siblings and make their lives hell… I meant it. But maybe there's a smarter way. Maybe I don't just go after them—I expose their lies."

"What do you mean?" Ginger asked, eyes steady.

"They've been telling everyone they grew up in the cult, in hardship, but clearly they've had it easy. I want to humiliate them both."

Ginger sighed. "I wish you weren't so angry. They're going to destroy you, sis."

Pepper looked at her little sister, no longer soft and scared but sharp-edged and steady, forged by years of quiet observation and forced obedience.

"We're going to burn this whole thing down," Pepper said quietly. "But not with fire."

Ginger smiled, just barely. "With the truth."

They hugged again—tight, certain—and Ginger stepped back into the night. Pepper gave her sister $200 from Maribel's secret drawer. She'd worry about replacing it later.

"I wish you could stay here, but I don't trust Maribel."

"Do you think she'd try and hurt you? Come with me! We can find somewhere close to home for you to hide."

Pepper smiled. "No more hiding. I'll be fine. I have…help. Don't ask more. Now you really should go before she gets home. There is a nice hotel two blocks from here. Go have a long bubble bath and order from the room service menu. They bring food right to your door!"

11

Wax, Wail... and Worry

Pepper sat curled on the old plaid sofa, knees hugged to her chest, staring at the dark square of the unlit fireplace. She hadn't wanted to come—she'd wanted to stay with Maribel, prove to her father, prove to herself, prove to the world that she wasn't the artistic one he dismissed at Sunday dinners. But she'd broken instead. Maribel confronted her about making backup drives of her personal files and the missing cash. Her face was bright red as she took Pepper by the arm and shoved her into the dark basement.

"I'll come back for you in a few days. We'll see how snoopy you are after a little starvation in the dark."

And then the door slammed shut.

Pepper cried herself to sleep and only awoke when she heard a tapping on the window above her head.

Her eyes scoured the dark room for something to use—and settled on an overturned bucket to reach the window.

Once again, he was her hero.

Pepper worked with feverish persistence trying to unhook the rusted latch. Finally when she was about to give up, it clicked.

"I'm going to pull you out," Joe said. Not questioning why she was in this situation or why he knew.

She allowed him to grab her from underneath her arms. She whimpered when her leg scratched as it was drug across the rough cement window well.

"Sorry. We'll tend to that when we get to my place."

"Won't she look there first?"

Joe flashed his trademark smile. It was like a light in the darkness of the night. "Not that one."

The door creaked. He stepped inside, snow dusting his shoulders, arms full of firewood. The cabin was small enough that when the wind sighed against the pines, the whole place seemed to breathe.

"You're still in the same spot," he said gently, setting the logs down by the hearth.

She rubbed her eyes. "If I move, I'll have to think about tomorrow."

Joe crouched, arranging kindling with steady hands. "Then don't think about tomorrow. Just tonight. Just the fire."

The match flared, caught, and soon the cabin filled with the crackle of flame. The light softened his profile—his square jaw, the faint scar at his temple from a tree-felling mishap last spring. He was ordinary in all the ways that mattered most: reliable, kind, steady as the mountains themselves.

He brought her a mug of broth, steam curling upward. "Soup first. Then maybe a walk if the storm calms down."

She tried to smile. "You make it sound so simple."

Joe sat beside her, arm warm around her shoulders. "It is simple. You're tired. You're hurting. The world can wait. Right now, you're here. With me."

She leaned against him, eyes closing, trying to let herself believe it. But even then—even wrapped in his steadiness—her mind ticked like a clock. The scoreboard loomed. Her father's voice calling her artistic. Forgettable.

"I just… I want to matter," she whispered.

"You already do," Joe said without hesitation. He kissed the top of her curly head. "Not because of what you do. Because you're you."

She wanted to hold him in her arms, but he pulled away. "There's something I've been wanting to ask you. We're both alone, we're both vulnerable to those who try and manipulate us."

He took her hands in his, and an electricity shot through her body. She nodded, wanting him this close forever.

"If you want to finally be free of your father and his oppressive rules, there is only one way."

She swallowed hard. "I don't think I'm ready to kill him. He's awful, but my mom and Ginger love him."

Joe's face twisted, first into a grimace but it melted into a grin. Dimples on either side of his mouth made him downright adorable. "Ohhh. You thought I had a great plan for eliminating him. No, I was going to propose to you, Pepper Plantz."

He pulled a band out of his pocket and in his palm was a ring containing tiny diamonds all around, and he slipped it on her finger.

Pepper gasped. "Oh, Joe! I..." He was more than she ever expected. Funny, beautiful, kind. But he was also at least ten years older than she.

For a fleeting moment, she let herself sink into it. The warmth. The pine-scented air. The silence. Was this the right thing to do? Going by the level of disgust her father would show, it was perfect. And if Joe could protect her from Maribel's wrath... "Okay. I'll do it. The sooner the better."

Pepper wore Joe's grandmother's wedding dress, which for some unexplained reason had been hanging in the closet at the cabin. It was simple, light pink flowers dotted the cream-colored fabric that only contained one coffee stain. It was perfect.

The next month was like some kind of fairy tale. Joe went to work for Maribel at the dock during the day, keeping Pepper's location a secret. Though she'd never been allowed in the kitchen to learn how to cook, she caught on quickly. Roasted chicken, rice, and glazed brussels sprouts. If there was one thing a Plantz did well, it was to follow directions.

But in her chest, ambition still gnawed. She wanted soup and fires and walks in the snow. But she also wanted the stage, the spotlight, the scoreboard tallying wins. She wanted her name to mean something. Pepper Plantz, now Friday, had a purpose.

They weren't expecting visitors.

When Pepper opened the door wiping her hands on an embroidered towel with the image of a chicken in three spots, she was shocked to find a snow-covered Maribel— resplendent in all white.

Pepper had prepared for this day, reciting her apology over and over in her head every time she couldn't sleep. "I'm so sorry, Maribel. After just learning how to socialize in Slackjaw Academy, I wasn't ready for marketing. It made me sick to my stomach."

Today, though, the words stuck in her throat like week-old bread.

"I'm sorry I left without telling you," Pepper began, uncertain of what she wanted to share. "I was scared."

Maribel sniffed. "May I come in? This won't take long."

Pepper felt helpless. This woman still had control of her. She stepped aside reluctantly.

"Smells like soup," Maribel commented as her eyes glanced around the small room.

If only Joe were home. He would smooth things over.

Maribel sat on their couch, a sacred spot where Pepper and Joe watched old movies she'd missed. Seemed like she missed out on a lot.

"You started out strong, Plantz. People took notice."

"Oh really? Who?"

Maribel cleared her throat. "Someone with power. He's interested in offering you a job."

Good old Maribel. Telling her just enough to hook her. "What would I be doing? And who is this mystery man?"

"Opening karaoke clubs for Moonbeam Enterprises. You wouldn't have to speak in front of large groups like when you were working for me."

"I'm really sorry, Maribel, I—"

Maribel held up a hand. "That's not our focus today. This is an opportunity that won't be there forever; you'd be a fool to pass it up."

It was exciting. Pepper could see herself climbing this ladder, away from her father and Maribel and anyone else who thought they could plan out her life for her.

As Maribel explained further, that Moonbeam was a powerful man who was responsible for many companies, Pepper felt a sense of pride. He wanted her.

"There's also the matter of the cult."

Pepper's eyes widened. "I would have to join a cult?"

"No. But you need to be aware the Mooners are his eyes and ears. They're everywhere."

"I'll have to talk to Joe first."

Maribel patted her thighs and stood. "Of course. You and your husband should be on the same page." She walked to the door and then paused. "This job is perfect for you. Sylvia and Nelson send their regards."

Pepper watched as Maribel trudged through the snow to her car. Joe scooped a path every morning, but people like Maribel did their own thing. When her car turned to go down the hill, Pepper asked, "did I do okay?"

"Perfect, darling. You said all the right things."

12

Love Hurts

He knew.

Knew the cabin wasn't enough for her anymore.

When she told him, Joe looked at her the way he always did with patience, with love. But there had been something else in his eyes that time. Resignation. "I'll miss you, Pepper Shaker. We always knew this day was coming."

"I'll miss you too, babe." She touched his face softly, suddenly feeling a pang of guilt. "I'll come home whenever I can. I promise.

And when Pepper left with Maribel, Joe didn't try and stop her.

The day Pepper flew to Atlanta, Joe drove her to the airport. He carried her bag, bought her a muffin she didn't eat, and held her hand until the last possible moment at security.

"I'll be here," he said. "No matter what happens."

But Pepper noticed something in his eyes then—a weight, a quiet sadness. She told herself it was nerves. She told herself he'd understand once she succeeded. Once she proved herself.

She didn't call him that night. Or the next. The days blurred into karaoke chaos, soft openings, and endless checklists. He never called either, just texted on occasion, something she tried pushing out of her head.

By the end of that month, Joe stopped asking when she'd be home.

By the end of the year, he quietly bowed out. No slammed doors. No bitter words. Just absence—like he had folded himself neatly out of her story, leaving only the memory of the cabin, the soup, the sound of pines swaying in mountain wind.

Pepper rarely let herself think of him after that. The ache was too sharp, the guilt too heavy. So she buried it beneath strategy decks, signage approvals, and a constant calendar of openings.

And yet, every now and then—on nights when the glitter settled too thickly or when Sybil's silence cut sharper than any critique—Pepper remembered the way Joe had carried her out of the dark.

And she wondered if chasing the scoreboard had already cost her the one thing she couldn't replace.

"DON'T LOOK him directly in the eye," Maribel began. "He is an entity. That means you show respect. And don't question his authority. He has vision like no other boss I've had. And the most important thing—DON'T disagree."

She nodded, pulling herself up tall.

Moonbeam's private office wasn't just an office —it was an *experience.*

Twice the size of the storefront, the room gleamed with maroon wallpaper flecked in gold, lacquered floors, and enough velvet to outfit a theater troupe. Rare records gleamed behind glass; framed photos of Moonbeam himself—crooning karaoke across the country—lined the opposite wall, each signed with a lyric and a date.

At the far end, behind a mahogany desk more altar than furniture, sat Moonbeam. Burgundy tunic, bolo tie, white boots. His curls glinted silver. His smile was equal parts blessing and warning.

"Pepper Friday," he said, rising with theatrical gravity. "You've outdone yourself."

"But I haven't worked for Maribel in years."

He chuckled softly. "Yes, I know. You were able to extract yourself from a situation you found untenable. Do you know what happened to her last protégé?"

She'd heard rumors. Mostly from Joe and mostly about a gruesome end at the bottom of a lake.

"He never spoke up. Not once. After Maribel

invested months into his training, he threw himself into a lake and drowned." Moonbeam shook his head. "All that time, all that expense, all out the window." His small brown eyes drifted away to another time. For a split second, she wondered if he had anything to do with the drowning.

"You made your feelings clear and marched out of her home without wasting anyone's time any longer."

"No…I…" she paused. If Maribel told him Pepper left because she was brave and not because she was locked in the basement, it was for the best.

"That's why," he continued, lowering himself onto his throne-like chair, "I'm offering you a promotion."

Her pulse skipped. A promotion. When she'd never worked a day in her life for the man. Was this what the business world was really like?

He tapped the silver-embossed folder on his desk. "The expansion project. Ten new lounges by year's end. You'll shadow my right hand, Sybil Screech. If she approves, you rise. If she doesn't… back to your desk job. No travel. No credit. No front-row access to the glitter cannon in Bend."

Pepper swallowed. "When do I meet her?"

He flicked a finger. A side door opened.

Sybil Screech entered like a storm contained in a navy suit. Clunky heels, leather portfolio clutched like a weapon, bun so tight it pulled her forehead taut, emphasizing a large mole. She circled Pepper once, hawk-like, before saying crisply, "Twelve percent increase in RSVPs when you added humor to emails. I don't like humor. But results don't lie. You'll come with me to Denver. Wear shoes you can run in."

And just like that, she was gone—leaving only peppermint tea or perhaps antacid in her wake.

Moonbeam chuckled. "Sybil doesn't do small talk. Don't take it personally."

Pepper clutched the itinerary Sybil had dropped into her hand. It felt like both a ticket and a trap.

That night, lying on an unfamiliar couch, the itinerary tucked beneath her pillow, Pepper's mind drifted—not to Moonbeam's velvet empire or Sybil's hawk-like scrutiny—but to the cabin.

The cabin where Joe had carried her when she'd broken.

She saw it as if she were still there: fire crackling in the stone hearth, snow pressing soft against the windows, Joe's steady hands coaxing kindling to life. He'd wrapped her in blankets, placed a steaming mug of broth in her hands. "Don't think about tomorrow," he'd told her. "Just tonight. Just the fire. And us."

She'd leaned against him on the old plaid sofa, the scents of pine and woodsmoke filling the air and whispered the ache she couldn't silence. "I just want to matter."

"You already do," Joe had said, without hesitation. "Not because of what you do. Because you're you."

It should have been enough. Soup, firelight, the quiet steadiness of a man who loved her.

But even then, ambition had gnawed. Her father's voice calling her artistic. Forgettable.

She turned over in bed, the faint sound of her neighbor mangling "Total Eclipse of the Heart" drifting through the floorboards. It felt like a sign. She would make this work. She would prove herself. Someone already thought she was important enough to carry this secret. To infiltrate this cult.

She whispered into the dark: "Sybil Screech, you haven't met this Friday yet."

Pepper lay awake long after she tucked Sybil's itinerary beneath her pillow. The walls of her apartment felt too thin, the ceiling too close. She kept replaying the cabin—Joe's steady hands, the soup steaming on the chipped enamel stove, the silence between the pines that had felt like a lullaby.

Joe had saved her once. Twice, really. He never asked for credit. Never asked for anything but time together, walks by the river, coffee that was too weak for her taste but perfect for his.

And now here she was, standing at the brink of something massive, glittering, dangerous. Moonbeam's empire. Sybil's scrutiny. The scoreboard she'd been chasing for years.

Joe had warned her gently, the night before she left for Atlanta.

"You don't have to prove yourself to people who never saw you in the first place, Pepper Pot."

She'd kissed him then, fiercely, as if to erase the words. "I just need to try."

And he had nodded because that's what Joe did. He steadied. He gave her space to chase what she thought she needed.

But even steadiness has a limit.

If they came for her again, she wouldn't be caught unprepared.

"Hold the ladder," a man called out, confused and hopeful. "It's wobbly."

Sybil didn't move.

Instead, she let out a huff so sharp it could've sliced drywall and spoke in a voice that was pinched, urgent, and laced with undisguised disgust. "You're using the wrong twine. That's going to snap under a sneeze."

The man froze in place halfway up the ladder, one hand reaching toward a banner that read "Soft Opening Karaoke Spectacular" in glitter letters, the other clinging to the top rung like a kitten stuck in a tree. "I got it from the emergency supply bucket," he offered meekly. "Nobody told me what kind to use."

Sybil arched a single hairless brow. "And what kind of emergency," she asked, voice dripping venom, "would require party twine, you reckless imbecile?"

He blinked slowly. "Uh…"

Three Mooners dressed in pale gray tunics with bright yellow treble clefs on the chest scurried by singing, "We love, love, love when we move, move, move," the nonsensical song of the day.

"Get. Down."

It wasn't a suggestion, and it sure wasn't maternal concern. It was a death sentence.

He clambered down the ladder so fast he nearly pantsed himself. When he hit the floor, he stood at attention like a schoolboy in trouble for sneezing during the Pledge of Allegiance. "I was told I'm co-running this location with you, Sybil?"

At that, the temperature dropped. Not metaphorically—literally. Pepper felt it the moment she stepped through the rear service entrance, the air heavy and damp like a walk-in freezer full of disappointment.

The scent hit her next: a pungent swirl of licorice lozenges, heavily starched polyester, and something unplaceable, metallic—like pennies and microwaved regret. She gave a polite sniff and shivered.

The two of them turned to face her.

The man so pale he looked photosensitive, his eyes blank and faintly moist, like peeled grapes. The other was Sybil, a small, hawkish woman with no visible eyebrows and a mole in the exact center of her forehead, as if the universe had stamped her for villainy at birth.

"Hello, Sybil," Pepper ventured.

The woman sniffed once and adjusted the thick, tartan scarf wrapped so tightly around her neck it could've been a medical device.

"Ms. Screech," she corrected. "Until you're promoted to minion."

"Until you're promoted to minion," the bald man snickered. "I know things that you don't."

Pepper blinked. "Right," she said, sticking out a hand with too much cheer, like someone trying to win Employee of the Month at their very first shift.

Ms. Screech stared at it like it had just stolen her parking spot.

Pepper let it fall. Her cheeks pinked. "I like your... scarf?"

"It's a neck weapon," Sybil said flatly. "Gift from Moonbeam. Worn with intent."

The pale man nodded solemnly in agreement, his head bobbing like a dashboard hula doll caught in traffic.

"I was told I'd be co–"

"There's no 'co' here," Sybil snapped, cutting her off like a butcher hacking a roast. "You'll be working *for me*, and you won't breathe unless I give you the okay."

"But Moonbeam said—"

"*'But Moonbeam said,'*" the pale man mimicked, twisting his voice into a cruel falsetto. He glanced quickly at Sybil, desperate for approval. It never came. But he relaxed, as if she'd smiled internally and that was enough.

They both chuckled, dry and humorless like paper cuts.

Pepper tried again, standing up straighter. "I was told I'd be involved in operations. Hiring. Marketing. Co-leadership."

Sybil stepped forward until the mole on her forehead was nearly touching Pepper's own. Up close, it seemed sentient. "Moonbeam sends me *fresh meat*. You, the fresh meat, can either learn the hierarchy, or we'll send you packing to your next minimum wage job—no lunch break, smelly bathroom, and worse coffee."

The pale man, who still hadn't introduced himself, cleared his throat. "That's not how we got rid of Randall. We blindfolded him and took him out in the woods. Remember? Two hours from town."

Sybil's mole twitched—*visibly twitched*—and a single vein in her diminutive neck throbbed. Without warning, she took her scarf and slapped the man across the face.

"That was an isolated incident, you idiot," she muttered. "Well, Ms. Friday," Sybil said, snapping back into full intimidation mode. "What will it be?"

Pepper hesitated, mind racing. She was still jet-lagged. She hadn't eaten. She hadn't even fully unpacked. And yet… quitting wasn't an option. Not with the promise of new information on her siblings so close. Not with a job she sacrificed her marriage for. Not with Sybil clearly hoping she'd bolt.

She swallowed, squared her shoulders, and stepped forward. "I'll stay."

The pale man snorted. "You'll have to do what I say!"

Sybil didn't respond. Instead, she reached into her oversized side-pouch and produced a clipboard with PEPPER FRIDAY printed across the top in aggressive, all-caps Sharpie.

"Sign here," Sybil barked. "Initial here. And if you're still standing by next Friday, we'll consider giving you access to the *Batter Room.*"

Pepper blinked. "The what?"

The pale man whispered, reverently, "It's not what you think."

Pepper Friday arrived at the Denver club opening two hours early, as instructed. Sybil Screech had sent her a calendar invite titled "Checklist Conformity Walkthrough – DO NOT ALTER OR RESCHEDULE," which somehow felt like a threat even though it contained no adjectives.

Pepper had worn her nicest gray slacks, a wrinkle-proof button-up blouse, and practical-but-flattering ankle boots. She had also packed four extra pens, a backup laptop charger, and a high-protein snack bar labeled "FOCUS FUEL."

She wasn't nervous. Not exactly.

She just didn't want to give Sybil any reason to dismiss her.

Not when she had come this far.

Not when she had so much riding on this job.

THE DENVER CLUB was sleek and modern—polished concrete floors, neon lights in muted jewel tones, and a glimmering karaoke stage framed by velvet curtains in a color Sybil referred to only as "eggplant but not obnoxious."

Pepper had spent most of the morning testing mic levels, coordinating with the social media freelancer, and making sure the signage featured both the correct font and Moonbeam's precise shade of crescent gold.

At 11:00 a.m. sharp, Sybil arrived, holding a tablet and a cup of black coffee that looked like it had been brewed with intent to interrogate. Derek za'Dimwit trailed behind her, walking on his tip toes like he was ready to pirouette.

"Three chairs are missing from the back lounge," Sybil said before offering so much as a greeting. "The photographer is using a filter I don't approve of, and there's a suspicious noise coming from the vending machine. I want a report."

"Already flagged the chairs," Pepper replied. "The vending machine's making that sound because someone dropped a bottle cap into the change return. As for the photographer, I've asked for raw files only."

Sybil narrowed her eyes. "Hm."

It wasn't a compliment. But it also wasn't a criticism.

It was, by Pepper's calculations, the closest thing to a nod of approval she was likely to get. Later that afternoon, after the fire marshal had signed off on the occupancy and the VIP lounge had been de-glittered per Sybil's no-glitter mandate, Pepper retreated to her hotel room for a brief hour of silence.

She kicked off her boots, wrapped herself in the waffle-knit robe, and opened her laptop.

The first thing she did was type: Is it petty to want to be more successful than your half siblings?

Then she deleted it.

Instead, she opened a private folder labeled PERSONAL.

Inside was a subfolder titled Dad's Other Kids —capitalized like a tabloid headline.

She clicked through a few bookmarked pages, pulled from social media and alumni databases. Her half-brother, Nochturn, had just been promoted at a financial firm in Piney Falls. He was still just as handsome as the day she'd met him. Often she'd pull up his social media to see what he'd written. Pictures of his model wife and his two children who resembled their mother dotted the page. Nochturn became not only her brother, but the example of the man she wanted to marry.

Her half-sister, November, was another matter.

She was living in California, the wife of a toilet

paper magnet. The entitled witch wrote a guest column for a local newspaper about the importance of ants in our diet. Pepper felt disgust and…was it jealousy?

Pepper studied November's photograph. They shared the same frizzy hair and upturned noses. Though she knew November and Nochturn grew up in a cult, they sure didn't seem the worse for wear. November always dressed monochromatically. Themed. Maybe that was what was missing? Pepper needed a theme?

Pepper wasn't jealous. Not exactly. At least not of that weird November.

She just wanted to win.

Not out of cruelty, but for the scoreboard in her mind—the invisible tally that had been climbing ever since she overheard her father, ten years ago, say, "Pepper's okay, sure. But Ginger's got drive. Pepper's more… artistic."

Artistic as in impractical.

As in not serious.

As in forgettable.

Well, not anymore.

Not after ten successful email campaigns. Not after traveling across the country, running high-stakes club launches. Not after Sybil Screech herself had said nothing negative for a full five minutes.

Pepper closed the browser and reopened her work dashboard.

She had three upcoming club launches to prep

and a marketing meeting with Moonbeam on Monday. She had branded napkins to approve and a jingle pitch to ignore from a man who kept rhyming karaoke with hokey pokey.

No time for distractions.

Pepper resisted the urge to scream into a pillow. "You've got this, Friday. And the best is yet to come."

13

Best Foot Forward

The next morning, Sybil was already pacing the club's lobby at 6:30 a.m., scanning QR codes on a clipboard and muttering things like, "Bathroom signage is half a centimeter off center," and, "Why are there three brands of seltzer in the green room when we agreed on one?"

"Pepper," Sybil said sharply. "Inventory count, front desk. I want confirmation that every lyric book matches the karaoke machine's internal system."

"On it."

"And make sure no one adds surprise confetti. I've been ambushed before."

Pepper jogged to the front desk, then circled back five minutes later.

"Two lyric books were swapped by a local comic who thought it'd be funny to change every third song to 'Barbie Girl'. I've fixed it. Also removed a disco ball someone tried to install above the women's restroom."

Sybil paused mid-step. "Efficient."

"Thank you."

Sybil squinted at her, lips pressing into something that almost looked like curiosity.

"What's your angle, Friday?"

"My angle?"

"You're working harder than anyone has a right to. You're two steps ahead, overprepared, and you've already figured out how to decode my mood based on the way I walk. I can see it in your face."

Pepper hesitated. "I just want to do well."

"You want to be seen."

Pepper flushed. "Isn't that the same thing?"

Sybil didn't answer. Instead, she tapped her tablet and walked away.

That night, after the club's soft opening went off without a hitch—no injuries, no songbook sabotage, and only one drunk uncle attempting interpretive dance—Pepper stood in the backstage lounge, watching the crowd laugh and sing.

Sybil approached quietly, holding a tablet, which she handed off to a passing assistant.

"You've earned your place," Sybil said.

Pepper turned, startled. "What?"

"I'm not warm, Friday. I don't say things to boost morale. But you've done what few others can. You've kept pace. You've asked smart questions. You didn't get flustered when the Denver reporter called the karaoke empire frivolous. That's worth something."

Pepper nodded slowly. "Thank you."

Sybil studied her. "But you're still distracted.

Pepper stiffened. "No. I—"

"I'm not interested in your personal life. But I've known dozens like you. Chasing something invisible. Someone's approval, someone's acknowledgment. Sometimes it's better to stop running and build your own scoreboard."

Pepper didn't reply.

She didn't trust herself to.

Sybil started to walk away, then paused. "Your half- brother's podcast is insufferable, by the way. He interviews other hedge fund managers as if they're astronauts."

Pepper blinked. "You looked him up?"

"I do thorough background checks on everyone. Including family drama. It helps me prepare for sabotage and oversharing."

Pepper laughed—short and surprised. "So I'm not the only one with a folder?"

Sybil gave her a rare, razor-edged smile. "Don't flatter yourself. Mine's alphabetized."

For one tiny moment in time, she respected her boss.

"What's this?" Derek inserted himself between them. "No chitchat without Derek. Right, Sibby?"

His love turned and walked away, shaking her head.by.

"I've got news, Sibby!" He called after her. "Real news! Not like the dolphins coming to close to the resort pool in Ibiza and scaring the rich ladies."

Sybil turned abruptly. "What?" she snapped.

Derek seemed unprepared for the spotlight. "I...um..."

"Wasting my valuable time. Again." Sybil shook her head.

"Someone died after the last club opening in Denver. Keeled right over in the alley. The manager said his rendition of *Total Eclipse of the Heart'* made dogs howl from a half-mile away. Right after the dramatic spin—he'd been practicing it for weeks—he clutched his chest and staggered outside."

"Hmm."

Sybil appeared to take his words into consideration. For once. "Sounds like he ate too many cheeseburgers and the ticker gave out. Not our problem."

Derek and Pepper watched as Sybil walked away, her heels clomping as her body released foul odors. When she was out of sight, Derek turned for a moment to glare at Pepper. "You don't EVER get between us, understand?"

14

Sweet Girl of Mine

Pepper envisioned an office party, and maybe some cake for learning her duties so quickly. Under Sybil's tutelage, it was either understand the first time she said it or have Derek berate her for an hour, going on and on about how impressed everyone would be with him someday. What she hadn't expected were the required restraints and blindfold, which Derek applied with glee, or the strange, rhythmic chant of Mooners echoing down the fluorescent stairwell.

"Don't lock your knees," Sybil hissed behind her. "It messes with the batter distribution."

The room looked like a kitchen had a baby with a laser tag arena. Chrome vats lined the walls, bubbling with unnervingly scented batter:

- Maple Oblivion

- Blueberry Bruise
- Sriracha Rings of Saturn

The hose dangled from the ceiling. The nozzle gleamed. The red button pulsed like a heartbeat.

On the side, Moonbeam sat on a giant throne next to a choir of Mooners, who sang a variety of songs Pepper had never heard before.

Pepper laughed—giddy from the absurdity. The walls pulsed slightly with karaoke basslines from above, and at the center of the room stood a control panel with two levers and a big red button labeled "SHOOT TO SOOTHE."

"You've done well, Friday," he intoned. "The Astoria opening set records. The karaoke frequencies are strong. As a reward, you shall baptize the Tender Mooners in... Pancake Exultation."

Sybil stood at the panel, arms crossed. "Don't make a mess of it."

Pepper blinked. "You want me to... shoot them? With batter?"

Moonbeam spread his arms. "Only the worthy shall be frosted in flapjack glory."

From behind a fogged-up glass wall, a dozen Mooners began to appear, dancing awkwardly to "Sweet Caroline". One wore a Viking helmet. Another had glowsticks in their hair. All of them were barefoot and vibrating with over-eager cult energy.

Sybil handed Pepper the nozzle.

"It's set to STREAM. For spray, flip the lever. For splatter, double-pump and twist."

"Do I... warn them first?"

Sybil scowled. "Don't make this dramatic, Friday. Just make the boss smile and then go to the decontamination room to clean up."

The lights dimmed. Disco ball glitter fell from unseen vents. The Mooners stomped in unison and chanted, "LET HER POUR! LET HER POUR!"

Pepper squared her shoulders, aimed the hose at the writhing dancers, and yelled, "Batter yourselves silly!"

She squeezed the trigger.

A blast of thick, golden pancake batter launched across the room with the velocity of a fire-hose at a state fair. The first Mooner caught it full in the chest and spun, arms out like a batter-soaked ballerina. The crowd screamed in glee.

She flipped to SPRAY. Pancake mist filled the air.

Then SPLATTER.

Another Mooner appeared out of nowhere and placed a syrup bottle in her hand like it was a sacred relic.

Pepper's arms shook from adrenaline and gluten. Her heart raced.

She'd never felt more alive.

Or more suspicious.

Because someone in the back wasn't laughing. And they weren't covered in batter.

Derek.

PINEY Falls

Piney Falls, Oregon

15

We Are Family

"Alright, Bean. If you're going to eat everything in the pastry case, grab an apron and get busy making more."

Cosmo shakes his head, his handsome salt-and-pepper locks unusually long. He refuses to go get his hair cut at a salon, waiting instead for Clips, the ancient barber who only works when he feels like it, to return from his fishing sabbatical. I can't complain though, watching my husband always makes my heart flutter.

"There are exactly six scones left," he says. "It's only 10 a.m. I expect them to find their way into the gullets of actual customers. Got it?"

November jumps up like she's been challenged to a duel, one hand gripping a half-eaten Buzz Aldrin Blueberry Scone, the other holding a Strawberry Cream Solar Scone. Her face is dusted in crumbs and streaked with pink filling, but the fire in her eyes is unmistakable. She's ready to pounce.

It's just another Tuesday for these two.

I touch Cosmo's chest—a subtle reminder that we're in public and married and he does love me, even if his pastries are under siege. "You always bake extra on Tuesdays," I remind him. "You said, 'Bean has consumed an entire days' worth of scones for the last time!'"

His gaze softens.

"I know she's your best friend, but she has food at home, right?"

I wish I could give him an answer he would like. He tolerates the one person who drives him completely mad because she is his wife's best friend. If that's not a sign of love, I don't know what is.

"Your scones would still be in the back of your freezer if it weren't for me buying enough to sell out, Astrological Armpit."

He narrows his eyes but says nothing. His focus is, as always, on the woman who knows how to take him from one to ten in an instant. Happily, it's me.

Though they both grew up in the Fallen Branch Cult and you'd think they had a kinship through hardship, these two are always at each other's throats.

The standoff stretches—Cosmo and November locked in an unspoken war over scone territory—until I realize it's going to be up to me to de-escalate.

I turn to Vem, who's decided that maroon is the color of the day. Her headband holding back wild frizzy hair, glasses frames, jumpsuit, and sneakers are all the same hue, and the effect is both alarming and impressively coordinated.

"Vem, honey, I know you're concerned that the new karaoke club might take away your moaning clients, but aren't they two totally different activities?"

"Money is money, Lanie," she replies, her tone icy enough to frost a Bundt cake. "Everyone's got a limited number of activities they can afford. If they blow their budget on themed cocktails and screeching contests—" she gestures toward the pastry case—"this entire community is in trouble."

Thankfully the phone rings, distracting Cosmo.

When we are finally re-seated at our table, each with a steaming mug of Piney Falls' finest coffee and Vem with her fourth scone, I notice for the first time that something green and gelatinous has taken up residence under her eyes. "Vem, honey, what's going on with your eyes?"

"I didn't sleep," she says dismally. "Didn't have time to remove the aspen leaf gelatin eye mask. No one will notice."

A group of local businessmen and women seated at a nearby table chat loudly.

"I can't wait for the karaoke club to open," says a man wearing a shirt emblazoned with the logo

"We Suck So You Don't," and on the next line, "Bixby Dryer Vent Cleaning."

"We really need someplace to just let loose. Someplace classier than another dirty old bar." This woman is wearing a ruffled shirt buttoned up to and including a portion of her chin.

Without warning, November hops on our table.

"Vem, what are you—"

"Woke up late but I'm feelin' right
Coffee in a cup like it's a date night
Mirror says, 'Girl, you're a whole vibe…

Even my cat gave me a high five…'"

The song is a familiar one, at least in more capable hands. I love this woman like a long-lost sister, but she couldn't carry a tune if it came with wheels and a handle.

Still, the patrons give her a standing ovation. Even the bank manager claps like she's just witnessed Broadway-level brilliance.

"I'd watch *that* at the karaoke club!" the ruffled blouse woman declares.

"You're missing the whole point!" Vem leaps off the chair with alarming agility. "We can sing wherever we want. I hummed all fifteen bars of 'Tic-Tack Got Your Back' last week on our drive to Tellum, didn't I, Lanie?"

I nod, though my smile is weak. I had to

mentally recite my entire grocery list just to keep from pulling over and shoving my fist in her mouth.

"You can express joy through song anywhere the day takes you. No need for a special club, especially one that has to destroy a local landmark. That place will be nothing but trouble, and you can't convince me otherwise. Oh, and I'm handing out fifty percent off coupons for your first visit to my moaning studio. I'll be giving lessons as well as moaning to de-stress while we wait for them to dissect our local landmark."

"Destress from what? The deafness your caterwauling will cause?" Cosmo mutters from the kitchen. "No one needs voice lessons from you, Bean."

"I prefer *Harmony Consultant,*" she snips.

"I bet you do."

The back doorbell rings, a sign that a supplier is here with product of some kind. Cos blows a kiss at me. "See you at home, babe."

"O…M…G…are you THE November Bean?"

I brace myself for some sort of angry comment about Vem's quirky behavior. She's been known to break out in a howl, moan, or off-key song at the most inopportune moments.

Instead it is the complete opposite. Two women dressed from head to toe in fluorescent orange track suits and coordinating shoes and socks practically beam as they approach our table. One woman pulls a visor up from her forehead to the top of her curly grey head and squints. "Yep, Bertha. You were right. It IS her!"

The women take a step back as Vem hops off the table, and then immediately they grab her hands. "We took your seminar Mono Moan Your Life into Focus at the World Moaning Festival!"

They look at each and grin. "We took our vacation out here hoping we'd run into you. Didn't I tell you we would, Bertha?"

Vem stands a little taller. It's rare to see her speechless. I have to enjoy the moment.

"She has moaning classes every other day. Tonight is Moan for Macaroni. She only does the carb class once a month, so you came at the right time."

I can't believe I know this.

After she signs their visors and hands them each a headshot she keeps in her traveling trunk of a purse, the women are on the way. I tap her arm. "Look at you! Am I still okay to talk to you? Or do I need to go through security?"

She rolls her eyes, but I can tell November Bean feels special. My bestie deserves every moment in the spotlight.

Once the normal hum of the bakery returns, I grab a napkin, lick my finger, and wipe pink filling off November's cheek. I'm not touching those eye masks. She's been known to slip animal excrement in her concoctions.

"There. Now that's the Bean I—"

"Shhh… Lanie. Look!"

Vem's eyes are wide as she points toward the pastry counter.

There, examining the remaining sweets, stands a woman in a black-and-white polka-dotted dress. Her skirt swishes like she's in a musical, and her shiny Mary Janes match perfectly, and they emit—glitter? That's a new one. Even her wristwatch is polka-dotted. Her frizzy black hair barely brushes her neck. She is definitely a vibe.

I stifle a giggle. "You don't see that every day," I whisper.

"What a magnificent creature," Vem breathes. And before I can stop her, she bounces to the counter and taps the woman on the shoulder.

The woman spins—maybe too quickly—and knocks Vem to the ground in a graceful, clumsy blur.

"Oh, golly Wally! I'm sooo sorry!" Her voice is high-pitched, squeaky, like a kazoo in a blender. The kind of sound that immediately takes up residence in the part of my brain labeled "Sensory Offenses."

Still, she reaches down and lifts Vem to her feet with surprising ease.

Then they lock eyes.

"I don't think I've ever seen a woman… quite as stunning as you before," Vem whispers with awe.

There is a startling resemblance. The women share the same frizzy hair, long nose with an upturn at the end, and tiny mouth. One in monochrome maroon, the other a human polka-dot.

"Roll me in dirt and call me Compost Carla. *YOU'RE* November Bean, aren't you? What a co-ink-ee-dink! I wanted to look you up when I got here. My father, Dill, used to live in the Fallen Branch Cult. I guess everyone there was kind of like family."

She winks, and something deep in my gut tightens. Danger. This woman is hiding something. I can smell it, and it's not coming from the scone tray.

"Gosh, and a real wordsmith too! Lanie, can you believe it? This pint-sized perfection and me have to be related!"

Before I can answer, November wraps the woman in a crushing hug and lifts her off the floor.

"Vem! Put her down! You don't want to find and lose a relative in the same hour!"

Still stunned, I step closer. My eyes don't deceive me—she's real. And familiar in a way that makes my skin crawl.

"My friend has a twisted family tree," I begin. "She doesn't know any cousins. Maybe you're—"

"Not a cousin, silly-willy," the Novem-bot insists. "She's my *sister!*"

16

The Plan

I'm halfway through reorganizing my spice cabinet alphabetically again (the way I relax when something disturbing like an unknown relative of Vem's is on my mind), when my daughter Piper barges into the kitchen like a tiny tornado with an agenda. Though she's barely five feet tall and has the milky-smooth skin of a baby, she is actually an adult. She's clutching a stack of papers, her lavender contacts shining and cheeks flushed with purpose.

"Mom," she says, breathless. "Emergency meeting. You, me, and Obie. Front porch. Now."

When your newly adopted daughter and business partner demands a meeting with the town deputy and includes you like she's chairing a board, you don't argue. You grab your lukewarm tea and a sweater and you follow her outside.

Obie Lumquest, son of Police Chief Boysie Lumquest and our daughter's fiancé, is already there, leaning against the porch railing like a thin cowboy who misplaced his horse. He taps the tip of his nose four times. Piper tells me this is his way of signaling something important is to come. It's a new movement for him. His OCD has improved since Piper has been dating him, but there are always new tics developing. We love him for loving our daughter. That's all that matters.

"Ladies," he says in his on-duty voice. "I've come to understand a new cult is trying to purchase businesses here in town. Moonbeam Enterprises is looking at local fixer-uppers. That includes historic sites."

Immediately I wrap a protective arm around my daughter. Just like Cosmo and November, Piper experienced a secluded and torturous life inside a cult. We're top-heavy with cult survivors and not excited for more.

"Not if I have anything to say about it. We protect our history just like it is another member of the family. It's why the Scheddy name remains on every building built before 1940."

Fiona and Faye Scheddy were cannery magnet widows who put everything they had into turning Piney Falls into a respectable resort town. There are still four buildings with their names attached: Scheddy Books and Saucy Brews Library and Bar, (located on the top floor of the police station) Scheddy Sutures Hospital, or as it is used now, Scheddy Or Not Museum of Oddities, Scheddy

Courthouse, Jail, and Library, and La Maison Scheddy Opera House.

I learned all that information when I became an official tour guide for the Fallen Branch Resort. My chest always swells with pride when I show tourists around town. "There's no way any of those buildings are in danger. They're all on the National Historical Register."

Piper drops her papers on the porch like they're evidence. "I'm sorry, Mom. But there is talk that they've already settled on a location, a historic location, and we need a plan. Before these awful investors turn a thing of beauty into a gawdy shrine to this Moonbeam person. Did you know he runs a cult?"

"Hold on. I will support you kids in just about any endeavor, but I need to know what, exactly, I'm supporting first."

Obie clears his throat. "Moonbeam Enterprises. It's an umbrella organization for these Pitch, Please karaoke clubs popping up all over the coast. Dad received a call from the Tellum police chief. Sounds like the whole town has gone gaga over karaoke. Bernie from Bernie's Magnificent Mufflers hasn't been to work in a week. And now this Moonbeam person is planning to build a karaoke club right here in Piney Falls. We can't let the town fall apart. We need a plan before everyone in town is in an uproar."

I swallow hard. Word has gotten around, which

takes approximately ten minutes in a small town. Piper is grinning from ear to ear as she gazes lovingly at her fiancé. "Go ahead, Obie. Tell her. It's genius, Mom!"

Obie nods and pats his shoulders three times. "The Tellum chief said they came in and claimed their purchase of the old Tulip Sloan Memorial Theatre was a part of the cultural revitalization initiative." He rolls his eyes. "Geoff Street is on the city planning committee. We both did props for the musical *Don't Diss Darla* in high school and became good pals. If there is a purchase of this magnitude for commercial use, there is endless red tape. He'll make sure there is enough red tape to keep this Moonbeam occupied while we find...financing."

Obie glances up at me quickly before Piper takes his hand and squeezes it. We sit in silence for a moment, soaking in the reality. Someone is attacking the very fiber of our city. The heart and soul.

"Oh, guys, you know I love you both with all my heart. But Cos and I don't have the kind of money needed for that kind of purchase."

"No, Mom," Piper shakes her head. "I wasn't asking for that. We've already come up with a great idea. Tell her, Obie!"

"Sabotage?" I offer.

"Legal sabotage," Obie amends. "I won't be involved in anything illegal."

Piper sighs. "You guys."

Then Obie leans forward. "My idea is simple. What if we can buy the building? Maybe go door-to-door collecting donations? The police department does a lot for people in this town. They'll be grateful enough to contribute."

I blink. "Which one?"

"Ideally all of them," he says. "If we own them, we control what happens to them. We stop them at the root. But we start with the theater."

Piper's mouth drops open. "Buy a historic, haunted, crumbling building? With what money? I thought you wanted to rent it. Dad and I put most of what we make back into our business. Unless we can purchase it for the 1920s prices used to build it, there's just no way."

I sip my tea, suddenly buzzing. "We could fundraise. Our city could purchase one building at a time."

"Sure," Obie says. "Classic bake sales. Haunted opera tours. Haunted bake sales—ghosts selling cookies. That will only take a few decades to raise enough money."

Piper's eyes light up. "What about something bold? Something Piney Falls-y?"

That's when the idea hits me like a poorly timed confetti cannon.

"What if," I say slowly, "we launch a fundraiser culminating in a carnival? We could have all sorts of different events that will end that day. Like men grow their hair and beards out—no trimming allowed—and at the end, the highest bidder gets to make the first cut?"

Piper's mouth spreads into a grin. "Like a hairy telethon!"

Obie chuckles. "We could call it, SUP. Save Unique Places. What SUP? On every promotional item."

"Genius," I say. "It's catchy, weird, and slightly uncomfortable. Everything we stand for."

"What if we're too late and the sale is already in the works?" Piper asks.

Our jovial spirits sink to the ground quicker than a deflated balloon.

"I'm not asking you to break the law, certainly," I begin, taking care not to stare Obie directly in the eye. His OCD kicks into high gear when that happens. "You and your dad could find out which building it is and go over that place with a fine-toothed comb and find some code violations to report to the city. That would buy us a few months."

Piper gives her fiancé the side-eye. "My mom would NEVER ask you to break the law, right, Mom?"

I open my mouth to reply, actually to lie, but thankfully Obie speaks first. "That's genius! That building has been empty for a long time. I'm sure something is out of order. Dad can go with the inspector. He wants to preserve Piney Falls history just as much as the rest of us."

We start outlining the details. Participants sign up with pledges from friends and family. Weekly photo updates. Mid-point challenges—maybe style your beard like a villain or dye your hair opera red. At the end, we host a massive Cut-A-Thon in the large courtyard of La Maison Scheddy, the opera house built by the women that was an architectural wonder in its day. Food trucks, music, and dramatic shearing under the stars.

Obie scratches his jaw. "We might run into some problems hosting the party there before we've been able to obtain ownership. But I'll think about it."

Piper is already sketching logos. "We'll need a poster. Maybe a slogan like 'Grow for Dough.'"

I can't stop smiling. For once, we're not reacting. We're creating. Building something real.

As the sky turns orange over the ocean, we finalize our plan. SUP will launch in one week. We'll announce it with a town-wide beard and bun challenge.

It's bold. It's ridiculous. It might work.

And with any luck, it'll be enough to keep Piney Falls safe—and karaoke cult free.

Still grinning, I hug my daughter and look over at Obie. "Let's save our town. One follicle at a time."

17

Winner Winner Tofu Dinner

It takes me the better part of the afternoon to convince Cosmo that dinner with a mystery guest at November's place isn't a bad thing. But by the time we're walking up Bean's porch, he's at least pretending to be civil.

"You promised we'd only stay an hour," he grumbles, brushing invisible lint from his flannel. "That's about when my indigestion kicks in. And why are we doing this on a Wednesday? Wednesdays are when we eat our leftovers. Emotional bonding should be scheduled for Saturdays."

"You look fantastic," I tell him. "That shirt makes your eyes look like something that could heal a small nation. Be nice."

He tugs at the collar again. "Is the casserole gonna explode? I'm not trying to be dramatic, but I saw it bubbling like lava."

"Totally normal. It's Cosmo-proof," I assure him, even though I can't say the same for the emotional temperature of this evening.

Vem opens the door before we can knock. She's head-to-toe in soft gray, even her glasses rimmed in silver. Her home smells like roasted rosemary and something citrusy—bright, comforting. I take that as a good sign.

"She's not coming," Vem says immediately, already halfway back down the hall.

"Who?" Cos asks, suddenly wary. He eyes me like I'm here to steal his favorite pony. "Is this an intervention? I've cut way back on the pizza rolls, Lanie."

I shoot him a look. "No one's intervening. Yet. Go put this in the kitchen, babe. Use the second oven."

He disappears just as Vem turns to me with that wide-eyed, trying-to-be-casual expression that means she's deeply invested and trying not to be.

"Have you seen my new painting?" she asks.

"Yes," I reply. "Six times."

She tilts her head. "This time I hung it vertically."

"I need to sit," I say, letting myself sink into her plushest couch. It's probably a $4,000 vintage antique, but she lets me use it like it's a recliner at the lodge.

"How did you convince the grump to come over? Is this a sex thing?"

"No!" I scoff. "The other day he was in the back when Pepper came to the bakery. I made the strategic decision not to tell him yet."

November pushes her glasses up her nose. "Hmph. Probably wise."

"So why did Pepper back out?" I ask gently. "Too much, too fast?"

Vem just shrugs, fidgeting with the sleeve of her cardigan. "She's late. My father believed in punctuality. If she isn't here at 7:00, she isn't coming."

Just as I open my mouth to challenge that logic, the doorbell rings.

Vem scowls. "7:03. Technically late."

"Don't say anything about the time," I hiss.

She opens the door anyway.

Pepper enters like she's coming in hot– stage left. She's polished, poised, and practically humming with performative charm. The color of the day is blue, with polka dots of course—headband to heels—and she greets Cosmo with a smile that could stop a train.

My poor husband is caught completely unaware and drops his beer when he sees them side by side. "There are *two* of them? Lanie, why?"

I roll my eyes. I knew this was coming. "She's here for dinner, not to ruin your life, darling. Be nice."

Cosmo mutters something about needing some air before disappearing out the screen door and on to Vem's deck. I don't stop him.

"Come in, Pepper," I say with a warmth I don't feel. There's something off about this kid. "It's lovely to see you. Quite the surprise, running into your… sister."

Pepper studies me, eyes sharp. "Laurie, is it?"

"Lanie," Vem corrects instantly. "Lanie Brimelda Anders-Hill. My best friend. My emergency contact. My ride-or-die."

"She gets it," I say quickly, before Vem starts reading from our friendship vows. "And that's not my middle name. It's Middle Madness March and November believes she should bestow a new middle name on me every day until she finds one that fits." I'm not even apologetic. I've grown used to Vem's quirkiness. Proud of it, even.

Pepper furrows her brow but says nothing. Thankfully.

Ten minutes later, we're seated around the table. I've retrieved my reluctant husband, pleading with him to be on his best behavior. The food smells amazing, but the tension could curdle milk.

"I appreciate the invitation," Pepper says, folding her hands in her lap. "It's been a whirlwind since I got into town." She looks around. "Will Nochturn be joining us?"

Cos and I stare at each other. This isn't news to deliver before dinner.

Vem hasn't said a word. She bounces her knee under the table like she's tapping out Morse code.

"I bet your father was bursting with pride when

you told him you were going to connect with November."

Both November and Pepper shoot me glares that could cut glass. Since she never talks about him, sometimes I forget that Vem has no happy memories of her father. Barely any memories at all since he lived in a different building on the other side of the Fallen Branch compound while she was growing up.

"My…dad and I don't have a good relationship anymore. I haven't spoken to him since I was in high school."

"You got my smarts then!" Vem says.

"So what brings you here?" I ask quickly. "Just visiting?"

Vem bolts from her chair. "Anyone for more walnut root tea?" Her abrupt movement causes her glass to spill a few drops before she grabs it.

"Sit, Bean," Cos groans. "If I have to drink tree bark, I want to see *you* suffer first."

I lean in to help mop the small spill and whisper, "What's wrong?"

Vem shakes her head. No answer.

Pepper smiles, all easy charm. "I'm here on assignment, actually. My company—Moonbeam Enterprises—is opening a *Pitch, Please* karaoke club."

Silence. Absolute and instant.

"YOU'RE the one?" Vem finally asks, voice like ice water. "Here? In Piney Falls? Nobody sings here.

We moan. Loudly. With intent." I bite my tongue, unwilling to argue that she hopped up on a table and started singing in protest of the karaoke club just yesterday.

She gives Pepper a sly wink. I blink. That's not nothing.

"I'm with Bean," Cosmo adds from the kitchen. "Remember the Founders Day Choir? I'm still half-deaf from Gladys Petrie's solo."

"I've heard," Pepper replies. "But that's why it's perfect. Karaoke isn't about talent—it's about joy. Confidence. We bring state-of-the-art sound systems, themed drink menus, and no-judgment vibes. In the communities where we're already established, there has been a marked decrease in violent encounter calls with the police. We've documented the evidence." Pepper smiles broadly. "Karaoke heals. You're very fortunate we chose Piney Falls."

Cosmo grunts his displeasure.. "Which building are you sacrificing for this pop nightmare?"

Pepper beams. "No demolition necessary. I've already put a bid on La Maison Scheddy, the Opera House."

I feel the air leave the room. Obie and Piper were right.

"That building is *historic,*" I say. "Fiona Scheddy hosted Lassie Flutterblast there in the 1920s. It's a landmark."

"And it's rotting," Pepper replies in a self-assured way that makes me cringe. "This way, it becomes something useful."

"You mean loud and commercialized," Cos mutters.

"And is that the *only* reason you're here?" I ask.

She hesitates. "That's the official reason."

"And the unofficial?"

Her eyes soften just a little. "I wanted to see where Dill came from."

Silence again.

"My…our…father never spoke of this place," Pepper continues, her eyes shifting. "Or of you, November. But Ginger and I always followed your lives from a distance. Your wedding photos were like something out of a movie. And Nochturn, he's so handsome and—"

"His name isn't Dill." November says sharply. "It's Elkhorn, Year of the E. Didn't he tell you that?"

Pepper's mouth falls open. "I…uh…"

"He was a particular favorite of Zion, our leader. We had to listen to endless lectures about Elkhorn's wisdom and bravery." Vem rolls her eyes. I sense Cos tensing as well. He doesn't like to discuss his time in the cult.

"But then when the cops infiltrated, he was the first guy out. Trampled women and children to escape."

The way Vem is winding up, I'm afraid she'll be at a ten before tofu chocolate pie and it will take a week's worth of Midnight Moans before she's right in the head. I've listened before. It's not a pleasant experience.

I place a hand on her muscular arm. "Vem, honey, I'm sure she didn't come here to upset—"

"No, Lanie," she says as she shakes free of my grasp. "If the kid wants to know about her father, she needs to hear the truth." She turns to face Pepper directly. "That's why you're here, right?"

Pepper nods, though it's unclear whether she's really happy about this turn of events.

"When people came into the cult, they were required to turn over all their worldly valuables. That included jewels and money. Elkhorn, Year of the E, got to choose his assignment, so he chose tending the garden. More specifically, the garden used only for Zion's food. Organic. Treated like royalty, if vegetables can be. He convinced Zion there was a way to control people's minds using roots of common fruits and vegetables."

Cosmo leans forward, clasping his hands together. "Bean, you have a right to be angry. But the kid hasn't done anything. She doesn't have to hear this."

"Quite the contrary." Pepper clears her throat. "I want to know everything."

Vem gives Cos a smirk fitting for a playground fight that she won. "Like I was saying, Elkhorn, Year of the E, tended Zion's garden and ALLEGEDLY cooked up a mind-control concoction. But that was also one spot where valuables were buried. When he heard Zion was missing and the camp would be raided, he headed straight for the garden. I caught him digging up people's money and jewels."

This poor girl. I don't think she came prepared to hear this. "I'm sure you're tired, Pepper. We should really call it a night."

The words are barely out of my mouth before Cosmo rises. "Yep. Early morning tomorrow."

"Our conversation got sidetracked. We've heard that your clubs in other towns are all housed in historic buildings. I would encourage you to take another look around. There are newer properties that require less work. I'm sure your boss would be happy to hear that." I give her my sweetest smile.

She nods, receiving my icky-sweet smile and sending one right back. "Our company prides itself on revitalizing buildings that otherwise would face the wrecking ball. You should feel honored we chose that majestic building to save. My boss saw great potential in Piney Falls ,and after researching the number of tourists coming through, I agreed. Crazy co-inky-dink, right?"

I cringe. Her cutesy language has returned.

Vem's hands are white knuckled around her glass. It's not out of the question that she'll shatter this one. Again.

Pepper raises hers in a half-toast. "Now I'm here. Singing for my supper."

"Please don't sing," Vem murmurs. "Unless it's 'Tator, Tator Sister Traitor.' Second verse only."

For the first time all night, Pepper cracks a real smile. Not wide. Not theatrical. Just real.

"Noted."

18

Secret Agent (Wo)Man

"Can I go on record protesting this idea?"

I lower the binoculars and rub my temples like that'll stop the headache steamrolling its way into my day. "You've already planted your fancy little listening device in her tote. Why do we also need to stalk her like a crazy PI with an expired license?"

"*Two*," Vem pipes up from the back seat, mouth full of something suspiciously cookie shaped. "You keep forgetting I'm here."

I adjust her rearview mirror, placing Vem's green Misty Cove Fight Tissues cap squarely in my view. Today's green ensemble also includes green-lensed sunglasses the size of an orange. "How could I forget? We're in your car! Snooping on your sister!"

"Lanie *GoodGollyMissWally* Anders-Hill, may I remind you that *you* are the one who insisted we not trust my *exquisite* sister?"

Middle Name Mania Monday strikes again. I groan. "When I said that, I didn't mean we needed to follow that polka-dotted princess all day. I have a life, you know."

She ignores me, as usual, sipping her hibiscus tea from a matching green thermos like it holds the secrets of the universe. Vem leans forward between the front seats, shoving a crumpled bag of sweet potato crisps in my direction. I wave them off.

We're parked half a block from the Scheddy Opera House, angled ever so slightly between a rusting hydrant and a newspaper stand that's become a home for spiders and bad headlines. Piney Falls still hasn't fully shaken off its morning hush. The fog's dragging its feet, and everything smells like cedar and secrets.

The opera house sits across the street like an old woman in a wedding gown—faded, regal, a little tipsy. Ivy curls up its flaking columns like fingers gripping at time, and a crooked banner hangs across the front: *What SUP?! Saving Our Opera House, That's What!* Someone added a string of faux autumn leaves to the railing. The effect is… charmingly desperate.

Pepper sighs dramatically and presses her forehead to the steering wheel. "We're bringing you back to life, old girl."

"She's talking to this building like it's her best friend," Vem mutters. "That tracks. She gets it from our side of the family."

There's a beat of silence.

Pepper sits up straighter. Her eyes narrow, locked on the opera house like it just whispered a challenge.

She pops her door open, steps into the crisp morning air, and crosses the street in her rust-and-lime polka-dot coat, boots crunching over frost-bitten leaves. She plops herself on a bench across from the entrance—one someone stenciled with "SESCH" for "Save the Scheddy," though it looks more like a gang tag from the Soft Crafts Club.

"She's gonna make her move," Vem says, licking sugar off her thumb. "You betting she sneaks in before lunch or after?"

"After," I say. "She's got a meeting."

And sure enough, after a few minutes of dramatic staring and whispered pep talks to abandoned architecture, Pepper heads down Main Street, likely following the smell of maple syrup to her next rendezvous. I wait two minutes, then signal to Vem, who's already sliding into the driver's seat.

"Wait here," I say. "I want a clean listen."

"You owe me a dozen day-old scones," she calls as I close the door.

I tail Pepper at a careful distance. She slips into *Pancakes, Pancakes, and Pancakes*—still the most aggressively named diner in town. The bell jingles as I step inside a moment later.

I take a seat at the counter, pull out my phone,

and quietly link into the audio feed from Pepper's mic. It's scratchy, but good enough.

I spot her in a back booth, unbuttoning her coat. She's already sipping coffee when *he* walks in.

Red Rooph.

Lumbering. Gray at the temples. Jacket collar up like he's trying to disappear into it.

He slides into the booth across from her, and they get straight to business.

"Ms. Friday," he says.

"Red," she replies. Her voice is all sugar and sharpened steel. "Golly, thanks for meeting me."

I don't even need to look to know she's just handed him the folder. I hear the faint shuffle of papers.

"Before you worry about permits," she says, "you should know I've already done half the work."

Red flips through the file. I imagine his unruly eyebrows arching into roller coaster form as he sees permits, blueprints, contractor lists, digital renderings—Pepper's signature all over everything. It's what she does. She overwhelms you with pretty visions and precision.

"You move fast," Red mutters.

"Piney Falls deserves better than a crumbling landmark," she says. "I'm not here to gut the town. I'm here to partner with it."

They talk more. About history. About restoration. About ethics.

And then she asks it.

"By the way, Red... Do you know someone named Nochturn?"

There's a pause.

Then Red lies. Smooth and flat. "Nope. Never heard of him."

The booth goes quiet for a beat too long. I don't need visuals to know what Pepper's face looks like.

"I can leave my bag here while I run to the girlie room, right?"

Red leans forward. "Well I wouldn't have much use for it. Polka dots aren't my thing."

Pepper excuses herself to the restroom, and I wait.

Ten minutes pass.

Then fifteen.

I'm still listening when I hear the phone come out of his pocket. The quiet buzz of a call being made. And then—

"It's Red. Just wanted to update you."

His voice is tight. Nervous.

"I met her. Pepper Friday. She's sharp. Slick but not greasy. Smart as a fox."

A pause.

"It just seems wrong to—"

Then I hear it. A clipped voice on the other end, sharp as a slap. Cold. Unforgiving.

"I make the decisions. Not you."

Red swallows.

"And I'll get paid, like we agreed?"

Another pause.

"A deal's a deal. $100,000 in small bills. Half tonight, half when you push through the sale and permits."

The line goes dead.

Red doesn't move. Just sits there, clutching his coffee like a man holding a confession.

I slip out the door before he sees me.

The air outside is warmer now, the fog finally giving way. The sunlight glances off the cracked windows of the opera house, catching on the flecks of gold in its peeling paint.

And me?

I'm already texting Vem.

> Red's selling her out. $100K deal. He lied about Nochturn. We need to head to the greenhouse.

She replies immediately.

> Oh! You've finally taken my advice about hanging plants over your bed so your hairy husband wakes up in a forest!

She's always insisting she comes up with these crazy ideas for his benefit. I think she enjoys tormenting Cos any way she can.

"No bed forest creations today. Red made a call that traced back to The Greenbean Scene."

And just like that, our quiet morning stakeout becomes something much bigger.

Because someone's pulling strings in Piney Falls.

And I think we just found the first knot.

19

Spies and Alibis

When she knocks on my door before using her key anyway, I'm just about to wrap my blonde locks in a towel. "Vem? Coffee's ready," I call as I put the finishing touches on my lime-colored knit top and black jeans. In all the years I worked for *Work Ahead Office Supplies, The Best Office Supply Chain in the World*, I never once wore casual clothing, not even on the weekends. I just couldn't get myself out of work mode. It feels good to be a more genuine version of me here in Piney Falls.

Vem snuck a tiny tracking device in her sister's black-and-white polka-dot purse before Pepper left and we held our breaths that she didn't find it. Luckily we were able to listen to her entire conversation with Red Rooph regarding the sale of La Maison Scheddy.

An afternoon trip to the greenhouse proved fruitless; the sign on the door said, "Gone for Edna

Throddlebum's funeral. Taking the whole day as her family will spill the tea after the punchbowl is empty."

"Oh yeah," Vem says. "I read that in the paper last week.

"LOCAL RESIDENT *FATALLY ENTANGLED BETWEEN TWO SHOPPING CARTS; POLICE CALL IT "A PERFECT STORM OF BAD WHEELS"*

"Whoever called must've done it from the alley. We can check, but I doubt we'll find anything."

We didn't.

WHEN I ENTER the kitchen this morning, Vem's mouth is full of Cosmic Cream Cheese Cinnamon Rolls. I'd be surprised if she wasn't in full-on garbage disposal mode after yesterday's spy adventure.

"Today we can do something fun to distract us from—"

She's sporting a camouflage green jumpsuit, sunglasses the size of cereal bowls, and a scarf pulled so high she looks like she's being eaten by a snake made of wool. I know exactly what she's planning.

"This is not casual wear," I remind her.

"It is when you're emotionally compromised," she replies, somehow keeping all that food in her mouth. As soon as she swallows, she reaches into her oversized pocket and stuffs ant jerky, that took over a year to make because of how long it took to collect all those ants, into it.

"Do you want to talk about yesterday? It had to be incredibly difficult for you."

Vem stares at me, wide-eyed. I'm not sure if she's planning to tackle me to the ground as she's done on occasion when she's feeling "wolfish" or if she's ready to spew everything in her mouth, projectile-style, all over my clean face.

"After a midnight moan, a two-hour mediation, and the tofu chocolate silk pie, I've come to a conclusion. That's why I called this morning."

"Yes, I remember that five a.m. call." I sigh. "We talked about these early morning calls before. Only if it's an emergency. A 'we're going a-spying, Lanie' is not an emergency. I was hoping it was another fever dream."

Vem places her hands on her slender hips. "It's an emergency to me. We're going to spy on Pepper today. Again. I want to see what she's really up to."

"Hon, I know that having her pop up out of nowhere is unnerving." I'm actually the one feeling uncomfortable. "We don't have to follow your sister every single day. I was hoping your call was another case of your vocal diary and an unfortunate butt dial. Gladys can get information on anyone without us lifting one finger. Maybe we hang back and just wait to see what happens. We could invite Pepper over for tea in a few weeks."

"Oh, Lanie. Don't you think trying out my little spy gadgets is more exciting than listening to that gas bag?"

Arguing when she's already fully outfitted is wasted energy. After a quick breakfast, I agree to meet her in one of seven garages she's recently built for her myriad of vehicles and spy equipment. "Meet me in *Oil Be Bach,* Lanie," she instructed. Like I know which one that is. I wander around the recently cleared land through corrugated buildings that all look the same.

"Vem!" I call out in vain.

Out of pure luck, a small door opens in the building I'm standing in front of. "Geez, Lanie. You don't need to scream. There are orange-spotted bubble owls nesting nearby. Do you want to be responsible for their offspring splattered all over the ground like common chicken eggs? Come on in!"

This garage houses a tank, yes, a tank, a sports car, and lots and lots of gadgets. Something tells me I've yet to reach the inner, disturbing layers of her brain.

After convincing Vem an armored vehicle would be far too obvious, we jump into her sport utility vehicle. "How do we know where she is?" I ask, somehow forgetting yesterday's session.

We trail Pepper from a distance as she heads downtown, clipboard in hand, a bounce in her step that seems oddly cheerful for someone who is about to destroy a local place of pride that can't be undone.

She stops in front of the boarded-up hardware store.

"I'd much rather she set up her karaoke club in that dump," I whisper for no real reason. "Vem, can you turn up the volume on your gadget?"

Vem points to her screen again, where she's tapped a button that says "audio." Pepper's annoying peppy voice comes in loud and clear.

"Thanks for meeting me here, Mr. Bentnail. It's a super cute location." She giggles. I know she's young, but that cutesy stuff is really starting to get under my skin.

"Yeah, when you called I was out back, trying to clear out the last of my hammers. You'd think they only come in one size, wouldn't you?"

Pepper giggles again, this time sounding forced and awkward like she's mimicking a flock of angry birds. "The reason I contacted you, Mr. Bentnail, is because I think your building will be a perfect location. I'd like to offer you a fair price so we could start construction immediately."

"Yup, yup. Your offer was fair. Thought you was buying with someone else?"

"She's...otherwise occupied, but still my business partner." Pepper clears her throat. "So, do we have a deal, Mr. Bentnail?"

“Guess so. Sure hate to let go of the old place. Where do I sign.”

“Here. Here. And here. And remember, part of our deal is that you aren’t to share the new ownership or its intended purpose with anyone. Got it?”

“Yup.”

“Good. It’s been a pleasure doing business with you, sir. You have until the end of the month to remove your remaining…hammers…”

Pepper chats with the owner of the building for a few minutes, gestures to the awning, laughs a little too brightly, then scribbles something on her clipboard. I snap a photo. Vem bites a piece off her jerky like it’s a detective novel in meat form.

“See, Lanie?” she asks, mouth full. “She’s just getting to know Piney Falls. Nothing to worry about.”

“You were the one who didn’t trust her, Vem. Remember?” I have to admit, now I’m starting to feel like there is something up. Some nefarious reason for the building purchase. “Who do you think this mysterious partner is?”

Vem shrugs. “Could be another mini me.” She elbows me in the ribs. “Wouldn’t it be something if there were three Goddesses of Refinement right here in Piney Falls? Your husband would flip his lid.”

We follow her as she walks to a coffee shop and grocery called Sip Happens, and we wait, somewhat awkwardly, out of view. She orders something with oat milk and turmeric and sits in the corner by the window—facing out.

"That's a power move," Vem notes. "She wants to make sure no one is watching her."

"Like two misguided women who should have much better things to do," I say.

"She's looking straight at us!" Vem yanks my body down behind a large dahlia bush, and we wait.

Pepper emerges from the coffee shop cursing into a phone. I know Vem's going to mention how that's a family trait that she's proud of, so I clasp my hand firmly over her mouth.

"Yes, Your Exaltedness. I DO understand why a death at a club opening creates bad optics. I can release a statement that—you what? I don't think it's legal to mess with death certificates."

Pepper's shoulder's fall as though someone has just deflated her polka-dot vibe in one sentence. "He's not telling the truth, sir. I would never— yes, sir. Of course I should respect Mr. za'Dimwit as an authority figure, sir."

When she's done talking, Pepper throws her phone into her large polka-dotted bag and huffs, "Gahhh! This can't end soon enough!" Before stomping down the street.

Five minutes later, Vem peeks over the fern. "All clear."

"She saw us."

"She did not."

"There's no doubt now, Vem. Your sister is involved in something shady."

Pause.

"I don't feel good."

The times November Bean has been ill since I've known her are numbers I can count on one finger. One. When she ate what she thought was beetle dung in a macaroni casserole and instead it belonged to a skunk.

"Before we go, I want to check inside and see if she left anything. You can wait in the car if you'd like."

She nods somberly. I have to push aside my concern for her and my allegiance to our bakery and coffee shop as I look inside. In the booth where she was sitting is a neatly folded paper napkin. There are words scribbled on it.

Stop following me! and 119 Birdsong Lane.

A man exiting the bathroom stares hard at me. He is wearing a bowler hat like the one Cos wore on Halloween last year (he refused to be a mobster, given his many years in prison for a crime he didn't commit), instead insisting his pin-stripe suit made him a 1930s movie star. No argument from me.

"I was sitting there," he said in a deep baritone voice I recognize as the other person sitting with Pepper. "Was there something you needed, you gorgeous blonde, you?"

I blush. Most everyone in town knows I'm married, and compliments, while usually not unwelcome, don't seem warranted. "Oh, I…a friend dropped this. It has an address on it that I—"

The stranger snatches the napkin from my hand so quickly I don't have time for the defensive actions Vem has taught me. He reads the message and then shakes his head.

"Does that mean something to you, sir?" I ask innocently, hoping he questions the sanity of a middle-aged woman picking up random napkins.

"Oh yes. Yes indeedy." He takes the napkin and shoves it in the breast pocket of his shirt before grabbing his coffee. He stares at me with an intensity that makes me feel naked. I hope I'm not blushing. "It's probably best you mind your own business now, pretty lady."

Odd.

"Okay," Vem says shakily when I tell her. "So she definitely saw us."

"No, she definitely saw someone. It wasn't us."

Vem is silent for the ride home, and I am eternally grateful. I need to think about the implications of our morning. I was careful not to give her the address on the napkin. I want to investigate this without her tagging along, at least until I know it won't cause her any more pain.

Back at my house, Cos is watching a documentary on dramatic 1880s train robberies and eating tortilla chips and cheese slices off a cutting board. He looks up as we enter, faces long.

"Please tell me you didn't confront her."

"No," I say.

"But she confronted us," Vem adds.

Cos sighs. "Bean I can understand getting mixed up in a mess like this, but you, Lanie, you know better."

That night, I can't sleep. I keep replaying the look in Bowler Hat Man's eyes when he read the message—part wink, part warning. I realize I wanted Pepper to be the only villain so Vem wouldn't be so fixated on this stranger. Now there are other players in this game.

20

Sibling Serenade

"I'm just looking out for you, Vem. Your sister is hiding something. We're up against the clock trying to get our What SUP?! Saving Our Opera House, That's What! campaign in full swing, and she's sneaking around doing non-karaoke-related things like purchasing the old hardware store. Don't you think that's odd?"

We had a *heated* exchange after spying on Pepper Friday three days ago ("she's dangerous and I don't want you around her, Vem!" "Don't tell ME who I can jabber with, Lanie Beulah Anders-Hill!"), and since then, I've successfully avoided Vem. Not an easy feat when she has government-issue spy equipment trained on our house 24/7. This morning, I made the mistake of taking the trash out in broad daylight. Rookie move. Before I'd even lifted the lid, she appeared like a crimson ghost.

Resplendent in rose red from headband to high-tops, Vem stands there, arms folded. "Yessirree, girlfriend. I know *exactly* what's going on here."

I toss the bag into the barrel and sigh. "Oh really? Please, enlighten me."

If I'm honest, this isn't just about mistrust. It's about hurt feelings. Mine specifically. We've always called each other sisters from another mister, and Pepper's surprise appearance feels like a wedge driven straight through the middle of our sisterhood.

"You're jealous, that's what." Vem's tone is almost gleeful. "You're afraid my magnificent baby sister is going to consume all my free time and you'll have no one but your husband to watch as he does pull ups at 9:17 p.m. every night."

I open my mouth, ready to deny it, but shut it again. What's the point?

"Pepper is lovely. Stunning, actually," Vem continues, ever generous with her praise. "She's funny, smart, and younger than you—"

"Are you *trying* to make me feel worse?"

She grabs me in one of her signature bear hugs—the kind that requires medical clearance beforehand. "Down, down," I wheeze.

Once I'm free and breathing again, I glance at her, my best friend, my family. Cosmo, Piper, and I have been her only real family for too long. Maybe it's time to ease up and just be there for her.

"You know what? You're right. I *was* a little jealous. I mean, how often do I get to experience two Vems at once? I'll support you, no matter what you decide about your sister."

"Promise?" Her arms twitch like she's about to hug me again.

I quickly grab the trash bin like a shield and roll it between us to the curb. "We're best friends. Nonnegotiable."

"I'VE NEVER BEEN fond of that Bean woman and her crazy moans and howls," Gladys Petrie, the oldest working person in Piney Falls and the town grump grumbles, "but this isn't something you do behind your best friend's back, toots."

Piney Falls' Land and Title Office smells like lemon polish, ancient paper, and macaroni salad that's been outside the refrigerator a little too long. Gladys has probably run this office since the town was founded. She's the original search engine. Dark web? She wrote the how-to manual. Her hacking skills outstrip every teenager and deputy in town combined.

Also ironic: her son-in-law and closest friend is the town's police chief, Boysie Lumquest. When I once pointed that out, she reached over her desk and knocked on my skull like a hollow pumpkin.

"Anybody home?" she asked. Not even pretending it was a joke.

"I'm not one to gossip," she says, clearly reveling in her title as Gossip Queen, "but the two of you are as thick as thieves, and everyone in town has noticed there's been an ice flow between you. I blame you."

"What? Why would you say such a thing, Gladys? That's so hurtful."

"That one's got a gaping hole in her noggin. But you've got a level head. You could fix this if you wanted," she replies, ignoring my question.

"Vem being my best friend is exactly why I need to make sure Pepper Friday is legit." I lean against the desk. "Spill it, Gladys. What do you know?"

She straightens in her squeaky swivel chair and adjusts her new glasses. The black frames magnify her eyes so large she can watch Carol Judson's affair with the pickleball coach from three blocks away. Owl eyes that could unearth your deepest secrets and then cross-reference them with your childhood vaccination records.

She motions me closer.

"There's no one else here, Gladys—"

"You want information? It comes with *my* direction!"

Sighing, I lean forward, bracing for a full assault of stale instant coffee breath.

"She came in the other day," Gladys whispers. "Wanted to know everything about the old opera house. And once she got what she came for, that walking exclamation point asked me what I knew about November Bean."

I blink. "That's not a secret. I already knew she was scoping locations for her karaoke club chain."

Gladys narrows her eyes. "If you don't want to hear the rest—"

"I'm late for my hair appointment!" I say with all the urgency of someone actively *not* late and actively *lying*.

Gladys clicks her tongue. "Fine. She asked about Ms. Bean but kept interrupting me. Seems like she's researched every moment of November's life, even back to her time in the cult. Only thing she didn't know was how little the parents saw the kids in that cult. She seemed shocked when I told her they barely knew their parents."

"Still not surprising," I say, standing to leave.

"First let me tell you what I found on the dark web."

Sighing, I take a look at my watch. The nonexistent appointment will wait. "Okay, but make it quick."

Gladys pushes her chair away from the desk, a nauseating squeaky sound. She walks slowly, allowing her orthopedic shoes to clunk harder than they should on the floor. Disappearing momentarily, she comes back with a ream of paper. There will be one page of useable information and gibberish on the other 99. Typical Gladys.

"Printed it out so you could see. She drops the stack with a dramatic thump, causing the glass figurine of Elvis riding a donkey I bought her for Christmas to jiggle. Luckily, the page with information is on top.

"See there?" she says from behind me. I can smell her tuna casserole breath so I know she's close.

"That little gal and her family own a greenhouse in Connecticut. They go by the surname of Plantz but never *legally* changed it. Sounds pretty fishy to me, if I were the suspicious type."

"Thank you, Gladys. I can read for myself." I turned to sit at an angle in my chair. The next thing that pops up is that her father, Dill, has been receiving large sums of money from a pretty unusual source. "This can't be right."

Gladys smiles like she just won the spelling bee. "Yup. Sure is. That man is filling his pockets with money from the US government. Can't figure out which department yet, but I'd bet Monday's blueberry scone that the November clone has no idea."

I think for a moment. "It's so strange they would pay an individual such large sums."

Gladys stares at me blankly. "Did I *say* it was just him? Don't think the noggin's needing serviced."

"Well who else? Don't leave me hanging!"

Honestly, that woman can be twice as irritating as Vem. The two women have so much in common, it's no wonder they are always at odds. Too many shared quirks lead to a lack of meaningful conversation.

"If you'd turn the page, you'd see for yourself," she snaps.

Bank transfers totaling several million dollars to something called Moonbeam Enterprises. She shoves my hand aside and points further down the page. "Here's several deposits from St. Slackjaw Preparatory School for the Mildly—"

"Pepper went to some fancy boarding school." Anger wells up inside me. Poor Vem grew up in a strict cult with no time to be a kid, while her sister lived in the lap of luxury.

"If you'd stop interrupting, toots, I'd get everything out at once. She told me all about the boarding school while I was looking up the hardware store's zoning. Seems her father and the headmaster had some kind of deal to pay her tuition. She never found out what it was though."

I frown. "She's far removed from high school."

The large clock on the wall overlooking her desk chimes three times. "You gonna be late for your hair appointment without even calling? Guess you haven't lived here long enough to learn some manners." Gladys's kids must've figured out early that you couldn't pull the wool over her eyes.

I blush. "What was the other thing you had to tell me? About when she came in person?"

"She also asked about the weaponry in Toodle Doodle's house. Handguns, to be exact."

I freeze. "Vern's house?"

"She wanted to know if any of it had *ever been used.*"

My stomach drops like I've missed a stair. "Why would she want to know that?"

Gladys grins, slow and dangerous. "Because. toots… your Pepperoni wants to *buy* one."

21

Don't Take Your Guns to Town

Gladys's news that Pepper is interested in purchasing something from Vem's stash of weaponry sends a cold chill down my spine. I don't dare talk to Vem about it yet. She would look at it as a compliment and then give her sister enough to blow Piney Falls to smithereens.

Vem isn't one to part with things she's collected. That's why they had to build a second Store-n-More on the edge of town. The first one filled up fast, mostly with Vem's "absolutely essential" collections: vintage Purple Chocolate albums, rare airhorns, velvet paintings of wombats, polaroids of Insects After Dark, and of course, her medieval weaponry.

She's enamored with her sister—and with good reason. Their father vanished without a trace, and their mother didn't stick around long enough to learn the girl's shoe size. Apparently, she couldn't handle raising kids after years of being told what to do in the cult.

Then there's Nochturn—Vem's brother. Sweet, stoic Nochturn. The poor woman has carried too much grief for one lifetime. She deserves a break. That's why I haven't said anything. Not yet.

There are currently much more important issues, namely our campaign to stop the sale of the opera house.

The campaign which has taken off like wildfire. There is no official record of the sale of the building yet, but it's clear we don't have much time.

What SUP is on everything from tablecloths to raffle tickets to homemade beard oil samples. Obie designed a logo featuring a cartoon opera house wearing sunglasses, and Piper—over at Cosmic Bakes—started a social media account that garnered three dozen followers within the first hour. By noon, someone has Photoshopped a top hat onto the building.

"We've gone viral," Piper declares, holding up her phone. "If you count 'Mildly Inflamed' as viral."

"It's better than lurking in the shadows, Pips," Obie insists.

The fundraiser is structured in levels:

- *Level 1: Grow Something Weird* – Entry-level donations earn attendees a new comb and one free hair product.

- *Level 2: Beard Buddies* – Sponsored pairs braid each other's beards while blindfolded. It's equal parts touching and terrifying. Top three entries get beard care products for a year.
- *Level 3: The Grand Trim Finale* – At the event's climax, the highest bidder gets to snip the first lock from our top beard-grower—live on stage. Possibly with a sword. Pending a last-minute safety approval from our insurance guy, who is currently judging a chili cookoff in Misty Cove.

Vem adds a special twist: Beard-omancy, a fortune-telling booth where she reads destinies using facial hair swirls. It's unclear whether she's making it up as she goes or if there's an actual system, but people are lining up.

22

No Revolution

I'm filled to the brim with excitement. I can't wait to tell Cos what we've accomplished so far. With Piper and Obie at the helm, I have full confidence it will be successful. When I reach the bakery, Doris, Cosmo's longtime employee, is mid-squabble with one of our most "colorful" regulars, Barney "Stabby" McNife. He's not dangerous, despite the nickname. He's just very...particular about his coffee temperature and the sharpness of his cutlery.

"I just filled your cup, Stabby. You're not getting more coffee until I deal with this line of *paying* customers," Doris barks.

Stabby turns around dramatically, where one teen is zombified by his phone and the last person in line is staring at the ceiling, mumbling something about alien blueprints. Not exactly the angry mob Doris is describing.

I scan the situation and step in. "I'm happy to fill your cup, Barney," I say, using his real name. Without waiting for an answer, I refill his mug and hand it over. Doris gives me a look that could curdle milk. Ever since Piper announced she was going on vacation, Doris has decided she's the de facto bakery manager, wielding a spatula like it's a sheriff's badge.

Once the line is handled and the gentle hum of cinnamon-scented conversation returns, I slip into Cosmo's office. He's hunched over the computer, squinting at Piper's new inventory software—some AI-based system that tracks every loaf, every scone, every single sprinkle.

There's a scowl on his ruggedly handsome face, made even funnier by the horn-rimmed reading glasses I left in his drawer after he "accidentally" sent a jam order to a janitorial supply company. We ended up with 60 door *jambs*.

I knock lightly. "Babe?"

He jumps like he's been electrocuted and spills coffee all over a stack of scone profitability reports.

"Dammit! Lanie, towel—fast!"

By the time I return with towels, paper napkins, and a mop, Cos has already taken off his shirt. And wow. That muscular build should come with a warning label.

"You don't need to worry, sweetheart," he says, catching my look. "This wasn't your fault."

"I know. It's just that you still take my breath away, Mr. Hill."

We kiss. Deeply. Thoroughly. Like we're teenagers behind the drive-in movie screen.

A knock interrupts us—sharp, insistent.

"There's a delivery for you, Lanie," Doris announces. "Says you need to sign. Also, Ms. Bean is here. Something about *Tickle Your Toes Day* or whatever."

"It's *Tickle Your Nose Day*," I correct, because of course I know. Vem insists we sync calendars now, and I have the aromatherapy-themed bullet journal to prove it. "We're supposed to keep track of the things we smell today."

"Come in, Doris," Cosmo calls. "It's just me and Lanie. You'll keep us honest."

Doris opens the door, then stops mid-step when she sees me perched on Cos's lap. "Two middle-aged people carrying on like they're sixteen-year-olds in a hayloft. Have some self-respect."

"Is there a question in there," Cos asks, "or are you just making sure we know you're disgusted?"

"Hmph!" She slams the door.

We dissolve into laughter. "I'd be sixteen again," Cos says while showing that heart-melting smile, "just so I'd have more time with you."

I've almost forgotten why I came. It's not uncommon to get lost in those ice blue eyes. "Oh, Cos—I just found out Pepper wants to purchase a weapon from Vem."

He sits back, his eyes narrowing. "Two of them with ammunition? That *really* scares me."

I nod. "Vem collects to collect, but Pepper? I don't know. It feels…off. Why pretend to build a relationship with Vem just for a business transaction?"

"I don't trust the young one at all," he mutters. "Bean is her own kind of nutty, but at least she has a good heart."

It's the first time I've heard Cos say anything even slightly kind about Vem. I open my mouth to thank him, but he gently presses his finger to my lips.

"Don't make me regret saying that," he warns. "What I *meant* is that she's harmless in her own wacky way."

"Yes. Right. Got it." It'll have to do.

"But the junior version…" he pauses, "she's got jealousy in her blood. You can see it in the way she watches Vem—like she's trying to measure how hard it would be to step into her shoes and walk away with everything."

Before I can respond, Doris knocks again. "Didn't I *just* say someone's waiting for your signature, Lanie?"

With a peck on Cos's cheek, I head out. "We'll talk more tonight, love."

The postal worker waiting for me has never once smiled. Her nickname is Stoneface, but I refuse to give in so easily. "I don't have all day,

Lanie," she grumbles, shoving a pen and form in front of me. "Sign here. And here."

"You look like you could use a coffee and a scone. What's new at the post office?"

She grunts, but I can't tell if it's in the affirmative. "This guy came into the post office the other day and asked how stamps work. Like in a condescending voice."

"A local?" I ask, surprised.

"Nope. He had a permanent shocked look on his face. Hope someone gets him some help. The way he was dressed, he comes from money."

"I wasn't expecting a delivery—especially not here at the bakery—can you tell me—?"

"I don't open the boxes, Mrs. Anders-Hill. That's a federal crime." She glances behind me. "That your last Marionberry Mars scone?"

"Would you like it? On the house. You look like you could use a pick-me-up."

Her mood improves instantly. "I'll take that. And an iced latte. Extra shot. Also, a Pluto Peach and Solar Strawberry for my mother and sister."

Once she's left with a small pastry empire in hand, I turn my attention to the box. It's large, heavy, with no return address—just a postmark from Virginia. Virginia? I rack my memory. I never traveled there during my marketing days with Work Ahead Office Supplies, The Largest Office Supply Chain in the World™.

I'm about to drag it out to my car when Doris

appears, bread knife in hand, and plunges it down the center of the box like she's carving a turkey.

"You're welcome."

Together we haul the box onto the center table. I peel back the packaging. On top, there's a neatly folded *turtleneck.* A very *plain*, very *beige* turtleneck. Beneath it? A strange, shiny contraption.

"Oooooh!" Vem squeals. I jump. "That's an original karaoke machine!"

"Where did *you* come from? And how do you *know* that?"

She crouches, eyeing the device like it's the Holy Grail of tuneless warbling. "Lanie, this thing has *never been used.* It's probably worth a fortune!"

"But why would someone send *this* to *me*?" I examine the bedazzled surface. It's covered in multicolored rhinestones, glued on in what can only be described as enthusiastic chaos. "I'm on the *committee* AGAINST the karaoke club. It makes no sense."

Before I can say another word, Vem shoves me out the front door. "Out! Everybody out! It's *ticking!*"

My blood runs cold.

"I have to get Cos!" I shout, pushing against her to run back inside. "And Doris!"

I burst through the door. Cos is already standing next to the blinking machine.

"Huh," he mutters. "Never seen anything like—"

"It's a bomb!" I scream. "We have to go—"

But it's too late. The ticking stops. The world goes silent for half a second.

"I love you," I mouth.

Then, an explosion.

23

Shimmer, Shake, and Sabotage

The sound of the explosion still rings in my ears—a high, insistent tone like a swarm of angry bees trapped in a tin can. It wasn't just loud, it was violent, slamming through the bakery with such force that even now, the world hums on a different frequency. My brain feels like it's underwater.

"Lanie?" Cos's voice filters in, far away, distorted, like it's traveling through a tunnel. His lips move, but all I catch is a garbled string of vowels—and maybe my name.

I blink once. Twice. Trying to clear both my vision and my head. The air is thick with silver. Every breath pulls in a powdery sweetness that coats the back of my throat. I can *taste* glitter—on my tongue, in my sinuses, embedded somewhere behind my eyes. There's glitter in my ears. In my nose. I run a hand through my hair and a sheet of sparkle sloughs off like I'm molting.

"Can you hear me?" Cos repeats, louder now—though it's hard to tell if it's him or if my brain is finally rebooting.

"I think… I think I can," I croak, my voice hoarse and clogged with more sparkle than sound.

Around us, chaos reigns in pastel shimmer. Vem is blinking rapidly, like she's trying to dislodge glitter from her tear ducts. Her glasses are packed to the brim. Doris is dabbing at her ears with pastry napkins, mumbling, "It's in my brain. I can *feel* it dancing."

November sneezes. No sound—just a fine puff of gold dust bursting from her nostrils like a cursed party favor.

Even Barney McNife, who once took a squirrel bite to the femur without flinching, is groaning from the floor, one hand clutching his glitter-clogged left ear, the other reaching blindly for his coffee mug. "I can't hear nothing but church bells," he mutters. "Glitter's gotten into my soul."

Cos stumbles toward the counter—and stops short. He just stares. The destruction is breathtaking in the worst possible way.

The bakery—his pride, his joy, his second home—is coated in shimmering ruin. No corner escaped. No surface spared.

There's glitter wedged into outlets, clinging to the ceiling tiles. The display case looks like a prismatic crime scene—every baked good twinkling like it's auditioning for a tap number.

Even the air hums with defeat. Cos… he crumbles a little.

He sinks onto a stool with a long, heavy exhale. His hands rest on his knees, fingers blackened with soot and shimmer. When he lifts one to his face, it comes away shining.

"I just cleaned the espresso machine," he says, quietly.

My heart twists. Not for the machine—for *him.* I know that tone. Hollow, tightly wound, the sound of someone trying to stay upright in the middle of something deeply unfair.

"The drains are going to be clogged for days," he murmurs. "We'll never get it out of the mixer gears. It's in the flour. The jam fridge. The yeast containers. It's in the vents, Lanie."

I slide onto the stool beside him, laying a hand on his shoulder. "Cos—"

"I had the weekend planned," he says, voice thin. "We were going to debut the bourbon pecan buns. Piper printed custom tags. Doris practiced her 'surprised customer' face in the mirror for an hour."

Silence settles.

Even Doris, never known for her restraint, slumps into a chair that puffs out a glitter cloud so thick it erases her from the neck down. "Can't hear a thing!" she shouts, still trying to clean her hearing aids. No point telling her it's not the batteries. It's the blast.

Cos steadies himself against the counter and leans forward. The note. The microphone. "P. F." he mutters, voice like gravel. "Do we know anyone with those initials, babe?"

"Maybe. I'm not sure," I reply. "I'm calling Boysie."

November steps gingerly through the wreckage, her usual monochrome wardrobe now confettied. She skirts a fallen coffee pot and a still-humming electric mixer.

Vem blows her nose into her hands, causing a glitter cloud to form over her head. I make a mental note to disinfect my car door handles. "Don't they understand that opening a karaoke club in a historic opera house is a crime against humanity?" she asks.

"What's that about a banana tree?" Doris hollers.

November scowls but doesn't argue. She's scanning the debris, expression strangely blank.

That's when it hits me. She's not startled. She's *scared*.

I move closer. "You okay?"

She nods too fast. "Yes. Fine. Just… Was it her, Lanie? I didn't think anyone with my genes would ever…" Her voice trails off.

"Don't think about that yet," I say gently. "If she's behind this, Boysie will figure it out. You've got a family in me, Cos, and Piper. Remember?"

Behind me, Barney McNife is trying to vacuum himself with what appears to be a vintage Dust-buster. It's working about as well as a comb in a hurricane. Mostly the glitter just clings harder.

"Guess we're closed," Cos announces. Understatement of the decade.

Doris's pocket explodes with horror-movie chimes, and we all jump. All except Doris, who remains free of hearing.

"Timer!" I yell, enunciating as clearly as possible. She reaches into her pocket and pulls out a glitter-covered box. "Guess I'd better check the oven," she mutters. "Sure would've been nice if someone told me the timer was going off."

Cosmo gives her a thumbs-up like a man who has just given up entirely.

I call Boysie, who makes me repeat the words glitter bomb *twice*. Then I call Piper.

"Cosmic Bakes, let us bake you happy, this is Piper speaking," she chirps, sounding more like a Girl Scout than a grown woman.

"Hon, we had an incident…"

"Oh no! Is it Dad's heart? Is he at the hospital? I'll close and be there in fifteen minutes."

"He's fine. Though he's covered head to toe in glitter."

Her laugh bursts through the line. "What kind of bet did he lose with November?"

"It was a bomb. A glitter bomb."

Silence.

"Piper? Hon? We're fine. The bakery… not so much. There's glitter in every crack and crevice.

Even stuff in the fridge. Doris thinks it rewired her brain."

"I don't find this funny, Mom. It was probably high school kids trying to outdo last year's homecoming prank of a cow in the library," she says.

"Probably. Which means you don't need to close up shop. We're fine here." Now I realize the benefit of keeping things to myself.

By mid-afternoon, the bakery is locked down and wrapped in bright yellow caution tape that neighborhood kids have jazzed up with signs: *WARNING: FAIRIES INSIDE* and *GLITTERY CRIMINALS AHEAD.*

Piney Falls doesn't have a bomb squad. What we *do* have is Marla Pickens—the middle school science teacher who once defused a suspicious lunchbox using salad tongs and a prayer to St. Newton.

Marla arrives in a lab coat over jeans, wielding a pair of tongs.

"Where's the device?"

"Mostly glitter now," I tell her. "Also trauma."

She grunts and heads inside without another word. An hour later we've all but forgotten about her when she re-emerges, lowering her ski goggles around her neck. "Simple explosive," she says matter-of-factly. "Any kid could make this if they listened to half the stuff I taught."

"Do you think a kid did this to me?" Cos asks, incredulous. "Why? I give them half-priced scones after school. I've never said anything out loud to offend any kid in this town!"

I place a calming hand on his arm. "What my husband is trying to ask is who do you think went to all this trouble?"

Marla shakes her head and places her hands on her hips. "Dunno. Boysie is better equipped to answer that. I'll email him my report and let him decide."

That evening, Cos and I collapse onto the front porch, still shedding glitter with every breath. There's a fleck stuck to his nose. I'm too tired to brush it off.

"Do you think it was really about the karaoke club?" he asks softly.

I wrap my hands around a mug of cooling tea. "Feels bigger. The note said, *Stop fundraising to buy the club or next time, no one survives.* That's not civic outrage. That's a vendetta."

"I don't like that it was delivered to *you.*"

"I don't like that it sparkled." I stir my tea absently. "And I *really* don't like that Pepper Friday is suddenly interested in Vem's weapons collection."

Cosmo grunts. "And I haven't even told you the weirdest part."

I turn toward him. "What could be weirder than a disco-themed death threat via explosive karaoke machine?"

He reaches behind his chair, pulling out a small,

glitter-smeared envelope. "This came in the mail today. From P.O.P."

I groan. "What now?"

He cracks the envelope. Glitter spills from the inside, and neither of us are sure if it came that way or is a casualty of today's mishap.

You've seen what I'm capable of. There will be casualties in my next performance. Is a broken-down opera house worth the lives lost?

A chill steam rolls its way down my spine. "I'll talk to Gladys. If anyone can track this lunatic, it's her."

We lapse into silence. Fireflies blink over the lawn. An owl hoots in the distance.

"Lanie, I…"

"Cos, I…" we say at the same time.

"You go," I offer.

Cos clears his throat. "Babe, saving an old building isn't worth losing your life. Maybe… maybe hand it over. Boysie's wife is always saying she's bored. At least she'd have him there to back her up."

I lean in, choosing my words with care. "Cos, I love that you want to protect me. But if all this person has is a glitter bomb, Lanie Anders-Hill can handle it." I lift his hand to my lips. I don't even brush the glitter off before kissing his fingers.

Time to dig.

Time to uncover secrets.

Time to protect our town—and our friends.

"I know it's just a building," he says. "I know it's just walls and ovens and a few thousand dollars' worth of gluten. But it was ours."

"We'll rebuild," I whisper. "But first we'll rest. You'll breathe. We'll deep clean and disinfect and get every last fleck of sparkle out, even if we're still finding it in our shoes five years from now. That bakery will never be quite so sparkly clean again."

He turns to look at me, and I see it then—just for a moment—a single tear cutting through the glitter pile on his cheek.

"It got in my *soul* too," he says.

And that's when I know: whoever did this didn't hurt a bakery.

They hurt the person who is my world.

And I'm going to find out who they are.

24

Glitter in the Air

Pepper's smile tightens, the corners of her mouth pulling up with all the sincerity of a mall Santa on their fourth cocoa-splashed shift.

Confronting her in her hotel room may not have been the smartest move on my part. She's much too comfortable.

"Oh, that's just terrible," she says in a voice so sugary I check the hallway to make sure I haven't stepped into a candied nightmare. "A glitter malfunction, you said?"

"No," I reply, folding my arms across my chest. "I said it was an *exploding karaoke machine* that just happened to glitter bomb an entire bakery, nearly give my husband a heart attack and leaving every square inch looking like the Scheddy Fairy Museum sneezed."

She laughs—quick, shallow. "Well, that sounds like… an insurance issue?"

"We *have* insurance, Pepper," I snap, stepping closer. "What we NEED is an explanation. You are the only person who oozes glitter, and suddenly it's exploding on our counter? Do you think we scare that easily?"

For half a second, something flashes across her face. Guilt? Shock? A split-second calculation? She covers it with a shrug.

"Lanie, I didn't send the machine. Do you know how much work is involved when we open a new club? I slept for three hours last night. Sometimes I don't even get undressed before I fall into bed."

I wait.

If you give people enough rope, they'll hang themselves. Finally, she sputters, "I could make a guess, but I'd hate to finger the wrong bomber."

She turns away, leaving me a full five seconds to admire her steely affect. With one quick flounce she turns back, her face now somber. "I wish I could help you, I really do. I feel…terrible… that my involvement with Moonbeam Enterprises might have been connected to your incident. The last thing I want is to leave my sister or anyone in this community worse off than I found them."

She speaks quickly, like she's trying to outrun the truth.

"It wasn't an incident, Pepper. It was a potentially life-threatening situation. Anyone, including your sister, could have been killed."

All the color has drained from her face now.

She flinches. Good.

"I don't know who did this," she says. "But if you want, I can use Moonbeam Enterprises vast resources to find the culprit."

She moves aside, gesturing for me to step into her room. I do, but I stay close to the door. Everything smells too expensive—designer perfume, lemon essential oil, and just the faintest whiff of panic.

Pepper pushes me aside and leans into the hallway, looking both ways before closing the door.

"Since you are my sister's best friend, I feel like I can confide something."

Her suitcase is still open on the floor, polka-dotted blouses in cobalt blue, cherry red, and aggressive polka dots spill out like fashion's version of a ransom note. On the desk, her laptop glows. Something about her concern doesn't hit right.

"I'm all ears," I reply, folding my arms across my chest.

"I don't feel safe in this organization anymore. I feel like someone is trying to get rid of me by any means possible."

"So what is all of this really about?" I ask, dubious. "Because it's clearly not about karaoke. Otherwise you wouldn't be looking to purchase Vem's weapons."

Pepper meets my eyes, and this time she doesn't flinch. She's got something to prove now. Or at least change the direction of the conversation.

"It *is* about karaoke," she says, voice firm. "And business. This town is charming in a vintage postcard kind of way, sure, but that opera house is *wasted* on history. We can bring jobs, music, tourism—"

"Noise, neon, and cheap booze in a building where world-class opera singers once stood," I cut in. "Great pitch."

She ignores that. "There's only one more hurdle. After this week's city council meeting, where we'll make our argument for removing the opera house from the historic register, Moonbeam Enterprises has won." She smiles in that ooey, gooey way I'm quickly finding makes my bile rise. "We're building this club whether you like it or not, Mrs. Anders-Hill. I was advised by our security team to carry protection in case one of your over-zealous friends decides to take matters into their own hands."

"You were saying you didn't feel safe?"

Pepper's gaze shifts. "No one involved in Moonbeam Enterprises can be trusted," she whispers. "I know I'm being followed. The other day I was at Pancakes, Pancakes and Pancakes and I found a bug in my purse."

My face reddens.

"I had to go into the bathroom to call my partner. Its spooky."

"And who is your partner? Someone local?"

Pepper shakes her head and laughs like she's a five-year-old. "No, silly billy; she's my boss."

Her abrupt change of demeanor. An unidentified "partner." Something about this smells like rotten eggs.

I reach into my coat pocket and pull out a Ziplock bag containing the gold microphone and the note, still faintly dusted with glitter.

"I'll give you one day," I say, holding it out like Exhibit A. "One day to tell your mysterious promotional team to come clean. Who sent this? Who wrote that note? Because if I find out *you* authorized it, I won't be going to the press."

Pepper raises her brows. "No?"

"No. I'll go to *Vem*."

Her bravado cracks just a hair. She nods once. "I understand."

I turn toward the door, but before I reach it, she calls after me.

"Lanie?"

I pause without turning.

"I'm working as hard as I can," she says, quieter now. "And then my sister will never see me again. And I really am. Feeling scared, I mean."

For the first time, I feel pity for this lonely Bean clone.

25

What SUP, Pussycat

The fundraiser is the perfect distraction. After the shock and sadness following the glitter explosion, Cosmo and his patrons could use a night of pure fun. And later this evening, we can attend the city council meeting and prove the citizens of this community have enough money to purchase the building, keeping it out of the hands of Moonbeam Enterprises.

The opera house itself is barely recognizable. Cos obtained the keys via an old friend from the cult who runs a security firm. Twinkle lights wrap around the marble columns. Folding chairs line the sides of the grand hall, leaving room in the middle for tables covered in succulents, donation jars, and facial hair accessories. Lush velvet curtains—borrowed from Doris, who claims they once belonged to a Titanic survivor—drape the entrance. And on the stage, the real star of the show: *The*

Beard Podium, a faux-gilded pedestal awaiting our town's most majestic chin fluff.

SUP Piney Falls—is supposed to be about coordination, community spirit, and me finally letting go of my control issues.

Instead, it's pure mayhem.

I arrive at the Scheddy Opera House at 8:00 a.m. sharp, clipboard in hand, wearing my optimistic jeans—the ones I only break out when I'm foolish enough to believe everything will go according to plan. The stuck zipper should have been my first indication they would not.

We sold tickets to just about everyone in Piney Falls. It was truly an incredible act of community unity.

Piper is already here, zip-tying a papier-mâché chandelier to the balcony railing like she's in a local production of a spy movie.

"Didn't we agree on battery-powered candles?" I ask, looking up with dread.

"They are battery-powered!" she calls back. "Ish. Don't worry—most of them didn't catch fire in testing."

Most?

Downstairs, Cosmo is locked in what I can only describe as a pastry-induced existential crisis. He's surrounded by no fewer than twenty trays of Opera Orange Scones. "Will this be enough, Lanie?"

"Cos," I say gently, "it's double the amount I asked for."

He looks up, wild-eyed. "My subconscious doubled trays because I panic-bake when I'm emotionally compromised, and I guess I'm still dealing with glitter PTSD."

"I know, love," I say, sliding into his arms. "Vem has promised a security detail will be walking the perimeter every ten minutes. We have to live our lives. We can't be ruled by fear. Of glitter."

Cosmo took over our second location, a lovely country home that doubles as Piper's abode and our commercial bakery, at least until we pass the health inspection. Our daughter is helping day and night, even though she should be packing.

In the main hall, Vem is straining under the weight of a giant prop harp she's insisting be used as the "Good Vibes" centerpiece. I don't ask why. If I've learned anything in my years of friendship with Vem, it's to limit questions to the ones that really matter.

She walks by muttering, "The subsonic frequency in this room is *off* again. You hear it? That hum? That's a death note, Lanie."

"It's probably just the chandelier shorting out," I say with just a hint of caution in my voice.

"Oh good," she replies, oblivious to the concern in my voice. "Then I won't worry about bad vibes."

In the lobby, the big hand-painted SUP banner refuses to stay up. Every time we tape it to the balcony, it slowly peels off like it's trying to make a dramatic exit. It finally gives up and crashes into the punch bowl, startling volunteer Sally Monella so much she sends a full tray of deviled eggs sailing into the grand piano. They land with a musical splat, B-flat by the sound of it.

"Oh no," she cries. "Those had decorative paprika!"

Meanwhile, the delivery truck Obie scheduled for sixty folding chairs shows up with... sixty topiary swans, driving his structured mind into hyper drive.

As soon as I see him walking in circles, mumbling something about dirty leaves, I signal to Piper. She takes his arm and lovingly guides him to a quiet space where he can calm down.

The driver hands me the clipboard and shrugs. "Says right here: 'Something decorative with a seat.'"

"He meant literal chairs," I say.

"You want me to take 'em back?"

I glance behind him at the truck of leafy waterfowl. "No. It's fine. I don't have time for anything else."

Cosmo tries to comfort me with an Opera Orange scone. It crumbles in my hand.

By noon, the lights start to flicker above the mezzanine. It's either faulty wiring or the ghost of opera past grumbling about the disruption. Either way, it feeds Vem's paranoia that her good luck centerpiece isn't enough to ward off bad vibes for the event.

Just before the guests start arriving, Vem

appears beside me in the lobby, holding a clipboard, a walkie-talkie, and what I swear is a glue gun holstered to her hip like she's crafting in the Wild West. She is monochromatically dressed in all black with a black kerchief covering her head.

"Perimeter is secure," she says. "The harp is stabilized with duct tape and prayers. Your husband is pacing around like a caged wildebeest. No sign of glitter bombers."

I scan the chaos and manage a half-smile. "It's fine. It's fine. It's all going to be... fine."

She squints. "That's the voice you use when it's *not* going to be fine."

She's not wrong.

But Lanie Anders-Hill doesn't back away from a challenge. I adjust my cardigan, square my shoulders, and get ready to raise funds for an opera house that might collapse under us *or* be saved by us.

It really could go either way.

BY 3:00 P.M., the opera house is transformed from "mildly haunted and in need of a good cleaning" to "mildly whimsical with an undercurrent of frosting."

Thanks to Piper.

Despite earlier zip-tie dramatics, she's come through like a sugar-slinging hero. She's carefully crafted crowns out of sugar, the centerpiece for each table. Her table of baked goods gleams under fairy lights: caramel opera cake, vanilla cupcakes with edible glitter, honey-almond tarts in the shape of musical notes, and her pièce de résistance—mini soprano cheesecakes with tiny chocolate mouths open in song.

"I call them Diva Bites," she says proudly, adjusting her lavender apron with the air of a general preparing for sweet war.

"Piper," I whisper. "If someone from television decides to sweep you away to stardom, you'll take your mother along, right?"

She grins. "Only if I get a dramatic backstory and one kitchen fire."

Portable cookers plugged precariously into a rickety power strip emit rich scents of soups and stews. Boysie and Obie will judge the soups and announce the winner at the end of the night.

Behind us, Obie is deep in tactical mode. He's in charge of all tables and chairs—*and he is not messing around.*

He's got a measuring tape clipped to his belt and a floor plan drawn in marker on a clipboard. At one point, I catch him using a bubble level to ensure the main table isn't slanted by even a millimeter.

"No one tips over a drink at my event," he mutters.

"Obie," I say gently, "don't fret. You're doing a great job." I pause. "And if you happen to see

Pepper and/or a cloud of glitter, will you make sure to call the rest of the police force?"

He pats his shoulders and tugs on one ear. "Yep. Already had it planned."

I leave him to it. Who am I to stand between a man and his perfectly aligned tableware? True to his word, Obie spoke to his friend on the city council who assured Obie the sale would be stalled for at least a month.

Guests start trickling in just after 4:00. The air is thick with the scent of SUP contestants' rich broths and human sweat. The theme is "Casual Elegance," but Piney Falls has interpreted that in its own way. Doris, Cosmo's faithful employee arrives in a sequin-covered gown with a feathered mask. Boysie's wife, Pamela Petrie-Lumquest shows up in a bedazzled velour tracksuit and heels. Someone's cousin is wearing a tuxedo T-shirt and actual spats.

A string quartet begins warming up in the corner. Except it's not really a string quartet—it's three violinists and one guy on a ukulele. They call themselves The Vibratos, and they specialize in "experimental covers of classic ballads." I'm choosing not to interpret that.

The fundraiser is officially in full swing.

We've set up booths around the hall.

"Name That Aria" (which quickly devolves into "Name That Commercial Jingle").

"Opera Face-Off" where two people must lip-sync an aria with exaggerated facial expressions and receive a digital copy for ten bucks.

A kissing booth, which is really just Piper letting people kiss a plush stuffed opera singer for five bucks, has a line as long as the one at Piney Plex when the second—or fifth, I don't understand the system—Stars Wars was released.

Vem, dressed in fully gypsy garb, tugs on my arm.

"I just told Barney McNife he's going to marry someone named Blenda and inherit three goats," she whispers to me. "He cried."

"As long as they're paying customers, you can tell them anything you want, Vem."

Patrons are seated around the fancy tables on swans. Women who weren't expecting such odd chairs are forced to sit sidesaddle in their fancy clothes. No one seems upset though.

Piper is running the concession stand (glitter-free, by special request), serving spicy candied pecans, fizzy juniper lemonade, and beard-shaped shortbread. Vem adjusts her headlamp.

"You're amazing, Vem. Running security and telling fortunes is quite the act of multi-tasking."

"Oh, you haven't seen me when I teach Moan, Loan, and Cone, where I teach people how to fill out loan applications while I moan and make ice cream cones."

There's also a silent auction for donated items: hand-knit scarves, a cruise to Hawaii, a bizarre sculpture shaped like a treble clef crying tears of rhinestones, and one framed photo of Cosmo playing Elvis at last year's New Year's Eve party that says, "No Reprints."

Speaking of Cosmo, he's pacing near the front of the stage, trying to avoid the folding barber chair we've set up.

"You promised," I remind him, gently nudging him forward.

"I also promised myself I'd never let a dog groomer with a pair of novelty scissors near my head again," he says.

"Again?"

"I'm going to look like a sad poodle."

"You're going to look like a heroic sad poodle."

Obie announces from the mic stand, "Ladies and gentlemen and undecideds of Piney Falls—prepare yourselves for the main event… THE CHARITY HAIRCUT." He sets the microphone on a chair he has sanitized and pats his shoulders three times. Once deathly afraid of public speaking, he glances at his fiancé for reassurance and Piper blows him a kiss.

There's polite applause. A few catcalls. One person throws a cupcake wrapper in excitement.

Cosmo sighs dramatically and settles into the chair. Biddie Binklestein, a local dog groomer who listed her qualifications as "available," appears with the scissors (glitter-handled, naturally) and fluffs his hair like she's about to shear a sheep with dreams.

"Who's a good boy?" she says in a voice that's sure to set my husband off if she doesn't start cutting soon.

"I'd like to dedicate this haircut," Cosmo intones, "to my dignity. May it rest in peace."

Just as Biddie raises the scissors and the crowd leans forward…

The creaky wooden double doors fly open, sending a sour-smelling breeze drifting across the room.

A small Asian woman appears, scowling like we've already disappointed her. "You all have to leave. This is Moonbeam Enterprises' property now."

Her plain, round face is hardened, maybe by years of hard work—or more likely the sheer effort of holding back opinions no one asked for but everyone was going to hear. Curiously, she has a large mole right in the center of her forehead, with wiry hairs shooting out. It seems to be…twitching? "I'm sorry. I'm terribly confused. We were under the impression the sale wasn't final. We were working with Pepper Friday and—"

She raises one small hand with razor sharp red nails. "She is my subordinate. I am the senior executive for Moonbeam Enterprises. I make all the decisions."

"She's number three," a bald man with gold-rimmed round glasses says with pride. "I'm the big number two."

The man accompanying her is her polar opposite. Bald, whiter than my best sheets, and staring at…well, I'm not sure. His pale blue eyes appear to have found a spot on the wall that is most interesting.

"You can say that again," Vem mutters.

"I didn't catch your name?" I'm trying to be polite. Even if it kills me.

"Sybil Screech. Derek!" She snaps her fingers, and instantly the doughy man opens a purple fanny pack and pulls out a business card to give me.

I glance at it briefly but it offers no clues to her real identity. "Nice to meet you, Ms. Screech. And you are…"

"Derek. za'Dimwit. I handle all the grunt work. Right, Sibby? You like it when I grunt."

I swear a growl comes out of her mouth and it's so fitting. "Go stand at the door and hand out coupons, Derek."

She watches him leave, and the corners of her mouth raise slightly. They must be in a relationship. Oddly enough.

"The city council is meeting tomorrow night to discuss the ramifications of declassifying this building as historic. We plan to present the funds collected tonight and urge the council to sell to its citizens instead of you. That way it stays in its natural state."

Sybil's hand goes in the air again, and for a split second, I'm afraid she might strike the odd man standing next to her. "You want to keep it run down and full of mold?" Instead, she points to a corner with a suspicious looking black substance.

"No, of course not."

"I'm here on behalf of Moonbeam Enterprises," she announces, her voice slicing clean through the air. "Which, as of 3:00 p.m. this afternoon, is the *legal* and *undisputed* owner of this crumbling slice of nostalgia you've all been trying to 'save.'"

A gasp flutters through the crowd like startled birds.

"Code 75. I repeat, code 75." Vem speaks into what I assume is a walkie talkie in her wristwatch. "Cranky woman on stairs. Proceed with caution. Flatten her like a mosquito. Watch out for the pulsing mole. I repeat: the mole. Is. Pulsing."

Instantly a group of heavily muscled men and women appear and march up the steps toward Sybil.

"Touch me and you'll regret it," she warns.

Though Sybil Screech is small, her voice carries so much power the security team stops dead in their tracks.

Sybil's heels click like gunfire against the parquet floor. The crowd quiets.

"Attention, patrons," Sybil Screech announces, her voice slicing through the cheer like a dull machete. "I'm afraid this little... get-together has not been sanctioned by Moonbeam Enterprises. You are all trespassing."

Derek grasps the clipboard with the solemnity of a priest holding sacred text. "You guys are so busted."

There's a gasp. Actually, several. Possibly even a dry heave from November, who was mid-beard reading when Sybil's words landed.

"There was no need to repeat yourself, strange mole lady. We heard you the first time."

I frown at Vem. "I'm sorry, what?" I say, stepping forward. "You got all the permits? But the city council doesn't meet until Thursday!"

"Correct," Derek replies, puffing out his chest like a baboon. "Money talks. And Moonbeam Enterprises could buy this whole town if we wanted. Course you don't have to worry about that; this trashhole isn't worth our—"

Sybil slaps his doughy face so hard it echoes in the quiet of the evening. "Silence, you twit!" She turns back to us, her mole pulsing to its own karaoke beat. "We arranged for a special council meeting earlier this afternoon." She smiles and leans forward. Immediately Vem yanks my arm. "Cloud of farts, Lanie! Cloud. OF. Farts."

Heeding her warning, I take a step backward. I don't want Sybil thinking I'm afraid of her, but my stomach has been unsettled all day.

Sybil doesn't blink. "You'll need to vacate the premises immediately. Renovations begin at dawn."

It takes everything I have not to lunge at her with one of the beard-braiding combs. Instead, I scan the crowd of friends and family. "Obie! Go call your dad and see if there's something we can do!"

He nods. Nothing excites Obie more than feeling useful. He pats both shoulders three times before calling, "On it!" and running outside.

The once-festive mood has become somber. Patrons begin shuffling toward the exits, some grumbling, some deflated. One man drops his Grow Something Weird packet and steps on it on the way out.

Derek gives a little wave. "Thank you for your... enthusiasm."

I can't believe my eyes when I see Derek…picking…his… nose. These two are an incredibly awful, perfectly matched pair. He is unfazed by his public humiliation and turns to walk away. Maybe he's skipping. Maybe he has a hitch in his giddyup.

The doors close behind him, leaving a stunned silence.

Piper, her eyes full of tears, walks over to where I'm standing, holding a melted opera mask in her hands. "What do we do now?"

I square my shoulders, blood humming in my ears.

"We regroup," I say. "Because if they think this is over, they clearly don't know who they're dealing with."

Sybil removes a shiny gun from her bag and points it squarely at the face of one of the volunteer security guards, causing patrons to dart underneath the tables, some screaming. The swan chairs swim gracefully into the middle of the room, forming their own alliance.

"Pa…pa…pa...Please don't shoot! I've got a wife and kids!" he whimpers.

"Then…LEAVE!" she shouts. Most of the security team scampers toward the exits, leaving only a handful of ex-military standing their ground.

"I knew I shouldn't have spent all that time making my tuna casserole!" Gladys harrumphs. "Now it'll just to waste."

"Doesn't have to go to waste," Barnie McKnife says, patting his round mid-section.

She turns and frowns. "Standing by what I said."

Sybil clomps down the remaining stairs, clapping her hands as she passes gas. *Does she think we can't hear the loud noise?* She cuts through the security staff like a hot knife through butter, waving her gun around wildly. "Out! Out! Out! You can come back when construction is done. Derek is at the door handing out fifty-percent-off coupons for your first visit to Scheddy to Rock."

When no one makes any effort to leave their hiding spots, Sybil whistles, startling us again. People dressed in matching sky-blue smocks with treble clefs on the chest filter in from the alley door. They are singing something it sounds like they made up. "Go now, go on now you. We'll be leaving, leaving too."

They surround one table and begin pulling frightened patrons out, one at a time. Doris's lovely sequined gown rips when one of the singers steps on it while helping her out from underneath a table. "My beautiful gown! "she gasps. "I bought it at an auction for $5,000 dollars! I'll sue this Moonbeam whatever, you watch!"

"Not true," Vem whispers in my ear. "She bought it at a costume shop in Tellum for $25. It had pizza stains on it from the cast party after the high school performance of *Mame* so she talked them down from $50."

I survey the room: half-eaten sloppy joes, Vegetables smashed into the carpet, and worst of all, Piper's beautiful cakes decorated with opera glasses in a heap around one table. What a waste.

The singers repeat their actions until they've removed every single person in the room. Everyone except us. Cos, Vem, Piper, and I stand our ground as the singing mafia approaches. Cos reaches in front of us protectively. "You put one hand on my family and you WILL be on the moon," he growls.

Sybil clears her throat and flicks a deadly finger. Somehow, these blue warblers understand this gesture and filter out the back door as quietly as they came.

The angry little woman steps closer to me, causing me to tremble slightly. She still has a gun in the opposite hand.

Cos has lowered his arm and his defenses. Is he scared of her too?

She only comes up to my shoulder, but I feel like she has experience poking out eyeballs with those nails of death.

"If you want to discuss this further, make an appointment with Derek on the way out. You've given me a headache, and now I have to hire a cleaning crew to remove this…this…"

"Deliciousness?" Vem says helpfully. "I'd be happy to eat—"

"Get... OUT!" Sybil screams, raising her gun once more. She shoots wildly at the ceiling, causing asbestos to fall like snow on a winter day.

Just as we reach the lobby, Boysie appears, looking flustered. "I stepped out to call Craig Countzel. The permits have indeed been issued. He said they received a nice donation to the high school gym refurbishment fund today."

26

Chew on That

Vem is at my door at six a.m. sharp. Luckily I was expecting her because she texted.

> Nose picker and angry farter have opened clubs before. Deaths, Lanie. Too many to be a co-ink-ee-dink.

Together we scour the internet and find a disturbing pattern. "I can't believe that people die within days of each club opening and no one has questioned what exactly is happening with Moonbeam Enterprises!"

I wait. Vem has to connect the dots—realizing that Pepper has been at every opening, right?

Instead, she taps both sides of her nose simultaneously, her signal that she'll be heading into a trancelike-state, a new method of meditation she's called Breeze Up My Skirt. Vem insists this technique she learned in Iowa gives her clarity that she's never experienced before.

I wait.

"Muh…muh…muh…muh…aaaack."

Her guttural sounds make it hard to keep a straight face. I love this woman so much.

Eventually she opens her eyes and stares at me. "Well? What did I say?"

"Just a bunch of gibberish. I'm sorry."

Her narrow shoulders drop. "Oh. Well I did see a dung beetle rolling his ball of turd up a hill and into the mouth of a Ms. Sybil Screech."

I can't decide if she's serious. "That's quite a visual. What, pray tell, did it mean?"

"That we have to keep the appointment you made last night. We're going to Otter's End to see a woman about a dung beetle."

"TWO HEART ATTACKS IN ONE CLUB," I mutter, breathless, as we pass the mural that greets visitors: *Otter's End: Where the Sea Meets the Mountains and Adventure Awaits!*

I chuckle to myself. They should add, *We're happy to welcome fresh victims.*

Piney Falls has its oddities, but Otters End seems to rack up deaths the way other towns collect parking tickets. The retired men who nurse their coffees at the Piney Perk have turned it into a running joke. Morbid but true.

Beside me, Vem adjusts her bag, jars of various unknown substances she calls snacks clattering softly. "And the one in Des Moines? Fell into the dry ice machine during a Bee Gees medley. You see the pattern, right, bestie? It's not the opera house we need to worry about. It's murder," she shouts. Vem was up all night researching Moonbeam Enterprises and their other karaoke locations.

"You're suggesting disco-related homicide?"

She doesn't laugh.

"Pattern or no, Vem, your sister has been at every opening. We need to face that."

The car jerks as she slams the brakes, seatbelt choking me in the process. She turns, glaring.

"Lanie Bartholomew Anders-Hill," she intones, finger poised like an accusing gavel.

"That's not my—"

Before I can protest, she presses that finger to my lips. "You've been far too judgmental about Pepper Friday. She's there because it's her *job.* You go to every event at Fallen Branch. What if I assumed you were behind the Frog Incident just because you were present?"

"That was *you*, Vem. And we're still finding frogs in the pool filter."

"It was a protest, Lanie. By definition, I had to contribute amphibians or my protest against manmade ponds on the property wouldn't have teeth."

We never do tension well. I soften my tone. "You're right. We need to investigate before judging. Let's park. I'd rather walk."

WAX & Wail is nestled into Otters End's oldest building, once a textile mill. Now it pulses with velvet curtains, vintage records, and too much vocal ambition.

I push open the brass-handled door. The scent of wood polish, peppermint tea, and nostalgia greets us. But beneath it, something sour hums.

"Let me do the talking," I whisper.

"You always say that," Vem hisses. "It's like you expect me to embarrass you."

Before I can reply, we're startled by an off-key version of "Footloose." We're definitely in the right place.

In blaring contrast, a woman is vacuuming the brand-new blue carpet while she sings with earbuds in her ears, oblivious to visitors. I've long since made my peace with the fact that I no longer have my finger on the pulse of what's hip. What does bother me is the fact that when my daughter explains what's hip to me, it takes two or three times before I retain it.

"Hellooo!"

I doubt if anyone is there they would hear me

over the vacuum. I turn to glare at the woman vacuuming, hoping she'll get the hint and go clean somewhere else. But she is just as oblivious to me as she is to the four pieces of popcorn she keeps missing.

Behind the record counter, a bald head pops up like a startled prairie dog.

"Hey, hey! Welcome to the *Wax!*" Derek spreads his arms wide, like a magician who forgot the rabbit. He radiates self-help video energy—Step One: Smile Big.

His light blue eyes buffer like a weak internet connection.

"I'm Derek za'Dimwit!" he announces proudly. "Regional something. Maybe Assistant to the Assistant Manager? Everyone else is upstairs." He waves vaguely upward.

Vem sniffs the air like she's testing him. "That's his real name. Poor thing."

"We already met you!" I shout over the sound of the vacuum. "The night of the fundraiser. You were handing out flyers at the door while your girlfriend threatened us with a gun. Remember?" I shout.

Derek shakes his head. "No, I'm not a hellraiser. I don't even know what that means."

"Can you ask her to stop?" I say, pointing to the vacuum and the bouncing woman operating it. Apparently I'm the only one perturbed by the noise.

"Susan?" he says in a voice that wouldn't attract the attention of a baby trying to nap.

"Susan!" All three of us yell at once.

The woman removes one earbud. "Huh?" She stares first at Derek, then at me. When her eyes come to rest on Vem, they instantly become the size of saucers. "You're…oh my goodness. It can't be…"

"Yes, yes, International Moaning Champion. That's me." Vem reaches into her bag and pulls out a facial mixture she carries everywhere, just in case she has ten minutes and wants to look twenty years younger. Attached to that is a signed headshot, Vem in her best maroon outfit. "I can offer you some of my secret recipe Fancy Face." She pauses only momentarily to take a breath. "Oh heck. I'll just tell you. It's made from squirrel dung, avocadoes, and siracha to give it a little punch."

The woman takes the jar without fear, something that gives me great admiration of her. "I was at the moaning convention in Iowa. I took your seminar, 'Midnight Mystery Moan.' I've been trying to set up a mystery club ever since, but no one wants to moan in the dark with sharp objects."

"It's fine. I can give you some pointers—"

"Vem, could we do that later? Sybil, remember?"

"Oh yeah. Give me your hand." She plucks my amber autumn lipstick from my bag before pulling the woman's hand toward her. "This is my number," she says as she's scribbling my expensive lipstick on this poor woman's hand, and I watch in abject horror. "Call me if you want to come to one of my classes in Piney Falls, m'kay?"

The woman nods eagerly before taking her vacuum to another room.

I steel myself. "We're here to see Sybil. She confirmed our appointment."

Derek's smile dims by one watt. "Sibby's on a very important call with Moonbeam. Strategy. Expansion. Balloons. Big stuff. Sibby'll make drawings for me later."

"She knew we were coming." I'm past irritated. Now I'm mad. Boysie did her a big favor when he didn't arrest her for threatening us with a weapon, because technically we were all trespassing on her property. And now she's playing these games, oblivious to the universe's gift. "And who exactly is Moonbeam? I know about Moonbeam Enterprises, but is it a man or an acronym for something?"

"Right, right. She probably said to wait. Or hydrate. I forget." He taps his temple as if his brain were more filing cabinet than bouncy castle. "Moonbeam. Oh man, where do I *even* start? The first time I saw him, I thought he was a mirage. You know, like when you're dehydrated, but spiritually. He was just *standing there* in front of the smoothie hut —robes flowing, beard glistening, surrounded by butterflies that may or may not have been trained.

"He looked at me and said, 'Your aura smells

like burnt toast.' And I was like, 'YES. FINALLY. Someone *gets* me.'"

I so badly want this to be a prank. Scouring the room, I don't find any cameras or people poised to jump out and yell, "just kidding!"

"Moonbeam handed me a flyer listing job openings for Moonbeam Enterprises," Derek continues. "They were looking for an Assistant to the Assistant of Vibrational Infrastructure. Then I met my Sibby and life got even better." He sighs like a twelve-year-old. I wish I could find it endearing, but this man is nothing short of bizarre.

"I make sure the office crystals don't touch. Because if the amethyst gets too close to the citrine? Boom. Spiritual static. We *can't* have that again.

"Moonbeam—sorry, *Revered Brother Moonbeam-Sage-Falcon*—says I'm a natural conduit for nonsense energy. I think that's good? He said my brain waves are uncluttered, which makes sense because I haven't really had a thought since Thursday."

Vem opens her mouth to reply, but this time its me nudging her to be quiet.

"Ow! Rude!" she yelps.

"He doesn't walk, by the way. Moonbeam *glides.* Like a mystical self-propelled vacuum of cosmic truth. He always smells like sage, rainwater, and a little bit like warm socks. Comforting. Ancient. Moist."

"Derek, this is interesting and all, but we'd like to see—"

"Sometimes he just *appears* in a room you swore was empty, whispers something like 'Follow the lavender,' and then vanishes into a curtain. No one knows how he does it. I tried once. Got stuck in a ficus."

There has to be someone here who can circumvent his trip down memory lane. I glance hopefully toward Susan, but she's lost in her modern drumbeat.

"Anyway, you should totally come to one of our Enlighten & Sip events. You get a free chakra reading and half-off on moon cheese puffs. I'll save you a beanbag next to the dolphin tapestry."

I exchange a look with Vem. I'm so relieved she hasn't found this word soup enchanting. We've been stonewalled before. "Where can we wait for Ms. Screech?"

He leans over the counter. "I've got a clipboard, a name tag, and an official polo. I can answer most questions."

"How reassuring," I say flatly. "Fine. Tell us about the Manlyville death."

Derek frowns, hard. "I had a breakfast sandwich there once. Real eggy."

Vem mutters, "Waste of time, Lanie." She taps her head. "Hollow as a chocolate bunny."

Grinding my teeth, I press on. "The Tropitanna Tanning and Karaoke in Misty Cove. A man died mid-'My Way.' The report says he 'ascended gracefully.'"

Derek slaps his knee. "Oh yeah! Stanley Badpitch. That was wild. Frank's a tough track. Emotional weight."

"He fell onto a chair that wasn't part of the property. He clawed at his eyes. Hardly song-induced."

Derek squints, struggling to comprehend my words. "Maybe metaphorical chairs, huh? Sibby says that all the time, but I don't really understand what it means."

Vem crosses her arms. "What about Tune Forks? The outage. Bella Foghorn. Frothing on the floor."

"Right, right. Tune Forks. Hacker hotspot." Derek giggles like an eight-year-old. He seems to be enjoying himself.

"No, it isn't," Vem snaps.

"Could've been ghosts. Or electromagnetic moon beams. Not a pun." He brightens. "But if it's a serial killer—kinda cool, right?"

"I didn't say serial killer," Vem hisses, advancing a step.

I try another tack. "Are you stalling, Derek?"

"Nope! This is my natural pace. Like a sloth after two coffees."

I bite down the groan. "Show us the incident reports from those deaths."

He claps once. Pauses. "I want to say yes, but… what are those?"

Vem inhales. Exhales. The howl is coming.

"Then let us speak to Sybil."

"She's probably whispering power phrases into her headset. Did you know she uses three screens?"

"Derek," I cut in sharply, "maybe you're not in the loop for a reason."

"Oh, 100%. I'm awful with secrets. Sibby once told me to shred a memo, and I used it to wrap my sandwich. Felt a little weird, eating something with the word dirty written across it."

I make a mental note: *Derek—possible distraction device. Unlikely mastermind. Too clueless to jaywalk alone. Or less likely, an Oscar-worthy actor.*

"Fine. Where was Sybil last Tuesday? There was a death in—"

"Trap-a-Troll Falls with Pepperoni. New club." He smiles and nods his head. Like there is some funny joke and I'm in on it.

"There was a death that very night, Mr. Dimwit," Vem says sharply.

"The ceiling collapsed during Britney Spears night," I say grimly. "According to reports, it happened during 'Hit Me Baby One More Time,' and several witnesses said they were, in fact, hit by ceiling beams."

Derek looks at us like he just caught us stealing money from the till. "*Technically* it was just the exercise bike area. Sibby says lies are like flies. Or maybe ladybugs. And no one got crushed—just sparkled on."

"But someone died."

Vem softens her tone, the way she does when interrogating beetles. "Derek, people are getting hurt. This isn't just glitter and playlists anymore."

For the first time, his grin falters. "You act like it's my fault. I don't control the bad stuff. I'm just the assistant. Nobody tells me anything."

Then—footsteps. Heavy, deliberate, echoing down the hall.

My pulse spikes. Even though I know she won't brandish a weapon in an open business (will she?), I'm still a little scared.

The diminutive figure rounds the corner. Derek's vacant blue eyes blaze with sudden recognition. His smile snaps back to full wattage.

And in that moment, I know—she is in total control.

27

Know Your Enemy

A tiny woman glares at me like she's about to challenge me to pistols at dawn. She has no eyebrows, a coat like an overcooked yam, and a massive mole in the center of her forehead that might be sentient. I don't flinch, but I *really* want to.

The mole is twitching. I swear.

She diverts her gaze to Derek, who stands slack-jawed beside her.

"Dum Dum," she says sweetly as though her words aren't a slur, "remember what I said about *strangers?*"

I try to smile like I'm not imagining her mole launching at me like a grappling hook. "We had an appointment, Ms. Screech. You confirmed by email. I have the chain if—"

She steps forward, extending a cold, pale hand. The moment it hits the air, the temperature drops ten degrees. I grip it quickly, afraid if I hesitate, I'll lose a finger.

"This is my best friend, November Bean," I say, gesturing toward Vem, hoping Sybil doesn't remember the spell Vem attempted to place on her the night of the fundraiser. Sybil slapped her hands out of the way mid-spell moan, and it ended before it began. "Vem was also one of your victims last night."

Sybil rolls her eyes, and her mole does a kind of wink. I'd think it was an interesting talent if I didn't already know her personality.

Vem closes her eyes, takes two exaggerated inhales, and reluctantly shakes the hand. I know that face. She's holding back a snark hurricane.

"Won't you join me in my office?" Sybil says, already moving toward a door that's not a door. It's a wall of laminated photos of famous singers, until she taps her heel and a section clicks open like a secret passage.

"As long as you aren't going to shoot us," I quip.

"Oh, that. I was just kidding around." Sybil's voice takes on a strange high-pitched sound. "Wanted to make my point and all."

Since we're needing information, I decline comment. Vem is blessedly silent too.

Inside, the décor is peak megalomania. Sybil sits behind a desk made for a Bond villain, perched on what is *definitely* a booster seat. Our chairs, by contrast, are so low they might as well be ottomans.

I feel like a child about to be told I've ruined Christmas.

"Scheddy to Rock will open in Piney Falls," Sybil says, folding her hands. "Whether the townspeople like it or not. Everyone will sing. Your fundraisers and town meetings and endless whining will mean nothing."

"It wasn't whining when the entire town gathered at the opera house to save it. Every single person in our community contributed something. We won't go away quietly." I straighten my spine. "You can't intimidate us."

"Oh, sweetheart." She leans forward. "This isn't intimidation. It's a *warning*. Keep meddling and your driver's license will be flagged for emotional instability. Your mail forwarded to a goat sanctuary. Your house—" she smiles, sharp as a guillotine "—the new site of a 24-hour yodeling retreat."

Vem puffs up like a balloon full of sarcasm. "Already is. I'm a local celebrity. International Moaner of the Year, two years running."

Sybil wrinkles her nose. "You smell like expired tahini and regret."

"You smell like a gas leak at a haunted sushi bar."

"The smell," Sybil says with a dramatic flourish, "is a rare digestive condition. I call them *whisper clouds.*" She taps her thick-soled shoes. A faint hiss escapes. "These cushion the ambiance."

I blink. "You're saying your shoes are soundproofing… for your gas?"

She grins like she's unveiling a new product on QVC. "Exactly."

Before I can formulate a response that won't get us kicked out, shot, or cursed, Derek shuffles in with two bottles of water. "One's from under the espresso machine, one from the copier room. Vintage unknown."

"Thank you, Der Der," Sybil coos.

He beams. "Did you tell them about the shoes?"

"We got there," I mutter, mentally noting: Sybil Screech: Gas-powered threat. Uses footwear as fart suppressors. Do not startle.

Sybil rises, folder tucked under one arm. "Now, if you'll excuse me, I have an expansion plan to finalize and a candlelit classic rock ritual with Moonbeam's strategic dream team."

With some effort and a butt boost from Vem, I stand. "This isn't over. People are getting hurt. If your empire has anything to do with it—we'll find out."

She waves like she's dismissing a server at a diner. "Then I hope you have excellent endurance."

28

Don't Fear the Reaper

Harmony Sungbad stares at the chipped teacup in her hands like it holds prophecy. It's not even tea anymore—just lukewarm mint water—but she keeps sipping it between cryptic verses like it's a holy ritual. Her eyes twitch every time Cosmo clears his throat, and I swear she's timing her breaths to the slow tick of her treble clef wall clock.

Harmony is Piney Falls' unofficial spiritual consultant, former choir director, and current proprietor of *Third Eye & Throat Lozenge*, the only metaphysical shop in town that also sells cough drops and emergency sheet music. Since she lost her lease, she's run her business out of this empty building. People say she can see the future. What she mostly sees is drama before it happens, which in Piney Falls makes her practically psychic.

We're here because Harmony claims she sensed "a disturbance in the alto range of destiny" last night and insisted it involved us, the greenhouse, and something "rolling with malevolent intent." She sent three texts, one voice memo, and a voicemail entirely in humming before we agreed to meet her for tea. If Vem had a daughter, Harmony would call her "Mama."

She smells faintly of patchouli and burnt toast, wears three scarves regardless of season, and speaks with the absolute confidence of a woman who once misread a horoscope and still built her life around it. Every sentence sounds like it should end with a gong. If she owned a crystal ball, it would be dusty and judgmental. If she didn't, she'd use the microwave door.

We sit in the back of the vacant Pizza Palace she calls home—if you can call a place lined with jars of nettles and old piano keys home.

"So," Cosmo says gently, as gently as a man who only came to see if she can call to dead trees, "how about we drop the riddles and you tell us why singers are dying after stepping on that stage? I've got a bakery to run and you're wasting time."

Harmony closes her eyes and sways slightly. "Only those who stray. Only those who deny the rhythm that binds."

"Harmony," I say, leaning forward, "who is this alto whatsa-more-ever? And why was it so important to tell us?"

"Red-man broke the contract," she whispers. "Red-Man broke the contract," she repeats, this time singing the words. "Red-Man BROKE THE CONTRACT!" she screams.

Cos puts one hand in the air, trying to calm her. "Okay, okay. We get it. Naughty Red-Man. What, exactly, was in the contract, and who is this Red--Man guy? Sounds like a real jerk."

I can tell he's being sarcastic, but at this point we need to light a fire under Harmony.

"Red-Man took the spotlight and gave no offering. He thought the song was free."

Her words send a chill crawling up my arms. I pull out my phone and type in "Red-Man" and "karaoke."

"Oh no!" I gasp. "It's Red Rooph, the realtor! He went to Tillamook last night and sang *Please Mister Please* before he finished, he collapsed onstage." I focus my shocked gaze on Harmony. "Is that who you're talking about? Red Rooph, the real estate agent who met with Pepper?"

"Did poor old Red forget to pay the cover charge?" Cosmo is enjoying this a little too much.

"Cos, it's real." I hand him my phone.

"Nothing sung in Moonbeam's oasis is free," she says, sharper now. "You pay with coin, with breath, with tone. Or you pay in silence."

I shoot Cosmo a look: she believes this. She isn't lying or being evasive—this is *doctrine.*

Cosmo shifts in his seat. "You said they only punish those who don't pay. What do you mean? Like… literal dues?"

Harmony nods once, dreamlike.

"The Circle of Tone. Monthly offerings. Some give money, some give voice. Some give gifts of their own design. One note, one tithe."

"And if you don't?"

"Dissonance comes for you. The Note bends back. It cuts the throat that denies it. The Mooners are all-powerful."

I bite the inside of my cheek.

Cosmo stays calm. "But someone's making sure that punishment actually happens, right? It's not just belief. There's tech. Frequencies. People like Sybil Screech are orchestrating it."

Harmony smiles, sad and slow.

"She holds the baton. But the choir sings its own revenge. Fear not, though," Harmony sways to the sound of the music in her head. "There are two. They wait in the shadows. They bring hope and nails."

"Nails? Like the kind you screw into the wall? Or the kind the overpriced nail salon gives me every two weeks?"

"You will know. All will know."

I try again. "Harmony… are you saying the cult *believes* they can kill someone through music alone?"

She meets my eyes—clear for just a heartbeat.

"Not the cult. Not believes." she says. "*Knows.*"

COSMO HAS BEEN quiet the entire walk from the library to the car. That's always a sign his mental gears are grinding at full tilt.

"Okay," he says, sliding behind the wheel. "We've been looking at this all wrong. People are dying left and right. No one is putting two and two together. And this whackadoodle-doo wants us to believe it's because they didn't pay their dues? The whole thing doesn't make any sense, Lanie."

"I agree. But not about the 'whackadoodle-do stuff. People pay Harmony big bucks for her readings. She just sat with us for close to an hour without charging a cent. Don't you find that interesting? Something she felt was so important, we needed to know without the use of our credit cards!"

We ride in silence until we're almost home. "Turn around, Cos."

"What? Did you forget something?"

"No. I need to speak with Harmony again."

"Babe, I—"

"Please, Cos! This is important! We have less than an hour before this gets around town, and then rumors will fly. Harmony will hide until it blows over like she always does when something catastrophic happens and people seek her out for the 'real' story."

29

Just an Illusion

We're surprised to find Harmony still seated in the same spot. Her eyes are closed, but her mouth curls into a smile when she hears us walk in. "I've been expecting you," she says.

"We're not staying. Just here for the wife to ask a couple more questions."

I move closer to Harmony. Before I open my mouth, she begins to sway and sing.

"She was the first to open the Hall. She was the note they shaped in flesh.

But flesh forgets. The Note does not."

Her voice drops to a whisper.

"I still hear her... inside me. She sings when I dream."

I've already forgotten the first rule of interviewing a suspect: record their words. With as much delicacy as I can muster, I reach into my purse and pull out my phone, hitting record immediately. "Is this Pepper? Is she the one killing people? We need to stop her, Harmony!"

"Harmony," Cos says carefully. "Who's next?"

She doesn't hesitate.

"The one with A sharp. The soprano. The one who thinks it's just a song."

"Who??" I'm ready to shake some sense into this girl.

"Go now!" She screams in a voice I've not heard before. "LEAVE!"

VEM IS IN FULL GEAR: bathrobe, platform slippers, a black clay mask smeared across her forehead like war paint. She's got one leg tucked under the other and is surrounded by open books on sonic theory and cult deprogramming.

"Bestie? I've been waiting all night!" she says with the clenched jaw of someone who has been caked in charcoal for too long.

"I know it's Monday Mask-er-ade night, and I wouldn't bother you before the spiked lemonade portion of the evening, but Cos and I just interviewed Harmony. Would you mind listening? Ignore the songs."

"She sang?" Vem asks, not even trying to hide her jealousy.

"Just a note," I say. "But it wasn't… normal. I felt it in my bones."

Vem listens to the playback, then pauses when the sound of a thunderous mewing cat fills the air. We stare at each other knowingly.

"Turn off the alarm. Go rinse and put your lemonade-fluff layer on. I can wait."

She returns a short time later with her face resembling a lemon meringue pie. Cos would have so many things to say.

"Okay. So she's not just nuts. She's deeply indoctrinated. That phrase—*the Note cuts the throat that denies it*—that's not a metaphor. That's *ritual language.*"

I take a sip of my blackberry tea, something I gave her as a gift so I would always have something safe to drink when I visited.

"She said singers who didn't pay their dues were punished. Killed. We thought it was a threat."

"It *is*," Vem says. "But one they believe they're manifesting. Through collective intention, performance, and resonance."

"It sounded like….like she was talking about someone we knew." I hope she can figure out who I'm talking about without my making it obvious. Vem announcing her sister is a killer will go over much easier coming from her lips.

Instead, she plasters a goofy grin on her face and we play the waiting game.

I stare. "So… like magic?"

"If these loony Mooners were capable of creating magic that killed. See, Lanie? I told you my sister wasn't involved."

30

Theories, Fog, and Very Bad Snacks

If I had a nickel for every time I broke into a condemned building with a woman who dresses like a grayscale cartoon villain and insists paper cups on a string count as viable communication equipment, I'd have exactly three nickels. Which doesn't sound like much, but it's enough to earn some kind of underground detective merit badge.

We're back inside La Maison Scheddy Opera House, which still smells like mildew, secrets, and Gladys's offensive casserole. Stale air curls through the shattered windows, winding between the rows of velvet seats like it's trying to find an exit. Vem walks ahead of me, flashlight bobbing, frizzy head bouncing like she's hiding a live squirrel under there. She's in charcoal gray again, which makes her look like a brooding librarian who moonlights as a crime lord.

"I have a theory," she says, which is code for

"there goes twenty minutes of my life I'm never getting back."

"Aliens?" I ask.

She turns and scowls. "Geez, you tell your bestie one time you were sucked up into the giant space goblet, and they never let you forget it."

"Sorry. Go ahead, Vem. I'm listening."

We're here to gather intel: karaoke equipment, evidence of tampered mics, or—my personal dream—a secret journal where Sybil Screech documents her descent from karaoke queen to poisoner-in-chief. No one is dying on our watch.

"So what's your theory?" I ask as we tiptoe past a heap of broken stage props.

"Pepper's not the killer," Vem says. "She's the control."

"The...what?"

"She's the one being tested. The whole program is built around her reactions. Every launch is a scenario. Every death is a variable."

I stop walking. "Oh, honey." I reach out to hug her, but she dodges my stubby arms. "All the evidence points to her. She's been at every club opening where someone later dies. Poor girl is furious she's been shoved aside by Sybil so she's sabotaging club openings and no one notices. And then there was that weird session with Harmony, chanting, 'She was the first to open the Hall. She was the note they shaped in flesh.'"

Vem rolls her eyes. "You don't have proof,

Lanie. Just theories in the old noggin. And besides, Harmony failed the entrance exam to B.O.O.B.S.—British Order of Oracle & Beyond Studies, Portland Campus. Twice. She's no expert."

We look at each other as we recite, "Our spirits are perky, not our science!"

"Point taken. It's just weird that we listened to Pepper's meeting with Red Rooph and then a few days later, he's dead. Then Harmony seems to point the finger…there are no coincidences, Vem."

I yank a crumpled paper from my coat pocket, one that I was hoping I wouldn't have to use. It was Cosmo's idea to have backup intel.

"All these people died after Pepper opened clubs in their cities. Twelve at last count. She walks away before they keel over so there is no blood on her hands. Sybil and that idiot Derek seem to live in their own world, probably trying to please Moonbeam. Just a theory."

"Or," Vem shoots back, "she's a traumatized employee in a corporate cult, just trying to keep her head above water. Poor kid doesn't want the big Moon Cheese—"

"Beam. It's 'MoonBEAM."

"Don't interrupt my thought train, bestie. We're reaching the age where, once out thoughts leave the station, they aren't coming back."

"Sorry. Continue please."

"Like I was saying, Pepper is afraid of whoever is committing the murders, like the Moonies. Think about it—would she want the boss thinking she's wreaking havoc on his clubs? Next thing you know, she'll be unemployable. I'll be forced to turn one of my garages into a refugee shelter and I'll have to teach her how to forage for scraps. My schedule's tight for that, Lanie. Much too tight."

As if on cue, a clatter upstairs interrupts us. Raccoon? Maybe. Sybil in disguise? Also possible. "I know what you're thinking. You aren't going to collect whatever animal excrement is up there for your next concoction."

She huffs. "You don't know everything that goes through my complicated brain, Lanie Cassandra July Anders-Hill. I'm a woman of mystery."

"I need coffee," I mutter.

We set up camp backstage: my laptop, a thermal camera Vem scored at a paranormal society auction, and three bags of trail mix I rescued from the vending machine. Two expired before aluminum cans were a thing.

"I found something," Vem calls. "Oh boy. It's a doozy!"

"Weirder than this?" I hold up the dusty trail mix.

She lifts a tin box with the lock hanging as if forgotten. It's filled with twelve green vials stamped in block letters: NOT FOR DEREK. Subtle.

The box contains a thick psychological profile.

Of Pepper.

"She's being watched," I whisper.

Vem reads:

Subject responds to authority with compliance followed by withdrawal. High pattern-recognition. Possible predisposition to counter-manipulation. One moment subject shows self-control and the next, is overemotional. Previous experience with mind control makes this subject perfect for our experiment.

"Pepper's mind," I say, "is going all directions at once, at least according to whoever is watching. She's a mess."

"Or someone wants it to look like she's a mess," Vem insists.

"Or both."

She picks up a vial.

"No! Don't touch! We don't want them to know we were here. I'll get a photo."

"Look, Lanie! There's something else."

Carefully I pull up the bottom of the box. There is a logo for *Frannie Fox Floricrine, Good for What Ails You!* We both gasp when we recognize a picture of a teenaged Pepper Friday on the label. She's wearing a white shirt and smiling.

"Vem, I…"

"Don't Lanie. Just don't."

A sudden pop makes us both jump. The vending machine spits out a ginger ale for no apparent reason.

"Let's finish up and get out of here. I don't want a repeat experience from the cancelled fundraiser evening. This time Sybil might aim directly at us," I say as I snap pictures of everything.

We pack essentials: the folder, the expired trail mix (for emergencies), the label with Pepper's picture on it, and a cracked piece of fog machine tubing that smells like eucalyptus and bad intentions. Maybe the coroner will take pity on me and agree to test the fog machine for foreign substances. As long as I bring him a dozen Ceres Cherry Chocolate scones, he'll do just about anything.

As we head out, Vem nudges me. "You still think Pepper's guilty?"

Her fists clench, breath sharp through her nose. Fire builds in her—justice, truth, her sister. I can't respond.

"She's not a killer," she insists. "She's just… complicated."

I hold up the folder. "Maybe she didn't start with murder. Maybe she was pulled in. But this?" I shake the paper. "This is someone trying to perfect it. Control it. Design it. How could she not know her picture was being used on the label?"

Grief and fury twist across her face. Something dangerously close to doubt. We ride home in silence, each of us struggling for words. We've never been on opposite sides in all the murder investigations we've done. It feels a little like a test.

Vem gets out of the car and slams her door. I follow suit, trying to match her energy. Like that's ever worked.

"You don't know her," she says, but her voice falters.

"No. And neither do you," I say softly. "Think about it—the first time we saw her, at the bakery? She acted surprised to see you, even though she showed up there and not your house. Think about it: How did she know we'd be there?"

Vem doesn't answer.

"I do think it's odd that report would be sitting in a box like that. Why isn't it on some flash drive somewhere? It's almost like whoever compiled it wants it found."

Vem turns her back. Her shoulders rise and fall like the air's too heavy. Then she kicks my ceramic frog across the garage. It smashes against the wall in a spray of ceramic shrapnel.

She storms out, charcoal sneakers squeaking, anger trailing behind her like smoke.

My heart is breaking.

31

Money Honey

"This appears to be a complex mixture of chemicals, Mrs. Hill."

Morty Fide Jr. adjusts his thick, black-rimmed glasses, refusing to look me in the eye as he consumes all ten scones in rapid succession.

"Uh-huh...you mentioned that when you were on your second scone. When you called you said you had received the full report from the state."

I feel guilty that Boysie wasn't included. He's been working hard on investigating the bombing of our bakery. I don't want to distract him from that.

"I did, Missus Hill." Morty shoots crumbs from his full mouth across his desk. He turns his computer screen so I can see.

"What in the world is ?"

He nods. "It's a new substance derived from mint leaves. The darling of the drug industry. I just heard last week that the drug sold to a big company for several million."

"And what does it do, exactly?"

Morty wipes his hands on his previously pristine lab coat, leaving traces of cherry. "Mind control. It's going to be a great way for the psychiatric community to control their patients. Prisons can send it through their filtration systems. Can you imagine a prison riot about to break out, and then they breathe in floricrine and poof! Everybody's calm."

"What if it got in the wrong hands?"

Morty sniffs. "That never happens. We are professionals."

"And yet I found this in a fog machine, which clearly is NOT something used by the medical community."

There is not one flicker of emotion on Marty's small face. It's like he's frozen, and part of me wants to leave him that way.

"Well, thank you, Morty. I appreciate your help."

I get up to leave, and just as I reach for the doorknob, he touches my back. I jump, unsure if he thinks I'm here for more than information.

"Missus Hill, this drug is so new…I had to do my own research when the report came back. These things take time and testing to reach the people they help the most."

"We don't know that, Morty. Fog machine—remember?"

He shakes his head. "Let me show you something."

Though this man gives off major "creepy dude" vibes and I'm out of food to distract him, I follow him to his computer.

After a few clicks, he says, "there. You see?"

On the computer screen are six boxes and in each one, an object or food with a bright, yellow substance visible. "Okay, so people are playing science with mayonnaise. What does that have to do with us?"

"Testing on animals is not well regarded anymore."

"Thank god."

"So people are getting creative. Scientists don't have the time to test every product. So they are farming the process out. Anyone with a little know-how and a lot of connections can become a researcher. And make big money while doing it."

I give this a moment to seep into my yellow mayonnaise-less brain. "What you're saying is that you think some bozo is testing this product by any method they have available to them, and it just so happens, they had a fog machine available to them. What happened to your scientific integrity?"

"Scientists are still professionals. Unfortunately, the other aspects of creating a safe drug have become a rather corrupted process. Money changes hands for all the wrong reasons if you get my drift."

Pepper or one of her team has been using the fog machine to test this new drug on unsuspecting singers?

If you take this to the police now, you'll slow down and possibly end the research. Think about the people you'll be hurting. There are a thousand reasons why it could have been on that fog machine. Don't make the mistake of assuming the worst."

32

Get in the Groove

Pepper Friday

The Portland club was just weird enough to be on-brand: an old movie theater-turned-karaoke venue, complete with red-velvet seats, a popcorn machine that had been converted into a fog machine, and soundproof booths decorated like miniature opera boxes. Pepper Friday loved it instantly.

It was Moonbeam's idea, of course—something about "the drama of cinema meeting the vulnerability of song," based on a three-hour lecture he gave his followers. But it was Pepper who made sure the permits were airtight, the lighting didn't trigger any migraines, and that no one accidentally built the stage two inches too high (as had happened once in Fresno).

Pepper had been left alone at the club for the night, her first full solo field oversight. The team had gone home. The lights were low. Her inbox was empty for the first time in three weeks. She could have gone back to the hotel.

But she didn't.

Instead she found herself wandering into Sybil's temporary office—an aggressively neat room at the back of the club, formerly the manager's projection booth.

The door wasn't locked.

Pepper stood in the doorway for a full minute before stepping inside. As she hesitated, her phone buzzed.

Glazed dozen…waiting.

She sighed before typing back: *I know!*

The desk was orderly in the way that felt almost… strategic. A slim silver laptop rested at the center, flanked by two color-coded folders and a coaster—already in use under a bottle of sparkling water.

On the wall was a dry-erase board with what looked like a launch timeline. But as she stepped closer, she saw there were no club names, no launch dates. Just dots. Arrows. Initials.

And something marked "Project Echo."

Pepper frowned.

She'd heard that name once before—in Denver, when a nervous intern mumbled it under his breath before quickly pivoting to discuss VIP wristbands.

She pulled out her phone and snapped a picture of the board.

Then she sat at the desk and opened the laptop.

The password screen blinked.

Pepper hesitated. Then she typed:

Sybil2024

Access denied.

She tried:

Eggplant1

Nope.

Then, after a moment's thought, she tried:

NotForDerek

The screen unlocked.

"Of course," she whispered.

THE DESKTOP BACKGROUND was a blank slate gray. No icons. But there was one folder in the bottom corner titled:

Do Not Access – Internal Only

It practically screamed click me.

Pepper obeyed.

Inside were dozens of spreadsheets, PDF contracts, and one strange document entitled, "USG crowd control, Seattle."

Her pulse quickened.

She double-clicked the file.

Nothing. There was definitely content, it was a large file, in fact.

She leaned in close and waited. Seconds turned

into minutes. Finally letters began appearing across the screen, one word at a time.

It was a contract. Standard-looking at first. Until she got to the rider at the end, buried in the fine print:

"Karaoke programming may include alternate background frequencies in accordance with Project Echo specifications, but ONLY after approval by Garden God. Client waives all liability."

Pepper scrolled back up.

The contract wasn't between Moonbeam's company and a karaoke equipment supplier.

It was between Sybil Screech and an entity listed only as G MASTER.

Those initials were familiar.

She opened a new browser tab and ran a search.

G MASTER.

—A shell company registered in Delaware.

—No employees listed.

—Mailing address shared with six other non-operational LLCs.

The rabbit hole was opening beneath her feet.

She clicked back to the folder.

This time, the entries were marked "Fog Machine Disbursement." Each with a city name attached: Denver. Toledo. Des Moines.

All the locations where strange accidents had happened.

She opened the Des Moines version. Same tone. Same eerie nothingness. The files were each between 3-7 minutes long, with names like:

Warmup_A3

PreShow_Hz67

CrowdAmbient, LowRider Observe substance released from fog machine.

Pepper's mind flashed back to the contract she'd signed, the one forcing her to keep her mouth shut about whatever she saw or else she'd never get another corporate job again. Moonbeam had warned her that he had "plenty of Mooners" to keep eyes on her at all times.

Could the fog machines be the cult's weapon of destruction?

In every club she opened, Sybil insisted she wear a high-quality mask. "No time for illness, Pepper Friday," she said.

Now it sounded sinister. Was Pepper protected in breathing the same air as everyone else because it was toxic?

She stared at the screen, barely blinking. With shaky hands, she inserted a thumb drive and saved the information.

Her phone buzzed.

A message from Sybil.

"Be in the lobby in 5. Shuttle arriving early."

Pepper sprang to her feet, pulled out the thumb drive, closed the laptop, and checked the door.

No one was there. When she looked the other direction, she ran smack into Derek.

"You can't scare people like that, Derek! People have weapons these days and you'll get shot!"

Though she felt bad for the way he was treated, some of it he brought upon himself.

"Everyone thinks I'm stupid."

His eyes were glazed over. Like usual. The man would fail a road sobriety test without ingesting one drink.

"No, they…" she stopped herself. "What did you need?"

"You'll all be surprised! Even you, Pepper!"

Some days, she actually felt sorry for him. He was probably making paper dolls for a shoebox karaoke performance. "We've got to get moving, Derek. We have to meet Sybil soon."

"You'll never be as close to her as me," he taunted.

Pepper blinked. "Derek, I don't want to date Sybil. She's all yours."

His body was firmly planted in place, giving Pepper no easy out.

"You want my Sibby to like you more, but I took care of it."

She debated. Do I want to wade in and ask what that meant? Or should I let it go and give it the burial it deserved?

"Derek, as much as you love…her, you know how angry she would be with both of us if we were late. Do you want to make her mad? Do you want to see that mole pulse?"

He drew what was left of his eyebrows together as he looked up towards the ceiling for answers.

On the van ride to the club, Pepper was lost in her thoughts as Derek prattled on about a kite he saw that he was certain was made of orange sherbet.

The setting sun did nothing to slow her thoughts that evening. Sybil was documenting the effects of the fog machine in excruciating detail. *Why kill individuals without including that information? Was she embarrassed? Was this a secret she was keeping from Moonbeam? And why?*

Pepper wanted to call the one person who might have the answers, but she knew calls were strictly limited to quick, pre-scheduled conversations.

When she finally looked at the time, it was almost two a.m.

The next morning, Sybil entered the club fifteen minutes before the final launch inspection. She was crisp, pressed, and unreadable as ever.

She glanced at Pepper, her mole pulsing.

"What's wrong with you? Did you forget the part of your contract forbidding you from guzzling drinks as strong as gasoline?"

"Didn't sleep well."

"Don't let it affect your performance."

Pepper nodded.

But her mind was racing.

She wasn't just working for a karaoke empire anymore.

She was standing at the edge of something much, much bigger—and possibly much more dangerous.

And her choice? Keep climbing the ladder.

33

Tea For Two

Lanie

If there's a worse way to start the day than a guilt headache, I haven't lived it yet. My head pounds in tempo with the slow-drip coffee maker while my ceramic frog's shattered remains wait for the proper burial they deserve. Vem hasn't called. Hasn't texted. She even left the group chat on mute, which is basically our version of filing for emotional divorce.

I replay our last conversation from two days ago over and over, chewing on every word I threw like it wasn't going to hit someone I care about. I had no right to accuse her sister of being a manipulative stalker without something more solid than a gut feeling and a folder full of conspiracy doodles. And I *definitely* had no right to say it like that.

Still. That vial. That fog machine. Floricrine. Was Pepper in over her head?

I pour coffee, strong and bitter, and dial the one person who can keep me from falling too deep into my own head.

"Lanie Frostine Anders-Hill," comes the voice on the other end. "I was just thinking about how long it's been since someone yelled at me in a parking lot."

"Hi, Vem."

A pause. "Is the frog okay?"

"No."

Another pause. "I'd offer to bury it, but my graveyard-yard is already full. I can get you on the waiting list in case something opens up." She pauses. "I'm sorry, bestie."

My breath shakes out of me in one long exhale. "Me too."

I can hear her moving around—probably pacing in mismatched socks. "Want to talk?"

"I have a kettle full of raspberry white tea and new evidence that could either crack this whole thing open or get us thrown in a very small, very padded room."

"That's the dream." Her voice is lighter now. "Be there in ten."

VEM ARRIVES with her hair tied up in one of her crime-solving lavender bandanas and a suspiciously shaped box under her arm.

"I brought snacks," she says.

"Your definition of 'snacks' scares me."

"I baked anti-anxiety muffins."

I raise an eyebrow.

"Chamomile, lavender, and a *hint* of mint chocolate. Warning: may cause hallucinations and deep personal revelations."

"Perfect."

We sit across from each other at the kitchen table, tea steaming between us. I push the folder of evidence toward her.

"I need to start by saying I was wrong," I say. "About how I said it. About pushing you like that. You've been through enough."

Her lips press together like she's trying not to cry or laugh. "You weren't wrong about being suspicious. I just didn't want you to be right."

She opens the folder slowly, her eyes scanning the contents. "Is this…"

"Floricrine," I say. "Morty confirmed it. It was on the fog machine. In the air. Probably in everyone's lungs at every karaoke club Moonbeam Enterprises has opened."

"Mind control." Her voice is barely above a whisper. "Why?"

I take a sip of tea. "Because it's not about killing. Not really. It's about *shaping behavior.* Making people do things—trust, obey, forget."

She frowns. "Then why are people dying?"

"That's the variable," I say. "Maybe it only works on certain people. Maybe some resist it. Maybe the deaths were... unintended consequences. Or worse—part of the experiment. Whoever is doing the testing is making lots of money. When you're getting paid, you don't want the money train to stop."

She shudders. "That means Sybil...or Moonbeam...or someone way up the food chain is testing it. On club members."

I nod. "And Pepper's in the middle. Either as the test subject... or the trigger."

"She wouldn't—"

"Vem, listen." I reach out, not to push, but to hold. Her hand is cold. "I believe you love her. I believe she loves you too. But that doesn't mean she's not being used. Or that she didn't get in too deep."

"She found me," Vem whispers. "I didn't tell anyone where I was. She just showed up. Said she missed me. But she had this way of saying it—like it had been rehearsed."

I nod. "She may be following a script. A psychological playbook."

Vem pulls out the psychological profile from the folder we found. "Subject shows high empathy response when presented with emotional distress."

I raise an eyebrow.

"That's me," she says.

A silence settles between us, full of fear and

realization. "What if this whole thing wasn't just about Pepper being manipulated?" I ask. "What if it was about *you*?"

Her eyes go wide. "Me?"

"She left her own version of a cult. They sent her to find you. To bring you back. Or at least get you close enough for… monitoring."

She leans back in her chair, the truth rattling around like loose change in her brain.

"I think she wanted to warn me," Vem says. "But she was scared."

"And now," I say, "we have something they can't ignore."

WE HEAD to the police station with the folder and a dozen Belatrix Blueberry scones. Boysie greets us like we're his two favorite trouble magnets.

"Ladies. I see sugar and danger are on the menu today."

"We found something," I say, handing him the folder.

Vem watches his face closely. "This is big, Boysie. Fog machines, a designer drug, and dead club members whose last breath might've been tinged with a research project gone awry."

"Oh. You heard about Red."

"It's been three days. The only people who haven't heard are people vacationing in Tibet. Do you have any updates on his cause of death?"

Boysie shakes his head. "State crime lab is still working on it. They did mention an unknown substance . Not conclusive yet."

"People are dying in every club they open because they inhale a poisonous gas. It's a group of people associated with Moonbeam Enterprises. They're testing a new drug in fog machines for some reason."

"No fog machines in Tillamook. The police chief there tells me it was contact poisoning." He flips through the report. "You realize this means the club launch events might've been staged environments for testing crowd control."

"Or brainwashing," Vem adds cheerfully.

"And you have this drug, I assume?"

"No," I say. "But we have photos, residue, and a coroner who's unusually enthusiastic about baked goods."

"Oh boy," Boysie says with a sigh. "This kind of case might be bigger than our little town. We may need to go federal."

"Floricrine is *new,*" I say. "It's not on any watch lists. The company developing it is private and tight-lipped. We won't get help from above until something explodes."

"Or someone *important* dies," Vem mutters.

Boysie nods, expression grim. "Then let's keep this quiet for now. I'll see what I can dig up on the company. You two stay out of trouble."

"I make no promises," I say.

"I make worse ones," Vem adds.

BACK HOME, the guilt headache is gone. Replaced by a *mission headache*, which at least feels productive.

Vem is curled on the couch, typing away on her laptop. "I think I found the parent company of floricrine's lab. It's a front. Registered to a fake address in Delaware. Classic."

"And what about Sybil? Is she listed on there anywhere?"

"No. But she's hosted every single club opening in the last six months. The fog machine appeared at the first three."

"But there were deaths at all the openings."

"People with no history of heart problems, stroke, or drug use. All sudden cardiac events. All dismissed as flukes."

I pace the room, nerves prickling. "Do you think they're testing doses? Or looking for the perfect combination of triggers? Or is it that they've escalated and now want to see what actual skin contact does with the drug? That's disturbing."

"Maybe all three."

"And Pepper?"

"She's… in the wind. No response to my messages. Her social media went dark last night after our meeting."

"What meeting? Vem, what aren't you telling me?"

"Oh, she wanted a sister connection," she says happily. "She asked to meet me in a dark alley. Kind of reminded of me Tulip Sloan in the movie, 'The Spy Who Did My Laundry.'"

"That's concerning. What happened when you got there?"

Vem clasps both hands together behind her frizzy head. "She was about to tell me something very sister-ish before a fan came up and wanted an autograph. When I turned around, she was gone. My public wants what it wants, Lanie."

I sit next to her. "We need to find her."

Vem leans forward. "You still think she's dangerous?"

"I think she's scared. And people who are scared are capable of anything."

She nods slowly. "So we find her first. Before they do."

"Exactly."

Vem looks at me, all the weight of the last few days on her face. "Lanie?"

"Yeah?"

"Thanks for coming back for me."

"Always," I say. "Even if you smash my frog."

34

In Too Deep

Pepper Friday

"I want to remind you, Ms. Friday, that you are under contract with me. Running away with your phone off doesn't sit well."

Moonbeam signals to a Moonie to fluff his robe. "I appreciate your taking responsibility for the glitter bomb. But your generosity was ill-timed. I had to pay off the sheriff as well as a number of state officials since Chief Lumquest wouldn't take a bribe."

Pepper let her breath out slowly. The less she said, the better. She waited as he stared hard at her, his beady eyes drilling a hole through her chest.

"I hope you'll find this information adequate for the time being. The longer you stay, the more information I'll give you, Pepper Friday. Just as I promised." Moonbeam's soft voice was barely heard over the sound of the disco music he combined with meditation tones. The odd mixture sounded like a 1975 horror movie.

Just as she reached for the folder, he placed a chubby hand in her way. "I will require something in return. You can't just run off like that again. Ms. Screech says you've been absent for three days. You know better than to leave in the middle of a club opening, Ms. Friday."

Pepper's cheeks turned crimson. "What…do you want, Your Holiness?"

"Not now. It's time for my weekly foot massage. Even the highest need attention to their corns." He chuckles. "But when I call for you, I expect an answer. No more flitting about like an aimless butterfly."

Moonbeam's voice echoed in her head like a bell rung too close to the ear. She clutched the envelope so tightly the paper creased at the corners. Her pulse roared louder than her footsteps as she sprinted down the hallway of the rented hotel suite in the Fallen Branch Inn and Spa, the slap of her kitten heels like punctuation marks of barely contained panic.

Once inside, she shut the door, locked it twice, and slid down with her back pressed to the wood, breath catching in her throat.

The envelope sat in her lap like a time bomb.

She opened it carefully, reverently. Inside, a thick stack of documents. Photos. Newspaper clippings. Birth announcements. A hand-scrawled note from someone named "Edelweiss" confirming blood ties. Probably a Moonie. She spread it all out on the bed, careful not to let anything slip to the floor like spilled secrets.

Nochturn was just as she remembered him. He looked younger in the photograph, but unmistakable. Same square jaw. Same coal-black eyes. He was smiling stiffly at a neighborhood barbecue, holding a beer in one hand and a toddler on his hip. It made Pepper's stomach twist to see it—he was capable of smiling like that? She ached to be near him again.

Her fingers moved, almost involuntarily, to the next photo.

November looked older than Pepper remembered—dressed in a bland beige suit, with tight curls piled atop her head. There was joy in her eyes, though. A kind of fearless, unfiltered joy. Her arm wrapped around her son, a boy with a sour little face and a stubborn chin. The kind of kid who probably organized his Halloween candy by brand.

Pepper stared at the images.

She wanted—no, ached—to feel something sharp. Jealousy. Rage. But instead, a hollow calm slid in. A recognition that this version of life—family photos, bake sales, matching holiday sweaters—would never be hers.

She stood, crossed the room, and opened her laptop.

With one click, she deleted the folder labeled *Dad's Other Kids*.

Not out of bitterness.

Out of peace.

She belonged elsewhere. Somewhere stranger, somewhere messier. Somewhere she'd carved her place with glitter, wit, and sheer will. Maybe that was enough.

"Pepperoni?"

Pepper huffed as she went to answer the door. "What, Derek? I'm busy!"

He moved to enter the room, and she blocked him. "Did you get in trouble with Moonbeam?"

Her mind raced. "No, why?"

"Because of the glitter bomb you sent." He jammed a tongue into the side of his cheek like he was ready to consume a human-sized cat.

Pepper's face tightened as the realization overtook her. "It was… you, wasn't it?"

Derek had been a thorn in her side since day one. For being a simple man, he sure caused problems. "Why would you do that, Derek? You could've hurt people! My sister was in that building!"

"Because you don't belong here. My Sibby is under your spell, and so is Moonbeam. I had to show them. Just like I'll show them—"

Pepper took a fist full of his slippery orange shirt. "Listen, you brainless twit! I'm only keeping your secret until we're done here. Then I'm telling the cops everything. It's not me who needs to move on. It's you!"

Luckily, for both Derek's safety and Pepper's sanity, a scheduled call with "M" was only minutes away. Her contact agreed to phone anonymously and tell Lanie about Derek's responsibility for the bombing of the bakery. "Can't call the police, Friday. Those are recorded lines. Sooner or later, they'll figure out my identity and then our cover is blown. It's too dangerous for us both."

HER FINGERS HOVERED above the keyboard, ready to resume her search for Nochturn. She'd forbidden herself from trying to contact him after their mysterious meeting years earlier. Did he resent their father enough to turn her away? Would Nochturn be angry that she was bothering his perfect life? She was trying to push those nagging questions out of her head when she heard it—a knock at the door. And why wouldn't anyone in Piney Falls talk about him?

Sharp. Unhesitating.

Pepper's pulse jumped. She glanced at the window—just enough to see city lights flickering like Morse code. Was it Moonbeam, already back? Had she failed some unspoken test?

She approached the door slowly, peered through the peephole—and nearly fell over.

Dressed in pea green. All pea green. Jumpsuit, headband, glasses frames, even her flats. Like she'd been woven together out of car interiors and museum walls. The long peacoat sported a lining with the words, "November Bean" written in curly cursive all over the shiny black fabric. And somehow, she was both elegant and terrifying.

November didn't wait for an invitation. She stepped inside, gaze scanning the room.

"Nice drapes," she said flatly. "Shame if they got holes in them."

Then, casually—as if reaching for a tissue—she pulled a revolver from between her breasts.

Pepper made a squeak that didn't sound like any human language.

"Gladys said you wanted some weaponry," November said, walking past her. "You should've come to me first, not the town loudmouth."

"I—what? I never said—wait, how do you—why do *you* have a gun?"

November turned to her, one eyebrow raised. "We're related, doll. You should know by now that comes with risks."

"Okay…"

"I have an entire storage facility full of things I acquired either through military auctions or the underground. The under-underground. Don't ask." November displayed a shiny pink gun. "Now this is Babs. She likes to chat with the others. I thought they could use a break."

Pepper blinked. Her heart thundered. The bright pink revolver looked absurd in November's manicured hand, like someone had armed a librarian.

"You're really giving me this?"

"No," November said. "I'm *lending* it. You look like the kind of girl who breaks things when she's emotional. Guns aren't for decoration. Or drama. Just promise me one thing."

"What?"

"That you won't shoot anything with four legs."

Pepper stares blankly.

"Hello?" November waved a hand in front of her face. "We do tend to veer off in this family."

"Sorry. I just thought you were a hunter, and that's why—"

"You think I collect these babies to hunt?" November shakes her head. "Sister-friend, I don't hunt anything bigger than a Hercules beetle, and I've only caught ten. Best stew I've ever made." She smacks her lips.

"Then why do you have so many weapons?"

Pepper wrapped her fingers around the cool grip. It felt like it belonged in her hand. Moonbeam was right. Her old family was holding her back from good things.

"Because I can. All the years I was married the Toilet Paper King, he never celebrated me. He was all about his appearance and our kid. But when it came to me, he was fresh out of attention."

She sniffed. "When I divorced him and got oodles of his TP cash, I decided I would never again live in the dark. November Bean is large and in charge. And all the auction houses know me and my tastes."

Pepper wanted to feel pride. Pride in a sister who survived hardship and now thrived. Instead, she felt resentful. Why did this silly woman own storage units full of weapons when she could do something good with her money? Why were Pepper and Ginger destined to suffer? Neither of them would ever marry someone like the toilet paper king.

She wanted to ask about Nochturn, but the timing seemed off.

That night, she didn't sleep.

The gun sat inside the drawer of the hotel nightstand, wrapped in a tea towel and humming with presence. Moonbeam hadn't even told her why she needed a gun. Just that she would know. And that when the time came, he'd call.

That call came the next day.

35

Wicked Game

Pepper Friday

They met at the rooftop lounge of the hotel. Moonbeam sat like a painted deity, robes pooled around him like fog. The sky behind him burned purple orange, and Pepper wondered if he planned it that way.

He gestured for her to sit.

She did, clutching her bag. The gun was inside, along with a change of clothes, a burner phone, and a small crystal that had come in her "initiate's kit."

"You have it?" Moonbeam asked, voice barely above a whisper.

Pepper nodded. She pulled the shiny pink metal object from her purse and sat it on the table.

He didn't smile.

"Your loyalty to our organization had to be

tested. That's why I sent you to Ms. Bean for the weapon. Now that you've passed that test, I'm going to give you another. Only those at the highest level of focus can achieve this kind of greatness. If you pass, I will consider making you Sybil's boss."

A pause.

"She has lots of weapons—November. I'm sure I can get whatever you need. Though next time I'll probably need to pay her."

He leaned closer.

"One is sufficient. But I need you to use it."

Pepper froze.

He went on, "You've proven your loyalty over and over again through the years. I've got one more test. I need you to kill November Bean with her own gun."

Pepper stared at him in shock. "But…why?"

"She's a hindrance. She and her friend have been asking a lot of questions. They got Derek confused, which isn't hard, but he almost told them about the full extent of our operation. I don't have to tell you how important the work we're doing is."

"I don't…this seems wrong."

Moonbeam's face remained neutral. "Doubt is the luxury of the unchosen. You are chosen, Pepper. And choices come with price. November Bean and her friend have been sticking their noses where they don't belong."

He reached into his sleeve and withdrew a picture. Pepper and Ginger, hugging and laughing, during Dill's birthday celebration. One of the few days a year that they were allowed to show emotion.

"You and Ms. Bean have grown close," he said. "That makes you ideal."

Pepper's mouth went dry.

"Can't someone else?" she whispered, thinking the whole time how she didn't want ANYONE harming her sister.

He leaned forward until his beard brushed the table.

"Are you going to prove your worth to the future of this company, or should I release you from employment and tell everyone, including your father, how you've failed? It's all up to you, Pepper."

She wished her father's approval meant nothing. She wished she could call her contact. But from the beginning Pepper heard, "you may have to do some things that make you very uncomfortable. That, under normal circumstances, could land you in prison."

"Ever since the glitter bomb incident, your loyalty to Moonbeam Enterprises has been in question. This is how you prove you're still part of the team. Part of our family, if you will."

THAT NIGHT, Pepper didn't eat. She barely breathed.

She walked through the streets of Piney Falls

with the revolver wrapped in velvet, the same way she'd carry an heirloom.

She'd asked Vem to meet her in the alley behind Stinky Feet Pete's, a local bar. Pepper arrived early, hoping to stake out the location and any cameras before her sister arrived.

What am I doing here? I've waited my entire life for this, and now I'm going to end her life? No, it's a mistake.

As she turned to leave, she bumped squarely into November, knocking her glasses to the side of her face. "Thought I'd come early and collect ants. They love nacho pretzels here." She pushed her glasses up with one elbow. Both her hands were encased in long rubber gloves, and she smiled warmly. "So what's the spooky reason you wanted to meet here?" Vem asked, her face slick with sweat.

"Hi!" Pepper called, voice too high.

Vem turned, suspicious. "You okay? You look like you saw a ghost. Or worse—Moonbeam in the nude."

Pepper tried to laugh.

"I just—I needed air."

She reached into her bag and felt the cold metal. She wrapped her fingers around it. Her thumb brushed the safety.

Vem took a step closer.

"You said you needed to talk about our unfortunate patrilineage?" she said, surprisingly gentle.

"Seems like we could have found a sanitary place to meet."

Pepper's eyes stung.

As she reached her hand in the bag, a voice called out, "Is that November Bean, THE winner of the world's best moaner contest in Keok, Iowa?"

November turned around. "It is. Who are you?"

"Brenda Talksworth. I went to your Moan for Mayonnaise class. I've never looked at sandwiches the same…"

And that was it.

She couldn't do it.

Pepper pushed the gun down into her purse. "I forgot something. I—I have to go."

Vem frowned. "Okay. But let me know if you want to talk again, okay, sister- from- the same-awful mister?"

All the way back, she thought of excuses—November didn't show, there were too many people watching—in the end, she went with honesty.

Moonbeam waited.

She placed the velvet-wrapped bundle on the table.

"I'm not doing it," she said. "You want me to kill someone who—who's never hurt me. Who might've saved me, actually." *Did she believe that?*

Moonbeam unwrapped the gun.

He examined it like it was a relic.

"You're not ready," he said finally. "But you will be. That was the point."

Pepper took a step back. "This was *never* about loyalty. It was about control."

He tilted his head.

"You're learning."

She picked up the gun and put it in her purse, walking briskly out the door before he could say more.

The next morning, she wrote Joe a letter.

It was long, messy, tear-streaked. Full of confessions about lies and cults and karaoke. She didn't send it. Not yet. But she wrote it, which was more than she'd ever allowed herself before.

She shoved it in her suitcase and looked at herself in the mirror.

No longer invisible.

No longer innocent.

But still hers.

Still Pepper Friday.

Pepper hit redial on the phone. Not the one she used for work, but the one she hid in the secret pocket of her purse.

The other party picked up but didn't speak.

"I have to get out of here. I feel like I'm suffocating. Can you pick me up?"

36

Hit Me With Your Best Plot

"That's plenty, thanks," I say as Ed Junior fills my cup with what I'm assuming is coffee, though it has the color and warmth of aquarium water. The Spruce Bark's addition of a breakfast bar isn't going to attract new customers unless it comes with a personality transplant and stronger caffeine.

Vem is already sniffing the syrup dispenser suspiciously.

I should have expected Derek to trip over his own tongue. What I didn't expect was for him to trip over it, fall down a mental flight of stairs, and then try to sell us a t-shirt commemorating the journey. Maybe asking to speak with him was a mistake.

Derek sniffles hard enough to concern a passing toddler. He wipes his nose on his sleeve with the defeated flourish of a man who once believed in happily ever after and now suspects he might die alone in a clearance bin.

"She betrayed me," he says again, as if repeating it will make it less humiliating.

"You think?" Vem says, arms crossed, one eyebrow firmly arched. "Was the betrayal before or after she had you delivering syrups labeled 'Do Not List Ingredients' in the middle of the night like some glitter-covered drug mule?"

Derek groans. "I thought Sybil loved me. I'm her Der Der. And why would she call and tell you about the glitter bomb when I never said anything to her? I kept a secret! Bigger than…the day we met."

I lean against the edge of the table and brace myself for the tragedy he's clearly about to unleash.

"She met me at the food court," he says, voice trembling with the gravity of a soap opera monologue. "I was wearing my Galaxy Snax hat—you know, the one with the space nacho logo? I dropped a tray of promotional cheese tubes and she—she didn't even flinch. Just stepped over the mess and said, 'You look like a man with access to storage.'"

Vem coughs to hide a laugh. I don't bother.

"And you took that as flirting?" I ask.

He nods solemnly. "She asked if I had a car and could take directions. I thought it was destiny."

"Derek," I say slowly, "that wasn't destiny. That was Sybil shopping for a patsy."

His face crumples like a damp napkin. "I don't mind being pastry. Filled with chocolate cream."

"No, patsy. As in 'you're too dense to know she's

evil," Vem says before turning to me. "Lanie, can you help? I feel like I'm talking to the twenty-foot Hemlock Pine in my backyard and it's giving stubborn two-year-old energy."

"She said I had knife-holder energy!'" he protests.

"She meant *you hold the knives for her,* Derek," I say. "Not that you were going to be handed the throne. You were the emotional Tupperware. Convenient. Reusable. Disposable."

He sinks deeper into his chair, eyes glistening. "But she made me her assistant."

"More like an *assistant to the sabotage,*" Vem mutters.

"You guys seem nice, but you don't know my Sibby. She's perfect. And if Miss Perfect chose me, then I'm Mr. Perfect."

Instinctively I slapped my hand over Vem's mouth, feeling the syrup ooze through my fingers. I'm also a little concerned she'll forget this is all a ruse and that we're trying to make Sybil the villain in poor dum dum's mind so he'll spill the tea.

He clasps his hands dramatically. "I just thought… if I showed her I could plan stuff too that she'd get rid of Pepper and I would be her only helper again."

"Again? What do you mean?"

Derek locks his mouth with an imaginary key and drops the key in his coffee.

"I have superhuman strength and nothing but time, dough boy," Vem warns.

"Randy. He was the last one. He didn't like me. So he's in the…is it desert or is it dessert? That always confuses me."

I exhale slowly. "We have to tell the police about the glitter bomb, Derek."

His head snaps up. "No! Please! Just—can you make it sound like a superhero? Like I was trying to save Sybil from the Grangonots from planet Venudia? Or bad Yelp reviews?"

Vem stands and levels him with a look so sharp it could slice a sponge cake. "We'll tell Boysie the truth. That you were duped by a woman who could weaponize mascara and once convinced you to hold a fog machine in your mouth to 'test diffusion.'"

That tidbit came out before we even sat down.

He groans. "It was good clean fun!"

It's clear he has no idea that Sybil is killing people. Maybe it's better that way.

"Derek," I say gently but firmly, "you didn't just fall for Sybil. You fell face-first into her scheme and rolled around in it like a golden retriever with no instincts."

His voice is small now. "No. I'm her Snuggle Biscuit."

"You were more like her seasonal scone special," Vem says. "Limited edition, low effort."

He whimpers, defeated.

And honestly? I almost feel sorry for him. Almost.

37

Dreams of Destiny

Gladys is listening to her favorite country artist, Tex Toaster, when I arrive. Normally, she puts on oversized headphones that still somehow plug in to her computer. Today she is singing and swaying like, well, someone other than Gladys.

I tapped her on her left shoulder, the one without arthritis. "Are you…okay?"

"Hmm? Good grief, toots! Can't a woman enjoy her music without interruption?"

She tosses her headphones on the desk for dramatic effect.

"I'd say yes if you weren't working in a public building that is open to the public. You know, serving the public."

"There's a contest, you know. Be the first person to sing at the soft opening of Scheddy to Rock. Boysie says my voice scares off the hungriest of cats, but I've got a plan."

"I'd love to hear, but—"

"I'm going to jazz things up. My grandson taught me how to use a beat box."

"If anyone deserves the first number, it's you, Gladys. I'm just worried there will be something in the filtration system that makes people sick. That, or some kind of contact poison. I think you should wear those long gloves you bought at the costume store auction and bring your own mic. Just to be cautious."

Gladys squints in the way that always makes me feel naked. "What gives, toots?"

It's never a question of whether or not to tell the fastest gossiper in town, it's a matter of carefully controlling the story. "We're concerned these Mooners aren't playing with a full deck. They might be jealous. Of your…voice."

Gladys's shoulders relax. "Oh. You should've said so to start with. I'll wear the gloves. I can wear Boysie's head mic that he bought to direct parade entries at last year's Piney Falls Proud Festival. Then I'll just put a gas mask over the top." She rubs her hands together and smiles. "Not so tough now, was it?"

LATER THAT DAY, I drop by Cosmic Cakes and Antiquery. Cos is wiping the counter like it owes him money. The place looks immaculate. The may be behind us, but he's still cleaning as if trauma comes off with lemon polish. My heart hurts for my husband.

He eyes me. "You look like you've been steam-rolled by a fog machine."

"Close." I collapse into a chair. "Is the new blackberry black hole scone still a controlled substance?"

"For you? Never." He reaches under the counter and pulls out a small plate covered in plastic wrap. Saved. For me. I didn't think I could love that man any more.

I take a bite and I sigh so hard it could inflate a bouncy house. "Cos, what if people are being *killed* through karaoke?"

He stares at me. "Like… song choice? Because I always knew 'You Light Up My Life' was a murder weapon."

"No, I mean *murder*-murder. Vem and I found vials of green liquid yesterday and in the same box there was a logo with Pepper's face on it. Pepper wants to buy a weapon from Vem. It's weird."

Cosmo takes my hands gently. "Lanie, don't repeat this. Ever. But I spent twenty years around real criminals. Neither Bean nor Junior Bean has what it takes to be true killers. They dress like they're auditioning for a cartoon, talk like they were raised by apes—well, technically Bean *was* raised by cult apes. But murderers? No. They're loud, dramatic, unpredictable—but not lethal."

"People are dying," I whisper, relieved he's given my best friend a back-handed compliment. "And either the higher-ups don't know… or worse, they do."

His face darkens. "You've gone back and forth with this one hundred times, babe. Now you think Pepper's involved? Again?"

"I think she's caught in something. I *hope* she's not the one behind it. But she's been present at every launch. She knows things she shouldn't."

Before he can respond, a voice behind me chirps, "Don't forget your backup!"

I jump. "Vem! Stop slithering into rooms. You're like a four-eyed ninja-snake."

"I've got intel," she says, sliding a greasy folder across the counter. The name Sybil is scribbled faintly on the corner.

Inside: names, dates, scribbled codes. A list. Cold. Methodical. Club goers—victims—cataloged like lab rats.

I scan quickly. "These aren't real names… 'Bob-A is the same name used in Tellum. These aren't karaoke fans. They're *subjects*."

Vitals. Emotional spikes. Vocal strain data. I feel sick.

"This isn't entertainment," I murmur. "It's *experimentation*."

"Project Echo," Vem whispers, her face pale.

"We have to confront her," I say. My voice shakes.

Vem freezes, her fists clenched so tightly her knuckles are white. “No, Lanie. I’ve been telling you all along. She’s not like that. She *can’t* be.”

“She’s been *everywhere*, Vem. She has access. She has motive. She’s using those vials—maybe to test fear, reaction, control. Hell, even her face is on the label. The only thing I don’t understand is why only one person in each club has died. Especially when it was spewed out through the fog machine.”

Silence settles like ash.

Then Vem lifts her chin, voice trembling but steady. “Dress rehearsal is in three days.”

I nod, heart pounding.

“There’s no time to waste.”

We’re stepping into the wings of a stage soaked in secrets.

And the curtain is about to rise.

38

Back Stabbers

Pepper Friday

Pepper stood just outside the doorway, half shielded by a curtain of tangled cords and discarded mic stands. She pretended to organize a bin of sound filters, though her fingers remained motionless. Her breath came shallow and slow. She didn't dare draw attention.

Inside the studio, Sybil's voice rang out—precise, polished, and as sharp as a straight razor.

"She's a liability, Highest Moonbeam. You need to cut her loose after the Piney Falls job. She's been asking questions. About the courier. Says she recognizes him as her father's friend."

Pepper didn't flinch. Not anymore. She'd spent the past few weeks expecting this moment. Her hands still trembled slightly, but she anchored them to the plastic rim of the bin.

From atop his massage table, Moonbeam let out a long, indecisive groan. A recent graduate from *Pressing Matters Massage Academy* worked diligently to untangle the knots in his enormous back, her fingers digging into layers of indulgence and secrecy.

"I mean it," Sybil continued, her heels clicking like an impatient metronome. "She's reckless. Her judgment's fraying. She was never built for this kind of operation. What happens when she finds out what we're really doing here and decides she wants revenge?"

There was a pause as the masseuse lifted one of Moonbeam's massive legs into the air. He gave a lazy grunt.

"You're getting emotional," he said finally. "Do you need my Mooners to accompany you into the sauna for a heat and healing session?"

"No, sir. I—" Her voice faltered. For the first time, Sybil sounded less like the puppet master and more like a nervous player afraid of losing the game.

Pepper's heart jumped at the shift in tone. It was quick, subtle, but unmistakable.

"You're right," Sybil continued, regaining composure. "I'll keep a close eye on her. I'm sure everything will work out."

Moonbeam shrugged—an infuriatingly noncommittal gesture. "So? You want me to fire her? And end our training? Seems like a waste. I don't think our investor would approve."

"After Piney Falls. Quietly," Sybil said. "Let her fade back into whatever vanilla life she crawled out of. Farm kids shouldn't play with fire."

Farm kids.

The words slid down Pepper's spine like a blade dipped in ice.

She blinked. Once. Then again, slower.

Dill's face rose in her memory. Not fondly. Not even with hatred. Just… there. Like a label. A warning. He'd said things like that too. Said she wasn't built for the mess. That she was all soft edges and naive dreams.

"Some might consider you sweet, Pepper," he'd mutter with that crooked smirk. "But that only means you're not made for chaos."

She thought it was a compliment, like she brought peace wherever she went. But one day her mother explained that Dill "thrived on the energy chaos provided." It was just another way for him to insult his older daughter.

She let herself believe she was lucky just to be here. Let Sybil shove her into shadows. Let Moonbeam dismiss her existence with a wave of his glitter-crusted hand. Let herself become something expendable.

But not anymore.

She turned away from the door, silent and swift, slipping down the hallway like a whisper. By the time she reached the basement break room, her mind was already racing ahead.

Pepper retrieved a flash drive from her bag, hidden beneath the lining of a knockoff purse Sybil once called "charmingly desperate." The drive was small, metallic, and held everything she'd collected over the past few months.

Courier logs. Staff rotations. Medical charts for club "performers." Data from Project Echo. Names. Conditions. Reactions. Songs sung and how long they stayed on stage. Some files were labeled only with code numbers, but others were more direct. Handwritten notes in Sybil's sharp print. Moonbeam's digital voice memos—some slurred, some chillingly clear.

All the vials she'd stored in a locked box while they were remodeling the opera house.

She shoved the drive into her laptop and began the upload. The cloud account she'd created was masked, password-locked, tied to no name. She'd covered her tracks. If things went bad, someone would find it.

The transfer bar crawled forward.

You're working for us now, Pepper. You'll a secret agent for the U.S. government. The mysterious lady who'd appeared in her bedroom all those years ago. Mystic. Maribel's older sister, who left the family to work for the F.B.I. and never told a soul. *We'll stay in contact through Joe Friday. He's been our operative but*

Maribel has begun to suspect him so he has to pull back before his life is in danger.

Pepper's chest tightened.

They'd been watching Dill. They'd been watching Mr. Gumb. The substance they were supposed to be testing was being bottled and sold to enemy countries. Even the supposedly innocent products sold at Teatimefest were designed to create an addiction to floricrine. Anything to make more money. And she was their secret weapon.

The night she'd escaped Maribel's home, Mystic and Joe took her to the cabin. They spent months teaching her how to take secret photos. Record conversations. When they thought she was ready, Mystic sent Maribel a message from Green Thumb. It said, "my daughter is a stray now. We need to bring her back into the organization before she starts asking questions." And then Maribel showed up at the cabin.

The upload finished with a soft chime.

Pepper ejected the drive, placed it back beneath the lining of her purse, and stood. Her hands were steadier now. Her thoughts more focused.

They thought she was the liability.

They had no idea.

She wasn't going to run. She wasn't going to be erased.

She was going to blow this whole operation apart.

. . .

MY DAUGHTER HASN'T SAID a word in fifteen minutes.

- She's been pacing the perimeter of her bedroom instead, like a caged wolf, the kind that's too restless to sleep and too stubborn to settle. Her steps leave faint indentations in the sunshine-yellow carpet, circling, circling, as though the act of moving might unravel the knot inside her head.
    - The air in here feels heavy. Even though we remodeled this farmhouse to use as a commercial location for our second bakery, there's still a ghostly tang of smoke beneath the lavender paint. And something else —something metallic—that never quite fades. The scent makes my skin itch, like we're sitting inside a memory that refuses to die.
    - She finally stops, arms folded tight across her chest, and turns to me. Her dark hair, usually pulled into a braid, has slipped loose during her pacing, frizzing into a halo around her face.
    - "She's not stupid," Piper says flatly.
    - I nod slowly, careful not to rush. "I never said she was."

- "She's not careless either," Piper presses. "Ms. Friday's a lot of things —messy, secretive, impossible to read —but she doesn't screw up. At least there was nothing you said that indicated otherwise."

I close the notebook in my lap. Pages of half-legible scrawl, names and dates, strange notes about chemicals and karaoke stages—my attempt to show Piper everything we've pieced together so far. I slide it across the fluffy purple comforter, closer to her side of the bed.

"I don't think she's screwing up, hon," I say softly. "I think she's escalating."

The word hangs in the air like smoke. Escalating. It hits me harder than I mean it to, knowing how sensitive my sweet daughter is to the pain of others.

Her eyes go distant, unfocused, as if she's picturing Pepper not as a schemer but as a frightened animal, cornered and lashing out.

"November must be devastated," she murmurs finally. "Do you think she'll be okay?"

The guilt slides in like a cold knife. I hate burdening my daughter with this—especially now when she should be excited about her upcoming cruise. A prize she won fair and square at the opera house fundraiser, her name pulled from the spinning raffle drum to the applause of neighbors. At least THAT part of the evening went off without a hitch. She should be thinking about sunscreen, not sabotage.

"Eventually," I say. "She'll be okay eventually. We're heading to the opera house soon for their business-after-hours social. It's a pre-opening, I guess."

Piper nods, her jaw still tight. "Of course, Mom. I just... I feel bad that we're leaving town when you need us."

"No, sweetie." I rise from the chair and cross the room, pulling her into my arms. She's petite—barely five feet tall—and her dark head fits neatly underneath my chin. Like we were always supposed to be family. My favorite place in the world. "I just needed a listening ear. There hasn't been a crisis yet that your dad and I couldn't handle. You go finish your packing. By the time you get back, this will all be a distant memory." But even as I say it, I don't believe it. This is more of a "I may never see you again, depending on the outcome of the evening," than a simple bon voyage. "Your dad and I, we... could never imagine a life with each other and with a beautiful daughter. We're so immensely grateful you came into our lives. Don't ever forget that."

We stand there for a moment, the room quiet except for the faint hum of her little desk fan. Her suitcase sits open on the bed, clothes neatly folded, a travel-size bottle of lavender lotion tucked in the corner. Piper has always been meticulous about packing—she says it makes her feel in control of whatever comes next.

"You don't think Pepper's dangerous," Piper says suddenly, muffled against my shoulder. "Not really. Do you?"

I pause, stroking her hair back from her forehead. "I think Pepper is… unpredictable. And unpredictable people can cause damage, even if they don't mean to."

"She means to," Piper whispers. "You can feel it. The woman is wrapped way too tight."

Her words settle like a stone in my chest. She's always had an instinct for people—an ability to sense what they don't say out loud. Sometimes I wonder if she inherited it from her biological mother.

I pull back enough to look her in the eye. "Do me a favor, okay? Don't carry this with you on your trip. Let yourself enjoy it. You've earned it."

Piper presses her lips together, reluctant. But she nods.

I linger as she showers. The air still smells faintly of her shampoo and history that won't leave this old farmhouse's walls. I glance at the notebook on the bed and feel the weight of it pressing down.

I think about November, holding herself together with stubborn dignity even as her world unravels. About Pepper—bright, capable, hungry for validation, and standing closer to the fire than she realizes.

The opera house is waiting, like a stage where one wrong note could kill.

And soon, someone will have to stand at the microphone.

I'm terrified for who will die next.

39

Tell Me The Truth

"Are you sure you won't join us?"

I don't want to put my husband in danger. *Do I?* No, I don't. But I'm also afraid to face this evening alone. More than any villain ever before, Sybil scares me. She has no soul.

"Babe, I say this with love," he begins. "I'd rather listen to Bean howling at the moon for six hours than show my face at this shindig."

"I can't say that I blame you," I confess. "Just know you'll be missed. I love you, Cosmo Hill." I hug him so tight he can't breathe.

He pulls away and cups my chin in his hand. "Don't worry, Lanie. I won't be cruising the streets looking for songless women while you're away."

Let the games begin.

The new carpet in Scheddy to Rock, the awful name placed on our historic opera house, is plush and maroon, designed to soak up secrets. It dulls the sound of our shoes as Vem and I approach the office, hearts pounding in unison like badly timed drumbeats.

Vem doesn't speak. She just nods once and opens the door with the key we "borrowed" from Moonbeam's office while he was away. I step through, trying not to let my emotions get the best of me.

Pepper is already inside, sitting at the desk, scrolling through a playlist on the office computer like she isn't minutes away from the collapse of her entire carefully curated world.

She looks up when we enter. Smiles like she's at a book club and not the edge of a cliff.

"Oh good," she says lightly. "You brought your interrogation faces."

"Don't joke, Pepper," Vem says, her voice a low, dark warning. "Not right now."

Pepper sits back in the creaky swivel chair, eyes moving between us. "You told her!" she cries. "I asked you not to tell, November!"

I close the door behind me, the click as final as a judge's gavel. I take the seat across from her, Vem leaning against the wall, arms crossed, recording device running silently in her coat pocket.

"Boysie has everything," I say. "We know Derek left the glitter bomb, and we found the labels for floricrine with your face on them. We know about the fog machines and your meticulous research. What I don't understand is why you would lead us straight to the source. It was so sloppy leaving that box in plain view. This would have taken months to pull together!"

"Speak for yourself, Lanie," Vem snorts. "I'm not easily tricked."

Ignoring Vem, I turn to Pepper. "There's no walking this back."

Pepper doesn't flinch. She folds her hands neatly on the desk like she's listening to a recipe for Bundt cake. But then she blushes.

A soft, fast rush of pink across her cheeks.

The exact same way Vem does when she lies.

I notice. Vem notices.

Pepper sees us noticing and straightens quickly. "I didn't have any knowledge of whatever fog machine issues you're referring to," she says, too fast. "Maybe you've confused the money ledgers with whatever research you're talking about?"

"This isn't about money," I say. "It's about murder."

She freezes.

"You know what Derek told us," I continue, putting on my best poker face. "The boss wasn't impressed by the lack of deaths with the fog machines. So you had to poison them individually."

Her lips part slightly. "I didn't kill anyone."

"You say that like it makes a difference," Vem says. "Sister-pie, this doesn't look good for you. I can afford a good lawyer, but they can't always keep you out of the stripes. And we don't look good in stripes. Well, except for great-aunt Lucretia, who liked to blend in with the wallpaper."

"What?" Pepper snaps, standing. "This is ridiculous."

I hold her gaze. "We know he about the drugs used on patrons. Enhancements, Derek called them. A way to keep patrons coming back."

"That's not true."

"He implicated you," I say.

"What?" She stands suddenly, causing her papers to fall to the floor. "Do you think I would tell that idiot anything important? He broadcast to the entire construction crew when he tore a hole in his underwear! It doesn't make any sense, Lanie!"

I'll have to admit, it doesn't. "Then why did you contact me and tell me about the glitter bomb?"

Pepper's mouth twitches. That blush again, climbing her neck like ivy.

"That wasn't me," she whispers.

"Do you understand how that sounds?" Vem says.

"I don't," Pepper says. "I don't know what you want from me. I didn't kill anyone, I didn't set off the glitter bomb. All I've ever wanted was to make my family proud. That's the honest truth. Clearly he lied to you."

The silence that follows is thick as cake batter.

"I came here to find you, November. I was so jealous..."

"You wanted to purchase one of her weapons to

kill her. Don't deny it," I say with more emotion than I'd like. Vem is my sister from another mister.

"I... yes, that's true."

Vem straightens. "You just confessed."

"No," Pepper says, shaking her head. "That's not what I meant. I meant—I—Maybe that was my initial plan, but the longer I was here, getting to know my sister, I changed my mind."

Something awful occurs to me. "Vem, did you sell her one of your weapons?"

Vem shakes her head with vigor. "Of course not, silly. I gave her one. Family doesn't charge family for weapons. Or ant jerky."

I try remaining stoic, but it is hard. Soo hard. "Which one, Vem? One that's still operational?"

"Violet Wren Mk VII is a concealed-operatives firearm developed under the *Covert Armament Elegance Initiative (CAEI)*. Designed for high-profile infiltrations, close-quarter neutralization, and civilian disguise operations, the Wren combines refined appearance with precise lethality," she recites. "Why? Did you want it? You should've said something, sister friend. I would have set it aside. I know your mister can be a handful at times, but I thought you'd decided to work things out with a series of kicks and giggles."

My astonished gaze moves to Pepper. "You were going to kill your sister with the weapon she gifted you. Were you getting some sick pleasure from killing Vem with her own gun?"

A look of confusion passes over her face. "Like I said, I came here with bad intentions, but I've studied up on my sister, and I realized I was wrong." Pepper's eyes well, but she blinks it back. "I only wish I could tell you guys. It's so unfair that this has to stay a secret."

A single tear escapes, trails down her cheek like a fissure.

Then—

Knock. Knock.

All three of us flinch. "Yes?"

"Derek wants you."

40

Watch and Listen

"Lanie Good Golly Miss Wally Anders-Hill, you look positively stunning. Did you finally get some sense in that head and leave your marcarooned mister?"

Middle Name Mania Mondays are not my favorite of her made-up holidays. "Not my middle name. Still. And thank you." I glance down at my maroon pantsuit. It's leftover from my days working as *The World's Largest Office Supply Company* and thanks to our daily hikes, it hangs loose on my body. I choose to ignore the dig about Cosmo.

There is still evidence of protest in the grand old theatre. Someone stenciled "Save the Scheddy," into the back of every brand-new chair in the row in front of us. I'm proud of those dissenters.

Glancing down at my watch, I see we're a mere fifteen minutes from show time. In more way than one. "Vem, I'm going to the —"

"I know," She says with a nod. And when I get to the bottom of the staircase, she yells, "Number one AND number two, Lanie. It's a long time till intermission."

Doesn't even faze me.

I'm halfway to the restroom, when I hear her voice—Pepper's—sharp and furious, slicing through the heavy hallway air like she's had *enough.*

I freeze outside Moonbeam's office, hand still hovering near the weird faux-gold bathroom door handle. I don't mean to eavesdrop. But I also don't mean to *not.*

"You knew," she says.

I lean back, ever so slightly, until I can hear better through the paper-thin walls of Moonbeam's velvet-covered kingdom of questionable choices.

Pepper slams something down. "Don't. This was in the bar crate. From Dill. Labeled for every club. It's toxic, it's addictive, and you're putting it in everything."

I blink. I've seen those bundles. I thought it was incense. Maybe eucalyptus.

Moonbeam doesn't flinch. "Darling, that's the entire point. The drinks are the hook. The music is the lure."

He pauses. "We're building dependence."

My blood goes cold.

"You're drugging people, overdosing them," Pepper says. "To build brand loyalty?"

"Innovation," he answers.

"Psychosis."

"Semantics."

I've heard a lot of bad ideas disguised as vision —but this is next-level cult capitalism.

"I'm not doing this," Pepper says. Her voice shakes, but only slightly. "I'm not selling poison for your little empire."

Moonbeam's chair creaks, and I picture him standing, dramatic and dripping in fabric like a wizard who sells essential oils at street fairs.

"You're not just selling it," he says. "You're *delivering* it. You scout the club locations. You open them. You distribute the product. You've even administered the drug yourself. We didn't ask you to get your hands that dirty. YOU wanted to open a club in Piney Falls, remember?"

Silence. Then Pepper again, small and dangerous, "What do you mean?"

Moonbeam grunts. "Did you really think we hired you for your marketing skills? For your clever little notebook full of colored tabs?"

He laughs, dry and bitter. "You were always meant to be the wholesome face of our organization and then our courier. Dill's idea. Clean enough to be trusted, edgy enough to be ignored. Plus, you've already got a record."

I wince.

"I don't have a—"

"Wilma," he says.

Pepper sucks in air, and I feel pity for her, even

though I have no idea who Wilma is. "That was boarding school," she says. "It was a prank and I was just a kid."

Moonbeam's voice drops to something almost… smug. "It was a test. Wilma, your ONLY friend in boarding school, was an operative too. Your headmaster recommended her because of her devious nature. Wilma was a conduit."

There's a long, painful silence. I press closer to the wall. I shouldn't be here. But now I *have* to be.

"She brought you to us."

My hand clamps over my mouth.

Moonbeam continues, soft and cold as a snake. "And speaking of deception, every time you've seen Dear Old Mr. Gumb, he was delivering more of your father's product. Bundles. Tinctures. Syrups. He tried avoiding you…" Moonbeam sighs dramatically. "…but you simply refused to leave him be."

Pepper's voice cracks. "You used me."

"We *invested* in you," he replies. "That's business."

"No. That's manipulation. That's predatory. And you tried to make a murderer out of me on top of that."

Moonbeam laughs. "Welcome to the real world, sweetheart. You've been in it the whole time. Everyone you've encountered is a part of the plan. Even your husband. You just didn't realize which end of the leash you were on."

I close my eyes. This can't be real. But it is.

"If anyone died on your watch, you've only got yourself to blame, Ms. Friday."

Poor Vem. She's going to be so hurt when she finds out her sister was the killer all along.

Then I hear the click of a revolver.

41

Lapdog, Loaded

I don't breathe. I don't move. The hallway suddenly feels about five inches wide and six miles long. *Don't do it Pepper, I whisper.*

"I'm not your lap dog," Pepper says with power in her voice I didn't know she had.

Moonbeam—still somehow unbothered—chuckles. "The lap dog gets the best snacks, doesn't it?"

He snaps twice.

And then I hear them—Mooners.

Dozens of them, spilling from god-knows-where like Broadway-trained termites. Singing in harmony, wearing matching smocks, chanting like we're one tambourine away from a full-blown cult revival.

"Miss Friday is trying her best to be fearless," Moonbeam booms. "She believes she can shoot me on my own property. What do you have to say about that?"

The Mooners keep singing. Some sort of musical nonsense—melodic brainwash.

"You see, Miss Friday?" he purrs. "You're always on the outside. If you'd join us willingly, they'd let you in."

I hear Pepper take a single step. It's deliberate. Defiant.

"No," she says. "I *don't* want in. I don't want your songs. Your snacks. Your syrup. I want out."

And then I hear her leave. Without a shot.

Polka-dotted shoes smacking the hallway like war drums.

I flatten myself into the shadow of the vending machine as she marches past me. She doesn't see me. She's somewhere else. Her eyes are fire. Her face is thunder.

I count to ten before exhaling.

Then I turn and sprint in the opposite direction.

There's only one thing I know for sure.

We're in *deep.*

42

Witness

I take my seat next to Vem just in time for the lights to dim. Pepper shocked, again, to be accused of murder. How?

There is so much to tell Vem and now I may never get the chance. The fog machine or however else the poison is being released will kill us before we get the chance to talk. I squeeze Vem's hand. She looks at me curiously before squeezing back. Our sign that everything is going to work out.

Sybil Screech takes center stage as if she were claiming ownership of the very foundation beneath her clogs. The velvet curtain framed her like a portrait in a museum, but the aura isn't elegance—it was ego.

The auditorium buzzes with energy, a dress rehearsal crowd made up of enthusiastic Mooners and local dignitaries.

"Syballus. Syballus. Syballus," Sybil says as her microphone test word without one note of irony.

Pepper Friday—frizzy-haired, wide-eyed, stands in the wings. She's obviously upset after her encounter with Moonbeam.

I rise, ready to intercept her before she hurts someone. "Lanie Punkin Pal Anders-Hill, what are you doing?" Vem hisses. "Don't make a scene!"

When I turn around I see Derek thrusting a microphone in her face before she steps onstage. "Could you give this to my Sibby?" he asks, unaware he's turned it on. "I'm afraid I gave her the wrong one. It'll cause all sorts of trouble in the sound booth."

Pepper narrows her eyes. "Why can't you give it to her?"

Derek's mouth curls into a sheepish smile. "Because... I don't want her to know I made a mistake. She'll make me sleep on the patio tonight."

Sybil's angry mole begins to pulse. "I can HEAR you, dum dums! The microphone I have is fine. Sybil's sharp voice lowers the temperature at least five degrees. "And where is my water? Room temp. Not glacier. I swear, if I wanted incompetence I would've taught preschool."

Derek disappears obediently.

With a sigh heard in row Z, Pepper stomps onstage, the microphone in her extended hand.

"If this is part of the show, I'm giving it one star."

"No, Vem. Don't give that shrew more venom to spit. We'll talk to Pepper privately, make sure she's okay."

My phone comes out and I send Boysie a text. This will just kill Vem.

Sybil reaches—Pepper yanks it back.

"I'll take an apology first."

The acoustics in the Scheddy Opera House are impeccable. A word whispered onstage will carry to the back row of the second balcony. At least where it used to be.

"She knows how to take care of herself," I whisper to Vem.

"You'll never get an apology from me!" Sybil snarls, then lunges. They wrestle for a brief moment, a tangle of gold lamé, polka dots, and righteous indignation. Finally, Pepper pulls the mic high overhead like a victory torch.

"Derek is tired of being your lapdog too," Pepper says, breathless. "He's always telling me that he wants to be known for his *expertise*, but all you do is berate him."

Sybil's laugh is enough to peel wallpaper.

"Neither of you could unscrew a lid without instructions. You're both USELESS. Moonbeam and I have decided to fire you! You've outworn your welcome, Ms. Friday!"

"I'm afraid not. I QUIT!" Pepper yells. The mic in her hand screeches in protest as she drops it to the floor. She storms offstage, her frilly skirt bouncing with purpose.

There is an audible gasp in the audience of local dignitaries and the wealthy who procured tickets through underhanded means.

Sybil, bathed in golden light, resumes her place at center stage. She is wearing a shimmering knee-length gold dress, and if it weren't for her smug face glistening with sweat and entitlement, I'd say she looked pretty.

Sybil turned toward the crowd with her usual dramatics. "You'll be entranced by a number I created. I call it, 'That final number again—'"

She stops.

Blinks.

A cough.

Then a choking sound.

Pepper freezes.

Sybil's eyes open wide. Her hands fly to her throat.

The microphone in her hand screeches as it slips from her grasp and hit the stage with a thud.

A horrible guttural gag brakes through the speaker system, then a gasp that sounds like she's swallowing glass.

She falls to her knees, scratching at her throat, eyes bulging. Foam gathers at the corners of her lips. Angry welts appeared like cursed ivy up her neck and across her face.

The audience erupts in chaos.

Screams. Gasps. Chairs scraped against the floor like panicked animals. Someone knocks over the fruit punch table. Councilman Chamberts asks, "Is this part of the show? Performance art is getting so real these days."

From the opposite side, I sprint down the aisle. In an impressive gymnastic move Vem launches herself up onto the stage with a speed athletes twice her age couldn't muster.

"Sybil!" Vem shouted, already kneeling beside her, unzipping the pouch at her hip. She reached for her phone with one hand and pressed two fingers to Sybil's neck with the other.

Pepper is still in the wings. A look of pure terror covers her face. Her hand is unclenched from the gun.

Sybil is dying—and Pepper didn't pulled the trigger.

Vem's now barking orders. "Clear the stage! Someone call EMS. Move!"

Pepper backs away slowly, her body trembling. She tucks the gun inside her coat before slipping through the side door just as the room plunges into chaos.

As if to get the last word, Sybil's body convulses once more. The sound technician muted the poisoned mic, but not before everyone had heard her last, gurgled cry.

Without a thought for my own safety I tear through the curtains and find no trace of Pepper.

"COME ON, YOU RAGEY WITCH."

Vem is still trying to save Sybil and neither of us have time to explain. I have to find Pepper.

43

Gummed Up The Works

The man wearing a red velvet suit is decidedly unpleasant and definitely not Santa. His round face looks waxy and cold. He blocks Pepper's path with the ease of someone who's been standing there a while, just waiting for his cue.

"Pepper," his voice is calm. Too calm.

She skids to a stop, breath ragged. "I don't have time for—"

"I told you I loved you like a daughter," he interrupts. "That wasn't a lie. But that doesn't mean I get to override your father's disappointment."

He reaches into his coat and pulls out a small, silver pin shaped like a crescent moon and holds it between two fingers. "Moonbeam Enterprises isn't just a chain of karaoke clubs. You know that now."

"You were supposed to dispose of that noisy one," he continues, gesturing towards Vem, who is straddling Sybil and bouncing on her chest while she moans.

"You... you were there, watching me?" Her voice is hoarse.

"I was there to *clean up* after you," he says quietly. "If you failed."

Then his face twists—something almost like regret surfacing.

"I gave Moonbeam the information on your siblings. The information your father fed us. The one thing he didn't tell you was that Nochturn is dead. No big brother for you."

Pepper's breath hitches. "You're lying."

"I'm not," he said. "I'm a lot of things. But I'm not a liar. Haven't you wondered why no one will tell you where he is? Some cult leader killed him years ago, and they kept it out of the news because they didn't want any copycat killings." He sighs, somehow making this her fault. "Unfortunately, you've made a mess here. It complicates things."

And then he reaches under his coat.

Before we have time to think, we hear the sound of a gunshot.

Mr. Gumb staggers back, eyes wide, clutching his side. He drops to one knee, wheezing.

Blood seeps through his shirt, warm and fast. Pepper stares at him in horror. "I'm sorry," she whispers as he falls to the ground. "I...loved you."

Moonbeam, unnoticed until now, is holding Pepper's gun. "I had such high hopes for him."

Moonbeam's high-pitched giggle startles us. "No matter. I will find someone better. Just as soon as I dispose of all of you. Now which one shall I kill first? One of the sisters?"

Without thinking, I move behind Moonbeam and shove him with all my might. His Rotundness lands on to fall on top of Mr. Gumb. November's gun skitters across the floor. For a brief moment, I lock eyes with Pepper. Then she's off again.

44

The Poisoned Pitch

I hear something in my pocket—wait, is it buzzing? I dig around and pull out Vem's listening device. She must've slipped it in this morning when she demanded that five-minute hug. I've never known five minutes to feel like a decade before now.

When I switch it on, Derek's voice spills out, cheerful as ever and dumber than should be legal.

I'm moving at a decidedly slower pace than Pepper, but luckily she's still in my sight range so I slow to a Lanie-sized trot while I listen.

"Well hello Mr. Floor Beam! You're all red and sticky. Are we making candy? That wasn't on my planner. Or maybe it was. I've been watching and it doesn't plan anything."

Moonbeam sighs. "I have a mess for you to—"

"I'm basically a genius," Derek continues. "I covered the mic in that mist stuff—what's it called —Fluffyzine? Florizine! The one marked 'Not for

Derek,' which means *definitely* for Derek. Right?" He laughs too loud. "Once Sibby started looking at Pepperoni like she was made of gold-plated salami, I knew I had to do something genius-y. So I started in Windy Ridge. With Buffalo Babs."

"I don't want to hear—"

Moonbeam has sighed continually. Guess even he gets flustered when he murders someone.

"You have to, sir. Derek za'Dimwit is on a roll. And not the kind that my Sibby says make me gassy. I did have one teeny problem—I didn't know how much poison to use. I just poured the whole vial into a spray bottle. I figured Babs could sing a little first, then croak. But she kind of… flopped before the first 'la.' Poor gal."

"Derek," Moonbeam says, strained, "you are catastrophically misunderstanding the mission. This is a government project. The serum is for tactical warfare. Not… open mic night homicide."

My eyes have to be the size of softballs. I can't believe what I'm hearing.

Derek's voice breaks again, suddenly weepy. I hear something heavy hit the floor with a thud.

"Oh nooo," Derek groans in a stunning moment of realization. "What have I done? My precious Sibby. I loved her almost as much as I love myself!"

In the background, I hear faint chanting: probably the Mooners, singing about rebirth and vocal transcendence.

"Get up, Derek. You're embarrassing yourself," Moonbeam mutters.

There's a thud. Some scuffling. "Why aren't you proud of me? I thought of this all on my own! I should get a raise! Or a raised donut! Please!"

"You've made a grave error," Moonbeam says, low and lethal. "You've jeopardized our mission here and our main source of income."

"This is all Pepperoni's fault!" Derek wails. "She was supposed to give Sibby the SAFE microphone. Wait—I just thought of something. I can fix this. Do we have… like, a reverse mist?"

"No. We don't fix spilled ink, Derek. We turn the page."

Derek pauses. I can almost hear the wheels in his brain turning. Slowly. Needing grease. "So… we're writing a book? Like a scrapbook of all the murders at the club openings?"

Moonbeam laughs quietly. "You're fired, Derek. I never should've let Ms. Screech talk me into hiring you. You've shown zero talent outside of massaging Sybil's corns."

"I liked her corns. I named them. Callous-y was my favorite."

"Get your things. Go back to your hotel room and sit on the bed. The police will be contacting you soon. And when they do, you tell them you are responsible for everything on your own. Moonbeam Enterprises has had nothing to do with any unfortunate deaths. Got it?"

That is highly doubtful.

A door squeaks.

"I took a little nap and woke up, and everyone was gone! Is it time for me to sing my song now?"

It's Gladys Petrie.

45

Run Run Run

I don't run.

Not for exercise, not for fun, and certainly not while wearing ankle boots with questionable arch support.

But here I am, breath already tight, legs cursing my life choices, and chasing after Pepper Friday like I've suddenly joined a reality show I never auditioned for. She's picked up speed and now appears to be trying to break the record for fastest escape in polka-dot heels. I'm sure it's been done before.

There have been no pauses, no red lights, nothing to slow her down since I listened to Derek shocking confession.

I catch sight of her up ahead—just a flash of long coat and fast feet. As luck would have it, the stoplight gods are in my favor. Finally.

But even so, I need her to stop.

"Pepper!" I wheeze. "Slow down!"

I don't think she hears me—or maybe she does and pretends not to. Either way, she keeps going until she reaches the end of the alley, where the streetlights flicker against the mist rolling off the hills.

Then, for a reason only apparent to her, she stops.

She's bent forward, hands on her knees, gasping for air.

I stagger up beside her, panting, feeling like every breath is made of gravel. A marathon would not end well for either of us.

She doesn't look at me. Just says, between breaths, "November told me that you didn't run."

"I don't," I cough. "I'm making an exception. For drama."

She lets out a soft laugh—surprised, maybe even a little human—and finally straightens up. Her eyes are red-rimmed. Her whole body is trembling like she's not sure whether to bolt again or burst into tears.

I don't say anything. I wait.

It works.

"I didn't come to Piney Falls just to work on the club," she says quietly. "I came… because of November."

I blink. "Because of her?"

She nods, eyes fixed on the sidewalk.

"From an early age, I was obsessed with my older siblings. They seemed so important in the world and my younger sister, Ginger and I were doomed to spend our lives in a greenhouse. I met my brother Nochturn and was in awe of his presence. I wanted to see more of him in Piney Falls."

"I thought you were here for November? You made a point of finding her at the bakery."

Pepper's breathing has slowed but now her face is the color of Sassy Lasses Radical Rose wine. "Yes, that's true. I was enamored of Nochturn, but as far as November goes, I felt…jealous of my older sister. Her life seemed glamorous and I wanted her to hurt the way I did growing up. That was on my mind when the F.B.I. said our target was setting up shop here."

My stomach flips. "The F.B.I.?"

"My old headmaster's sister, Mystic Glare recruited me. She's been a secret agent for two decades. Before I was recruited, they were getting intel from Gregory, Sybil's last assistant. But Sybil found out and took him out to the desert and let Derek torture him to death. Mystic and Joe—that's my husband—told me everything, about how Mystic's brother and sister were involved in mind control research and my father was developing serums. I was angry enough with November that I took the job going undercover without hesitation. I wanted to find a way to hurt her while I was here."

"Oh. Wow. That wasn't at all what I thought you'd say." My head is reeling. "So wait a minute. You were always planning to hurt Vem?" I ask carefully. "Did the F.B.I. approve? She's got contacts on the inside, so that would surprise me."

She shakes her head quickly. "No—no, not like that. I just thought… if I could undermine her, just a little, maybe I could make things even. Maybe she could experience some hardship in life. She and Nochturn had it so easy."

"That's the furthest thing from the truth, Pepper. They both suffered greatly from their time in the Fallen Branch Cult. Neither one had any social skills, nor did they understand who to trust. That's how November ended up marrying a smooth-talking toilet paper king. Did you know he was abusive? So much so that November had to leave under the cover of darkness without her son. Can you imagine how painful that was?"

She pulls her coat tighter around her, the blue polka-dot fabric bunching at her fists.

She laughs bitterly. "But she wasn't forced to endure hours of mindless lessons about plants and middle-of-the-night studying. She didn't have to give up her entire family in exchange for the promise of a new life, and then find out that was all staged too."

I watch her face as she speaks.

She's not deflecting.

For the first time, I believe I'm seeing the real Pepper Friday.

"None of that is Vem's fault. She's a good person, but she's had to overcome enormous obstacles to get there. You should give her a chance, a real chance. And I'm sorry that you had to hear of your brother's death that way. Vem says he was a good person. And he was the mayor!"

Tears form in her eyes. "Why wouldn't anyone tell me? Why didn't Mystic tell me? She has access to that kind of information. I don't understand."

"It was a dark chapter in Piney Falls history," I begin, not sure how much to say.

Before I can process any of that, I hear footsteps—fast, heavy, chaotic—pounding toward us.

First Derek, hair wild, shirt stained, eyes manic, sprints past without even seeing us.

Then—

"Lanie!" Vem shouts, charging around the corner like she's been waiting her whole life to tackle someone. "Catch him! He's our killer, and he's on the lam!"

I blink. "He's on what?"

"THE LAM!" Vem bellows as she barrels past.

Pepper and I look at each other.

I sigh.

"I don't run," I remind her, already turning to chase.

"Me neither," she says, already following.

But we do.

Because Derek has to be stopped.

46

I Fall to Pieces

We're too late.

By the time we round the corner—me gasping, Pepper trailing behind, and Vem running like she's auditioning for a post-apocalyptic sports league—Derek is already halfway across the parking lot, flailing his arms like a wounded duck and barreling toward the only four-lane street without stoplights in Piney Falls.

And he runs towards it.

No hesitation.

No plan.

Just full sprint, arms windmilling like a caffeinated inflatable tube man.

"Derek!" Vem yells. "That's not a sidewalk!"

But he doesn't stop.

A horn blares. A car swerves.

I'm at once grateful and envious of Vem's athletic prowess. She's right on his heels until I reach her and pull her back. “No, Vem,” I wheeze. “Don’t follow him into that crazy traffic. He’ll figure it out.”

He’s surprisingly fast for someone who eats five waffles a day.

“Stop, Derek!” I yell with all the breath left in my body. “You’re just making things worse!”

“Derek, please, don’t do this!” Pepper pleads. “the federal government likes to make deals with people who have inside intel!”

“The…what now?” Vem asks. Her shoulders are steady. Mine are heaving up and down like I’m on the dance floor under a huge disco ball. Lanie doesn’t run for a reason.

Derek , seemingly oblivious to the danger, veers into traffic.

Vem screams, “NO! NOT THE ROUNDABOUT!”

It’s too late.

Derek darts between two cars while another car slams on its brakes one moment too late. Poor za’Dimwit is sandwiched between its bumper and the car in front of him with a sickening whomp. Sybil’s plaything is wedged between the two like a slice of off-brand cheese in a roundabout panini press.

Pepper gasps beside me. “Oh my god—”

“Wait! Is he…?” Vem sputters.

“The doughy man is still alive!” a spectator next to me gasps.

One of the drivers opens his door and screams something unintelligible before throwing his car into reverse so fast that he knocks over a traffic cone. At least Derek's body can be recovered.

But instead of watching as a lifeless body crumbles to the ground, we witness a miracle. Or a horror movie yet to be written. Derek stumbles, walking sideways with eyes wide and unfocused.

"How's that guy still alive?" the spectator's husband asks me. "Is this some of that crazy performance art? It's hard to tell what's real these days."

"No, I'm pretty sure he's a zombie," his wife replies with the authority of someone who has given an accident play-by-play. "Next thing you know, the city council will want funds to support them. They think we're made of money!"

"I'm okay!" he yells. "You can't catch the wind!"

"That doesn't make any sense, buddy," the guy next to me says. "Okay. Now I'm *positive* it's performance art. Otherwise that guy would be in pieces in the roundabout."

"No. He's a zombie. Told you," his wife replies.

Derek is still staggering in traffic, his arms swaying like cooked spaghetti as his body struggles to remain upright. Horns are honking and tempers flare.

"Get out of the road, you drunk!" A driver new to our predicament yells.

Somehow, he makes it past the traffic circle. Derek is headed for the highway, where weekend traffic is heavy and unpredictable. He shouts mostly gibberish over the blare of car horns.

"I'm smarter than all of you! Derek za'Dimwit is the master -mastermind! You'll never catch—"

And that's when an army green minivan with a dented driver's side door and plastic over one window enters the scene. He's driving at least twenty miles over the speed limit and doesn't put his foot on the brake until Derek's body has been tossed in the air and lands on the hood of his van with a dramatic crackle.

The accumulating crowd gasps. Those of us who've been here since the prelude wait to see if Derek rallies for the finale.

The van screeches to a halt and Derek, or what's left of him, slides off the hood and onto the highway like a fried egg.

No one moves.

Vem makes finger binoculars. "Do we… check?"

I glance around, hoping someone else volunteers.

They don't.

As we approach, the driver of the minivan, who smells like he smoked the entire marijuana shop this morning, emerges from his van to assess the damage.

"Whoa, dude!" His bloodshot eyes grow large. "Is that his head? Man, I hope I'm trippin.'"

Neither Vem nor I respond as we are both

afraid to look. Our role here is just to make sure the chase is done.

"I've gotta get out of here," the driver says. "My probation officer told me the next time I tested positive after an accident, he'd make sure I got locked up. Again. Sorry dudes."

The sliding door opens, revealing six adults who look like they've given up showers and clean clothes to make a point. "Is that November Bean?" One of them calls.

"It's me!" Vem replies with a bit too much vigor for the current situation.

"Oh wow! I wish we could stay! I did your Moaning for Microwaves class in Iowa. It was awesome!"

Without any warning, the van speeds away as two of its' occupants pull the door closed.

The silence that follows seems worse than the conversation that just took place. Derek's vacant eyes protruding from a detached head stare at us. In death, his expression is exactly the same as it was in life.

Consistency. At least he had that going for him. After a few moments trying to process the grisly scene, Vem salutes. "May he rest in… several pieces."

"Amen!" someone shouts.

The coroner later confirms that Derek za'Dimwit perished from what he termed "a traffic-themed crescendo."

47

Don't Fear the Reaper

The sterile lighting of the hospital waiting room flickers with the kind of hum that makes every breath feel borrowed. It smells like antiseptic, grief, and too many bad vending machine choices.

Vem paces.

I sit on the edge of a plastic chair, flipping through notes on my phone with hands that can't quite stay steady. Watching Derek's demise was horrifying.

"Where is he?"

I turn quickly to see Derek's lovely ex-wife, looking as though she's in between a fashion show and a toothpaste commercial. I'm not sure if this is my responsibility or if I should leave the bad news to Boysie.

"He's flat as a pancake," Vem says matter-of-factly before I have a chance to think about it. "The mortician will probably get you a good deal on a coffin, since you'll only be using half of it."

She gasps, and tears flow from her big blue eyes.

I place an arm around her shoulders while directing Vem toward the vending machine with the other. "I'm so sorry you had to find out this way, Jasmine."

"He's been an awful husband and an even worse father. But when you've been with someone for a long time, it doesn't matter, you know?"

She even smells fantastic. Like lavender and roses.

"I wasted so many years trying to prove myself to someone who wasn't even paying attention. My brain wants to stay at the beginning instead of where we are now."

She blows her nose hard, in the manner of a construction worker. I have mad respect. "And my kids and I are back to square one. No money. I work two jobs, and still we suffer."

"Jasmine, listen to me." I take her exquisite face in my hands. It would be easy to get lost in her crystal-clear blue eyes, and I have no doubt someone very special will. "I'll do everything in my power to make sure you and your children are cared for. Don't worry about that now. Call your family. Get some support."

"Lanie? Honey?" I turn quickly and jump out of my chair, throwing my arms around my husband.

"What happened? One of the regulars said there was a shooting! Why didn't you call me?"

There aren't enough words left in me. Instead I nuzzle my face into his plaid shirt, drinking in the scent of fresh scones and Me Manly cologne.

"Don't move, okay?" I whisper.

48

Reckoning

I was nominated to watch Vem's sister. Boysie has everyone else waiting outside the nurse's lounge he's confiscated for impromptu interviews. Pepper insists she's not ready. So here I am.

Pepper stands at the window in the waiting room, arms folded. She's hyper-focused on the emergency room doors like they might fling open and erase the last twelve hours.

They don't.

Instead, a doctor steps into the room—young, pale, and clearly rattled.

"She's deteriorating," he says. "Rapidly. We've never seen anything like this. Her entire body is inflamed. Her skin's turned a… deep purple. Eyes are bulging from pressure. Shallow respiration. We've intubated, but… I don't know how long she has."

No one speaks.

The weight of it settles like wet wool over the room.

"I'm going to see her," Pepper announces.

The doctor hesitates. "She's not fully conscious—"

"I wasn't asking," Pepper says firmly.

I give her a soft, unreadable look but say nothing. She needs this.

I follow her until we reach the door. Pepper raises her hand, almost clipping my nose. "I don't need a babysitter, Lanie."

"Not saying you do. I promised Boysie I would stay close until he has a chance to question you. So like it or not, you've got a shadow."

Pepper huffs but says nothing as I follow her.

Inside the ICU, the room is silent except for the hissing rhythm of the ventilator and the soft beep of machines counting down a body's last obligations.

Sybil is barely recognizable.

Her skin looks like rotten grapes, bulging in places it shouldn't. It's stretched tight, as though it doesn't quite belong to her anymore. Angry purple welts cover her limbs, her neck, even her eyelids. Her face is grotesquely bloated, her eyes bulging unnaturally. Her fingers twitch beside the rail like they are still arguing with the universe.

Pepper moves to the edge of the bed.

She doesn't cry.

She doesn't tremble.

She just stares.

And then says, "I hate you."

Sybil's eyelids flutter slightly. *Can she really hear in this state?*

"For what you did to me. For what you did to Derek. For the way you lied and used and manipulated everyone—like we were all chess pieces on your personal toxic game board."

Pepper steps closer, lowering her voice as her confidence grows.

"You underestimated me. Just like everyone underestimated Derek."

That gets another reaction. Sybil's eyes twitched slightly.

"You remember him? The one you mocked? The one you used like a broken tool and tossed aside like dull scissors? Turns out, he wasn't quite as dumb as you thought."

She's laying it on thick. He is *exactly* as dumb as she thought.

Pepper leans down, close enough to feel the rancid heat coming off Sybil's damaged skin.

"He poisoned you," she whispers. "The mic was for Gladys, sure, but the dosage? That was just for you. Double what he gave anyone else."

Sybil's lips move slightly. She couldn't speak even if she wanted, not with that tube down her throat.

Pepper doesn't pull away.

"I hope that means you're suffering more," she says matter-of-factly.

Sybil's cracked upper lip twitches again. Suddenly her eyes pop open like something out of a horror movie. I jump and instinctively grab Pepper's arm, but Pepper shakes me off. She doesn't need comfort the way I do. There is more of Vem in her than I realized.

Sybil motions for her tube to come out, but neither of us making any effort to contact the doctor.

Then, her body goes still.

The machines begin to shriek.

Pepper backs away slowly, her face unreadable as nurses rush in.

She doesn't look at me as she leaves the room.

And just like that… Sybil Screech is gone.

Murder leaves holes. Not loud drums or fanfare. Just silence.

Down the hall, in the cramped break room that now serves as an impromptu HQ, I find Cosmo sitting across from Boysie. "Boysie, Cos has nothing to do with this. Don't you have other folks to interview?"

My husband looks up, surprised to see me, and grabs my hand. "He did, babe. Now we're just shooting the breeze. We're on the same page about Gladys's song. Derek did us a big favor."

"So Derek was our one-per-club killer," Boysie says, pinching the bridge of his nose. "It's the darndest thing. The few times I met him, I wasn't sure he could tie his own shoes without a map and a spyglass."

He and Cos chuckle.

"It's a tragedy, really," I say, feeling sad for all that's been lost today even though there were villains. "Derek had this beautiful wife and kids and a nice life. He gave it all up for nothing. I'll never understand it."

49

Jailhouse Blues

The moment we step into the jail's holding area, we're greeted not by silence or hostility—but by chanting.

Low, breathy, rhythmic chanting.

"Hoooaaaahhhmmmm... moon... mooOOOON... beam..."

Vem freezes mid-step. "Is he leading *meditation circles* in jail?"

"I think they're humming," Pepper whispers.

"They're *moaning,*" I correct, my stomach doing a small pirouette of dread.

There are four of us— Vem, me, Pepper, and her F.B.I. counterpart, Mystic Glaze. She's voiced her adoration for Pepper and has given us this final interview with Moonbeam as a thank you.

As we're escorted down the corridor, we pass three holding cells where half a dozen inmates are sitting crisscross on the floor, eyes closed, arms in loose spirals above their heads like knockoff yogis. One has drawn a treble clef in toothpaste on his bright pink jumpsuit. Another is wearing what might be a pillowcase tied like a ceremonial scarf.

And there, perched in the center of the activity, is Moonbeam himself—serene, glowing with smug enlightenment, and looking like a spiritual leader who just got promoted for excellent behavior.

He spots us immediately and raises his hands, cutting off the chant.

"These are my wayward flock," he says, beaming. "And they've returned."

One of the inmates—bald, tattooed, and holding a cup of instant noodles like it's a sacred relic—does a double take.

"Hey… HEY! Are you THE November Bean?" he shouts, squinting. "I took your Moaning for Money seminar in Iowa. It was great!" He looks down at the floor "Except…I wasn't so good at it. I got impatient and robbed a bank."

Vem shakes her head. She's not used to people complaining about her methods. "You signed the release. No refunds."

"Girl, you taught me the power of breath grief!" he continues.

Moonbeam clasps his hands, delighted. "I *knew* you had a past life on this plane."

Vem glares at him like she wants her eyes to slice him in half.

Moonbeam seats himself like a man at peace

with his legacy. "You see?" he says, gesturing to the hallway. "The path finds us all in time."

"Let's be clear," I say, setting down my tote bag with force. "You are in JAIL, your so-called moon followers are moaning in stripes and one of them just outed Vem as a—"

"—vocal healing pioneer," Moonbeam supplies helpfully.

Vem opens a tin of cookies my daughter made for the fundraiser and slides one underneath the bars. "We've got questions."

Moonbeam bends down and inhales deeply and closes his eyes like a monk experiencing pastry-based revelation.

"Blessed be the snickerdoodle."

"Mr. Moonbeam," I begin. "We're here to ask what you knew about floricrine. And how deeply you were involved with Pepper's father."

Moonbeam bites into a snickerdoodle like it's communion. Crumbs cling to the corners of his mouth, and I almost forget we're here to interrogate him and not watch a food review.

I lean in. "We need to know about Dill Plantz," I repeat. "How deeply was he involved?"

Moonbeam's expression shifts from sugary bliss to cautious amusement. "Ah. The pharmacist with the ironic name."

"Don't play coy," Vem says. "We know he developed floricrine. Did he know you were using it in your clubs?"

Moonbeam sighs dramatically. "The Mooners were growing…restless. I was losing control. People kept finding themselves and then finding the *exit*."

Vem frowns. "So you wanted mind control?"

"*Mild* control," Moonbeam corrects. "Floricrine was meant to open the third eye, quiet the noise of independence, and eliminate the urge to question robe distribution policies. But early batches were too strong. Made Janet think she was a cloud. She floated into traffic. Metaphorically."

"Seems to be a popular activity," Vem says.

I blink. "You dosed your own members to stop them from deserting?"

He shrugs. "I was tired of chasing people down and…well. Making adjustments. Floricrine was cleaner. More scalable."

"And Mr. Gumb?" I ask. "Where did he fit in?"

Moonbeam chuckles. "Henry came to me with the idea of selling our product to the government. You know, for use on prisoners of war. He saw…potential. He said we were limiting ourselves with just Mooners. He wanted expansion."

"And that's when he brought in the others?" I press.

He nods. "Maribel with the healing crystals—she already had a customer base of gullible rich women."

I shift my gaze to Mystic, wondering if she feels pain hearing this about her sister. She is leaning against the cement wall with her arms folded across her chest. She's already interrogated the failed cult leader and shows no interest in the conversation. Still, I feel sorry for her. Family ties aren't easily forgotten.

"Nochturn had those weird light therapy saunas," Moonbeam continues, clearly relishing the spotlight once more, "…Sylvia had a line of edible bath salts and a warehouse full of influencers. And Hollowhead—"

"*Headmaster* Hollowhead," Pepper corrects him.

"The very one," Moonbeam says with a sly smile. "He'd just lost funding for his experimental etiquette academy and was looking for a way back into the inner circle. He saw floricrine as a way to keep his students obedient and invested in proper dinner posture."

"And what about the missing Mooners?" I press. "The ones who tried to leave before you had floricrine?"

Moonbeam's face darkens, just slightly.

"They were…harder to manage," he says. "Some went quietly. Some didn't. You can't run a community on good vibes alone. Sometimes you need consequences."

"Consequences?" Vem echoes.

Moonbeam shrugs. "Nature has predators. The Mooners had me."

There's a long, awful pause.

Then from the adjacent cell, the inmate who recognized Vem earlier chimes in, "He tried to consequence me with that stuff in kale-peanut smoothies , but I faked a nut allergy."

"Quiet, Barry," Moonbeam mutters.

I take a breath. "So what happens now?"

Moonbeam raises his chin. "Now you girls turn the page."

Vem frowns. "Are we back to metaphors?"

"No," Moonbeam says. "You have the names. The formula. The network. I'm just the roots. The real tree's out there."

He leans forward. "You want to stop it? You'll have to go deeper. Dill, Hollowhead, Sylvia—*they* took it further than I ever did. I was just trying to keep my people *still.* They're trying to sell the silence."

I shiver. "That's…poetic and horrifying."

Moonbeam smiles. "That's cult leadership, darling."

50

Carnival, Confessions, and Clippings: a Coda

The air smells like fried dough, kettle corn, and poorly made choices.

The rescheduled Piney Falls Carnival is in full swing, scattered across the green lot behind the fire station, under a sky so blue it looks like someone photoshopped it. Streamers flap. Kids squeal. A llama with mysterious connections to the town council is eating someone's funnel cake.

And at the center of it all, seated like a reluctant woodland deity on a stage built from plywood and borrowed church risers, is Cosmo, grimacing beneath twenty-four inches of unforeseen curly, unruly, fully-grown-out-for-charity silver hair.

A crowd of what I can only assume are hair enthusiasts has gathered.

One person has brought a cordless hedge trimmer. Uninvited.

I lean against the lemonade stand, sipping from

a suspiciously sour cup and watching it all unfold with a strange blend of amusement and pride.

Cosmo winks at me, and I blow a kiss in return.

"Ten thousand dollars, Lanie." He flicks a sweaty curl out of his eye, —he refused to wash his long gray strands for one last time this morning. "Ten. Thousand. Dollars. For this."

"You look like a very tired folk singer who regrets the last twenty years of his career," I say cheerfully.

"I look like I've been living in bush country."

"It's for the opera house. Soon to be a community arts center, thanks in part to the departure of your luscious locks."

Before he can reply, Gladys Petrie, who complains daily about missing her big moment at the karaoke club, steps forward and ceremoniously snips a lock of his hair with way too much glee.

The crowd cheers.

I glance over toward the wellness tent, where Vem stands in a wide circle of locals, leading a community moaning session with serene authority and a hand drum.

"Inhale… release… allow your inner discontent to vibrate through your spleen…"

Half the group is humming like malfunctioning air conditioning units. The other half is giggling. Someone is weeping into a crocheted shawl. A stray curly-haired dog joins in with a high-pitched howl that somehow harmonizes with Vem's singing bowl.

It's so… Piney Falls.

Then the mic near the main stage crackles.

Pepper is there, standing in a loose, breezy linen dress consisting of pink-polka-dotted fabric and what might be confidence—or possibly heartburn, but I'm choosing to believe the former.

She adjusts the mic like a pro and flashes a smile that's a little sheepish and a little triumphant.

"Hi. So... I wasn't going to speak," she starts. "Because, let's be honest, most of you still believe I was the Pepper Friday who orchestrated the karaoke club murders. Newsflash: I didn't."

Laughter bubbles up from the crowd.

"But there are things—important things—the people of Piney Falls need to know."

The crowd falls into a hushed silence.

"Months ago, my husband, Joe Friday and I purchased the former hardware store. In fact, he's there right now, supervising the remodel. As you all know, Piney Falls seems to attract cults and the ex-members can really struggle to find their way back into society."

She pauses and smiles directly at me. I give her the thumbs up.

"We want to create a safe space to come and relax. Where you can talk to other survivors, get help, or just sit and be comfortable. We're calling it -Nuts and Bolts and New Beginnings."

There is a smattering of applause. Most people

in our community don't like talking about our history. They'll come around.

"Also, when the F.B.I. inventoried the theatre, they found a wad of cash stuffed behind a seat in the balcony."

Vem insisted on wearing her night vision goggles and breaking into the place in the wee hours of the morning instead of just handing over the cash. She said it was more fun if they had to search for it.

"Since they couldn't find any ties to criminal activity, I asked if the money could be used to help restore the theatre to it's previous glory."

This time, there is vigorous applause.

She grins. "And with that, we are officially over our fundraising goal to purchase the old opera house! The Scheddy Sisters Community Performing Arts Center will open next summer!"

The crowd erupts. Someone throws confetti. Someone else weeps openly into a corn dog. Cosmo sighs deeply as another lock of his hair hits the grass.

I look toward Vem, who is already moving through the crowd, beelining for Pepper.

They meet at the edge of the stage, the cheering still echoing around them. I follow out of curiosity.

"Sticking around?" Vem asks, a little breathless, a little hopeful. "Maybe we could… I don't know… try the whole sister thing, round two?"

Pepper smiles, soft but clear-eyed.

"I love the idea," she says. "But I need to carve my own path. No more contracts. No more cults. No more anyone telling me what to do—even if they do mean well and own a ceremonial drum. I'm going to take a few months off with my special someone and then see if the F.B.I. still wants me."

Vem bites her lip and nods.

Pepper takes her hand.

"Ginger told me you offered a place for her to stay if she wants to work at the bakery this summer. I know she'll be thrilled to meet her oldest sister! Now that Dill is facing serious charges, he had to shut down the greenhouse, so Ginger has no obligations at home. I wish we could convince Mom to come too. She's been under Dill's thumb for so long, it's going to take time before Sage is ready for change."

"And then there were three," Cosmo says, squeezing my shoulder. "Just asking for my own peace of mind; there are no more frizzy-haired powerhouses out there, right?"

"Cos! Stop it!" I scold. His hair is now slightly below his ears, longer than normal. But his handsome face is more visible, and his blue eyes still take my breath away. How did I get so lucky?

"Not for long, though. Ginger's gonna fit right in. I'll show her the ropes like any big sister. Like, how to howl properly, make bug jerky and talk to most of the forest trees. Some will be purposely left out. They know why."

"Yeah," Pepper says, looking out at the carnival. "Piney Falls is right where she belongs."

I wait for Vem to walk away before my surprise. She enters the moan tent to teach a bonus session titled "Grunt Through It: The Emotional Release of Disappointment with Dark Chocolate Pricing."

Pepper raises one brow. "You look like you have something else to say, Lanie."

"Cosmo Hill, please report to the food tent!" the loudspeaker blares. "That's my cue!" He blows me a kiss and I return the gesture.

We watch as a group of children begin gluing his fallen hair into a bizarre tribute mustache on a paper plate.

I laugh.

She laughs.

"Lanie, I…"

"You've said you were sorry a million times. We've moved on, Pepper. You're Vem's sister, and that makes you family. Now and forever. It took so much courage to do what you did. That's what I wanted to say. As Vem's 'sister from another mister' I'm incredibly proud of you."

"Did you tell her, toots?"

I turn to see Gladys wearing breast-high jeans and a floppy hat. "I was getting to that, Gladys."

I turn back to Pepper. "Gladys surfs the dark web. She's really good at finding people, probably better than the F.B.I. There is someone here who might interest you."

Gladys motions to some unrecognized face in the crowd. A handsome, dark-haired man steps forward and offers his hand to Pepper.

"I'm Nochturn's son, Nochturn Junior. I guess that makes you my aunt."

Pepper lets out a small cry. "I can't believe you're…oh, give me a hug!"

The two of them embrace and I swear I see Gladys getting emotional. She'll deny it for the rest of her life.

"Mrs. Anders-Hill?"

Jasmine approaches us with three children in tow. Two possess her stunning good looks and one has the same vacant look as his father.

"You asked me to meet you here? I've got fifteen minutes to drop off the kids at daycare and get to my second job."

While I hate to take Pepper away from this emotional moment, she has one more important task so I motion for her to join us.

"Jasmine, this is Pepper Friday. I'll let her tell you."

I wink at Pepper, knowing the secret we share is worthwhile.

"I was going through some of Derek's personal effects, and I found this."

Pepper hands her a very thick yellow envelope. Written on it in orange marker are the words, "Not For Sybil. Money for my kids."

Jasmine looks inside, blinking hard. "Is this

real?"

"Two million dollars. In tens. He put some away every month for you and the kids, Jasmine. Oh, and he left you this note too."

As she hands Jasmine a small card, I frown. That wasn't part of the plan. Just tell her the money Moonbeam stored in his robe drawer was actually from Derek.

Jasmine reads the note and then wraps her arms around Pepper.

"Mommy? What's wrong?" The smallest child asks.

Jasmine bends down and takes her daughter's face in her hands. "It's not what's wrong, Abigail. It's what's right."

The sun starts to set behind the carnival rides, throwing streaks of gold and pink across the sky like someone spilled watercolor over the town.

And just like that, Piney Falls breathes again.

Also by Joann Keder

Piney Falls Mysteries

Welcome to Piney Falls

Saving Piper Moonlight

Tales of Naybor Manor

Lavender's Tangled Tree

The Twisted Stitch Society

Kinundrum

Charming Mysteries

Oceanberry Blues

Tangerine Troubles

A Lime in Time

Emory Bing Mysteries

The Case of the Half-Baked Bing

The Case of the Rootbeer Bungle

The Case of the Fudged Features

The Case of the Chunky, Funky Monkey

The Case of the Clairvoyant Carrot

The Case of the Vegan Vixen

The Case of the Cream Cheese Caper

Pepperville Stories

The Story of Keilah

Secrets and Sunflowers

Franniebell and Purple Wonder

Be the first to hear about new releases! Sign up for my newsletter here:

http://www.joannkeder.com

About the Author

Joann Keder is a USA TODAY Bestselling author who writes award-winning novels full of heart, humor, and just enough trouble to keep things interesting.

After spending her 40 formative years on the flat, windy plains of Nebraska (where the gossip travels faster than the wind), Joann relocated to the Pacific Northwest—and promptly agreed with her soul that it was time to start writing down all the stories taking up space in her head.

Today, she brings to life unforgettable women, their wonderfully quirky companions, and the crooked, scenic routes they take toward healing, hope, and occasionally homemade scones and cookies. Her award-winning novels are a mix of mystery, wit, and heartfelt mayhem.

When she's not writing, Joann enjoys walking among trees that don't bend sideways, savoring good chocolate, and spending time friends and family. And yes, they will all eventually find their way into a story.

www.ingramcontent.com/pod-product-compliance
Lightning Source LLC
LaVergne TN
LVHW050924080826
845145LV00001B/199

* 9 7 8 1 9 5 3 2 7 0 4 3 6 *